D1581477

RUN
AND
HIDE

ALSO BY ALAN McDERMOTT

Tom Gray Novels

Gray Justice
Gray Resurrection
Gray Redemption
Gray Retribution
Gray Vengeance
Gray Salvation

Trojan

RUN
AND
HIDE

ALAN
McDermott

 **THOMAS & MERCER**

Text copyright © 2018 Alan McDermott
All rights reserved.

Published by Thomas & Mercer, Seattle

www.apub.com

Amazon, the Amazon logo, and Thomas & Mercer are trademarks of Amazon.com, Inc., or its affiliates.

ISBN-13: 9781503903081
ISBN-10: 1503903087

Cover design by Tom Sanderson

Printed in the United States of America

RUN
AND
HIDE

CHAPTER 1

It hadn't been hard to find Rees Colback. The electronic trail he'd left all over New York had been easy to follow, and he was now walking down Fifth Avenue without a care in the world.

If only he knew.

The hunt was always easier when the prey didn't know they were in the crosshairs. A deer might be naturally cautious and take heed of every twig snapping in the undergrowth, but a man with no known enemies was oblivious to the dangers around him.

And they were closing in.

The rider watched him stop and admire the display in a department store window, one of millions of people in New York City, going about his business unaware that death was stalking him. For most, the end came naturally, but Rees Colback was a marked man. Someone had decided that his time on the planet should come to a halt, and now it was all about waiting for the right moment.

She sat astride a powerful motorcycle at the side of the road, a hundred yards behind Colback. Any closer and he might notice the machine and spook, so giving him a head start was the best option for now. On foot he'd have no chance of outrunning the mechanical beast, making patience the order of the day.

The strike would come, she could sense it. It was only a matter of when.

Lifting the visor of her helmet, she scanned the avenue: nothing out of the ordinary, no threats sensed. Simply a huge crowd enjoying another sweltering evening in Midtown Manhattan.

A black SUV crept around the corner. Nothing sinister in that, but when it stopped and a passenger got out and walked purposefully toward Colback, she knew it was time to move.

That was when a yellow cab chose the most inopportune time to double-park and drop off a fare. Trapped between it and the sidewalk, she kicked out angrily at the cab's door. The driver rolled down his window to yell at her, but the rider wasn't listening. The man from the SUV was closing in on Colback and that was all that mattered.

The cab driver was still shouting and gesticulating, but the rider wasn't hanging around. She had business to attend to. She twisted the throttle and the bike leaped onto the sidewalk, scattering pedestrians in her way. Others were slower to react, making it difficult to avoid striking them with the heavy street bike. At the first opportunity, she cut back off of the sidewalk and onto the crowded avenue.

Now Colback was struggling with the man as the big SUV pulled up to join the fight.

Eva Driscoll hated being right.

CHAPTER 2

A light breeze blew in from the east, taking the edge off what had been a scorcher of a day. The temperature had reached and then exceeded the forecast 98 degrees, and even for Rees Colback, who'd grown up in Florida and served in some of the hottest hellholes imaginable, it had made for an uncomfortable day.

It was his first visit to the Big Apple. He'd followed the obligatory tourist trail, paying more than fifty bucks to take in the view from the top of the Empire State Building, then walking to Times Square for more pictures before having a sandwich in Central Park. As the evening wore on, his appetite had grown and he was heading down Fifth Avenue to an eatery his closest friend had recommended. Pricey, but the best steaks in New York, according to Jeff Driscoll.

Driscoll had left the army a year earlier, the lure of private sector money too much to resist, and he'd been working for a security firm based in Manhattan for the last nine months. He'd described it as mainly babysitting foreign executives while they enjoyed a few days of booze and strippers. It wasn't the kind of assignment Colback had been hoping for, but under the circumstances, he had little choice. It would also mean relocating from Okeechobee, Florida, to the New York metro area, which he felt more than a little ambivalent about.

He was due to meet up with Jeff tomorrow, but had arrived a day early to arrange temporary accommodations and to try to get a feel for the city. So far, it was much as he'd expected: loud and extremely busy, a far cry from his quiet hometown.

Colback was picturing the mouthwatering plate of juicy steak and baked potato that lay a couple of blocks south when his sixth sense kicked in. Years of Special Forces training and working in war zones had honed his personal alert system. Tilting his head slightly to the right, he identified a black SUV out of the corner of his eye. No telling how long it had been cruising slowly next to him; the tinted windows meant he couldn't see who was inside. He kept a subtle eye on the vehicle and quickened his pace a little, but jerked to a stop when he felt the hard object dig into the small of his back.

Shit. He had been too focused on the vehicle and had missed the real threat. He turned his head slightly to see the man who controlled the pistol behind him. The short-cropped hair and bulging biceps under the white shirt told Colback that this wasn't a typical street robbery.

Acronyms flashed through his mind. CIA. FBI. NSA.

Whoever they were, they'd gone about making his acquaintance the wrong way.

Colback saw the SUV come to a complete stop and the side door open. He had an instant to decide what to do. Given the way this was going down, he saw only one choice.

Fight.

Colback pivoted quickly at the waist to face the threat, spinning his right arm around in an arc as he turned and trapping the assailant's arm just below the elbow, the pistol now safely under his own arm. Dropping slightly at the knees and then thrusting up, he palmed the man under the nose, breaking it bloodily. He followed through with his right arm, delivering a vicious punch to the throat, then grabbed the man's gun hand and snapped the wrist backward. The weapon clattered to the sidewalk, but any thoughts of retrieving it were tempered by the sight of two more bodies exiting the vehicle.

Instead, a single word leaped into his head.

Run!

Colback's legs were pumping before his own mental warning even registered. A round from a silenced weapon slammed into the front of a building next to his head, and he took that as his cue to leave the sidewalk and run into the traffic. He almost collided with the hood of a yellow cab as he crossed Fifth Avenue, hoping to make his pursuers think twice about following him. A glance back told him he was mistaken, their tenacity confirming that these weren't simply thugs out to rob him.

At the corner of Fifth and East 49th, he took a left, dodging more traffic as he crossed to where a gaggle of pedal-powered rickshaws converged outside a department store. At eight in the evening, the pedestrian crowds remained as heavy as the street traffic, which only made the brazen attack more worrying.

Colback crashed through a large throng of Asian tourists and stole another look behind him. Two figures in leather jackets were hot on his heels, and at the intersection he saw the black SUV tearing down Fifth Avenue, no doubt to cut him off at the end of the block. The armed pair were closing in fast and he was quickly running out of options. He turned right at the corner of Madison and 49th and found himself outside a Starbucks, its outdoor seating area cordoned off by half a dozen metal poles supporting red ropes.

Colback had a better use for them.

He unhitched two ropes and picked up the pole. It weighed at least fifteen pounds and the base made it unwieldy, but it was all Colback had. He held it over his shoulder like a baseball bat, listening for the sounds of rapid footsteps approaching the corner.

Colback swung the pole, its round base catching the first of the pursuers square in the face, stopping him in his tracks. The second one couldn't stop in time and barreled into his companion. Both hit the deck hard, and with a couple more swings Colback made sure they'd stay down.

It still wasn't over. The SUV would be nearby and Colback's first instinct was to get as far from the scene as possible. He picked up the attackers' pistols and saw the comms units in their ears, but there wasn't time to take them. A crowd had seen what he'd done and he needed to get clear of the area. He ran out into the road, stuffing one of the guns into his waistband.

A female driver slammed on the brakes, stopping inches short of him. She threw up her hands and gave him a "what the fuck?" look, but her expression changed when Colback wrenched her door open and pointed the gun at her head.

"Get out."

He dragged her from the small Honda, got in, and hit the gas, the woman's screams lost in the wake of the whining engine.

As he slalomed through the traffic, Colback's only thought was putting distance between himself and the SUV, but a glance in his mirror told him it wasn't going to be that straightforward. The black vehicle was closing in fast and he had no idea how many men remained inside.

Desperate times, desperate measures.

Colback swung the wheel, and the car screeched around the corner onto East 53rd and into oncoming traffic. Horns blared as he jinked between vehicles, sideswiping a bus and narrowly avoiding a head-on collision with a Mercedes. Crossing Park Avenue, he leaned on the horn for another block and ran a red light before taking a sharp right onto Lexington, but it wasn't enough to shake the more powerful SUV.

Realizing he wasn't going to lose them on the street, Colback looked for the nearest subway station. He hoped it would have more than one exit so that he could double back onto the street and disappear in a department store.

Maybe then he could figure out what the hell was going on.

CHAPTER 3

The traffic on Lexington Avenue proved too slow, but Colback was so preoccupied with the men chasing him that he missed the chance to abandon the car outside the 51st Street subway station. He took a sudden left on 50th Street, his smaller vehicle pulling away from the SUV thanks to its superior maneuverability. Pressing his advantage, he took another immediate left onto Third Avenue, then another onto 51st Street. While he kept an eye out for a subway station, a better opportunity presented itself: the New York City Police Department's 17th Precinct, with squad cars lined up on the street and a couple of officers chatting near the entrance.

Colback hit the brakes and jumped out of the car, leaving one of the pistols on the passenger seat. He still had the other tucked into his waistband, and saw the SUV some fifty yards behind him. He ran into the building, seeking sanctuary. The people on his tail might be brazen enough to take shots at him in the street, but they'd be foolish to try to take him out in a police station.

The man behind the desk—Sergeant Daniels, according to his badge—was booking a woman who'd clearly had too much to drink.

Colback stepped up next to her and placed his hands on the desk. "Someone's trying to kill me."

Sergeant Daniels threw him a glance, then looked back to his paperwork.

"I'm serious!" Colback said, raising his voice enough to get the attention of a few officers in the room. "I just had guys shooting at me and they're coming here now."

The sergeant looked at him again, then waved for another uniformed officer to take the woman through for processing. "And who exactly is trying to kill you?"

"I don't know. I was walking down Fifth Avenue and suddenly this guy sticks a gun in my ribs and tries to force me into a black SUV. I managed to get away, but two men from the vehicle followed me on foot. I took them down but the ones in the SUV chased me here."

"You outran an SUV on foot?"

"No. I stole a car. I had to. Those guys were shooting at me."

The admission that the black guy standing in front of him had committed a felony was enough to get Daniels's full attention, and Colback wondered what kind of city it was where vehicle thefts raised more eyebrows than shootings.

Daniels pulled out a fresh report sheet. "Care to tell me your name?"

"It's Rees Colback," a voice said, and Colback turned to see two men in black suits and white shirts approaching him. One of them held up an ID card. "Agent Wills, Homeland Security," he said. "This man's coming with us."

"That's them!" Colback told Daniels. "They're the ones who tried to grab me!"

Before the sergeant had a chance to answer, Agent Wills stepped up to the desk. "Colback is wanted in connection with a planned terrorist attack. We tried to speak to him earlier but he took out two of my men. We'll take it from here."

Colback could sense that Daniels was going to agree to their request, but he couldn't let that happen. The terrorism story was bullshit, which meant that they had another agenda—and from their actions so far, it apparently involved removing him from the face of the earth.

"If I was a terrorist, do you think I'd come in here and hand myself in? These guys weren't trying to talk to me, they were trying to *kill* me. Check the CCTV at Fifth and East 49th!"

"Sergeant, a cell is planning an attack in New York and Colback has information that can stop it. We need to take him. *Now*."

"Then why did you try to kill me?" Colback asked. He turned to Daniels. "Take a careful look at their IDs, then check the CCTV. If they wanted to speak to me, they could have called, not shot at me in the middle of the street."

Daniels looked from Colback to Wills and back again, seemingly undecided. Eventually, he picked up a phone. "Captain, it's Daniels on front desk. We have a situation down here."

He put the phone down and leaned back in his chair, eyeing the three men before him. "This'll all get figured out in a minute."

Colback could see that the two goons looked slightly frustrated at the prospect of a short delay, although it gave him time to think. If they got their way, he would end up in the back of their vehicle. Once they had him behind the tinted glass, they could do what they wanted to him and no one would ever know.

He considered drawing the pistol he had tucked into the back of his jeans. If he could force the cops to arrest him, he might be safe for the time being. But would it put an end to things? He doubted it. Paperwork would be sent over and he'd eventually be released into their custody. All he'd be doing was delaying the inevitable.

The captain appeared at the desk, a tall man in his fifties with silver hair in a military cut. Sergeant Daniels explained the situation and sat back in his chair once more, clearly relieved to have handed the matter off to his superior.

"I'm Captain Hicks. What can I do for you gentlemen?"

"We need to take this man in for questioning in relation to a terrorist attack," Wills said.

Colback knew he had one chance to convince the police that all was not as it seemed. "Captain, if you check CCTV in the area you'll see that they never tried to speak to me. The first thing I knew was when one of them put a gun in my back and tried to force me into a vehicle. When I resisted, they started shooting. Those aren't the actions of people who want information from me. If you let them take me away, they'll kill me. Don't ask me why, because I don't have a fucking clue."

The suit named Wills had taken a couple of steps back and was on his phone. Colback could feel the captain's eyes drilling into him as he sized up the situation.

"Did you fire at him?"

"No, sir," the other suit said. "We tried to speak to him, but he must have known who we were. He took out two men and stole a car at gunpoint. Hardly the actions of an innocent man."

Hicks stood with his hands on his hips, staring at Colback and clenching his jaw as if in deep thought. "Daniels, prepare a cell for this man." He turned to Wills, who had finished his phone conversation. "Get me the paperwork and he's all yours."

"Authorization will be faxed over in the next couple of minutes. You might as well leave him here."

"I'm telling you, Captain," Colback said, holding up his hand, "if you let them take me away, I'm a dead man. The least you can do is check out my story before you hand me over."

The captain shrugged. "If they have the correct paperwork, it's out of my hands."

Colback let out a frustrated sigh and glanced to his right. The exit was tantalizingly close. He could either wait here for someone to fax over his death warrant or make a move. He saw no other officers in the lobby, so now was the time.

He shuffled his feet as if anxious, subtly maneuvering himself closer to Wills, then struck with lightning speed. As Wills fell to a blow to his temple, his partner went for a weapon, but Colback whipped a foot into his groin and, as the man bent double, grabbed the back of his head and brought his knee up to meet the man's face.

Colback didn't pause to study his handiwork. He dashed for the exit and out into an artificial twilight, the sun descending beyond the skyscrapers. This was as far ahead as he'd planned. He needed transportation, a way out of the immediate area and ultimately away from New York.

Perhaps even the United States itself.

He ran to the end of the block, his gait normal thanks to the custom-made orthopedic shoe he was wearing. Ahead, he finally saw a subway station, but now he faced more than a couple of guys in an SUV: New York's finest would be launching a manhunt for him too. If he took the subway, they'd have officers waiting at every station.

A deep buzzing sound made him turn, and he saw a black motorcycle heading toward him. The rider skidded to a halt next to him and flipped up the visor.

Colback stopped in his tracks and stared at the woman dressed head to toe in a black leather one-piece. He'd never seen eyes like hers. They looked like emeralds, the brightest green he'd ever seen, and the shape hinted at Asian ancestry. He was so lost in them that he didn't realize she was shouting at him.

"Get on!" the woman repeated.

Colback glanced back at the station and saw half a dozen cops charging at him, and he didn't need a third invitation. He leaped onto the back and threw his arms around her slim waist as she revved the bike and shot them across the intersection.

Colback soon lost his bearings as the rider weaved between vehicles, barely slowing when she made a left or right turn. All he could do was hold on tight and lean when she did. Sirens seemed to converge from every direction as the rider turned down a street. Colback thought she was going to drive them into a store, but instead she headed for a down ramp into a parking garage.

The bike roared through the concrete cavern and stopped at the farthest end. The rider kicked down the stand and Colback jumped off.

"Who are you?" he asked.

"Later," the woman said, removing her helmet. Jet-black hair cascaded over her shoulders, and once again Colback could only stare.

She was stunningly beautiful, but not in a conventional way. She had the slightest of overbites and her top lip rose at the center. Her nose also seemed a little pointed, but her imperfections somehow came together to create the most captivating face Colback had ever seen.

She took a key from her pocket and pressed a button to unlock the ancient Nissan sedan parked next to them. She opened the trunk. "Get in."

Colback looked at her as if she were crazy, but the woman ignored his gaze and unzipped the leathers, revealing a plain white T-shirt. It was drenched in sweat and stuck to her, accentuating the curves of her body.

"Last chance," she said as she pushed the leather one-piece down to her ankles and stepped out of it. Her legs gleamed with perspiration. "Get in the trunk or you're on your own."

Salvation stood in front of him, wearing only a T-shirt and navy briefs.

Colback shook his head. "I've just had the craziest thirty minutes of my life. I'm not about to make it worse by getting into the trunk of this piece of shit."

She took two steps toward him, her face inches from his. Colback could make out a hint of perfume behind the scent of sweat and leather.

"The people chasing you. What are their capabilities?"

"I have no idea."

"Exactly. So we assume they have satellite coverage, or at least CCTV with facial recognition. If I'm seen driving with you in the passenger seat, we're screwed. So be a good boy and pretty, pretty please, get in the fucking trunk."

Colback was used to taking orders but never from civilians, no matter how alluring. Still, if she'd wanted to kill him, she could have done it by now. "Okay, but when we get somewhere safe, you owe me a huge explanation."

"You'll get one. I need your phone too."

Colback reluctantly handed it over and climbed into the confined space. He was trying to make himself comfortable when he saw her remove the back of the phone and discard the battery and SIM card. She dropped the handset and stomped on it, grinding it into fragments under her heel.

"Hey!"

The trunk thumped closed, leaving him in complete darkness. He felt her weight sink the car slightly and heard the door slam before the engine caught at the first attempt. Colback felt the pistol pressing into the small of his back, and it provided him with a little comfort.

As the woman drove smoothly and slowly through the city, he tried once again to make sense of what had happened. Even if his pursuer's ID had been real, Homeland Security's assertion that he was involved in terrorist activities was ludicrous. He'd spent years fighting for his country, and while he'd done unsavory things in the name of its military, his worst violation of US law had been a speeding ticket five years earlier.

If they really just wanted to speak to him, why had they tried to bundle him into a vehicle at gunpoint? It couldn't have been a case of mistaken identity: the one called Wills knew his name.

No, it all pointed to a snatch squad, but he was still no closer to figuring out what they wanted him for.

After what felt like an hour, the sound of traffic thinned, and approximately thirty minutes later the car stopped and the engine died. Colback readied the pistol in case the woman had lured him into some kind of trap. When the trunk opened, she didn't seem the least bit surprised to find herself staring down the barrel of a gun.

"You can get out now," she said, standing aside to give him room to extricate himself.

Colback eased out of the trunk and stretched his legs. They were parked next to a cabin, and in the moonlight he saw nothing but trees in all directions. A single-lane dirt road provided the only means of access and led up to a garage.

"You owe me a phone and a damn good explanation," he said, keeping the gun trained on her.

"You'll get the explanation when we're inside. The phone can wait."

She walked past him, ignoring the threat of the weapon, and he had no choice but to follow. As he did, insects sang their nocturnal chorus and an owl gave fair warning to the local rodents.

"Do I even get a name?" he asked.

"Eva," she said over her shoulder as she unlocked the garage door.

The name was familiar but Colback couldn't place it.

The interior of the garage was pitch-black and Eva used the flashlight on her phone to light the way. The garage looked barely large enough to house the Nissan with enough space to open the doors. There certainly wasn't room for anything like workbenches. In fact, the only things Colback could see were an old V8 engine on a wooden pallet in the corner and a couple of empty cardboard boxes.

"Nice place you've got."

Eva ignored him. She walked over to the engine and stuck her hand into a hole in the drywall. Seconds later, the pallet rose a few inches off the floor and swung to one side, revealing an illuminated set of metal stairs. She gestured for Colback to make the descent.

Colback walked down the steps and into a room that was at least three times the size of the garage above. In one corner was a camping bed and sleeping bag, next to a kitchen area complete with sink and small refrigerator. The rest of that wall was taken up by a gun cabinet containing everything from pistols and knives to assault rifles and an assortment of grenades. The far wall hosted a desk, upon which sat a laptop connected to two monitors.

"I'll say it again: you've got a nice place."

Eva hit a switch at the side of the staircase and the trapdoor swung back into place. Colback took a seat on the bed.

"Now that we're here," he said, "would you mind explaining what the fuck is going on?"

Eva took a pair of jeans from a door-less closet and put them on, then sat at the laptop and hit a few keys before swiveling the chair around to face him. "To answer your question as bluntly as I can, I have no fucking idea. I was hoping you could tell me."

"You mean you picked me off the street at random?"

"No, dumbass, I've been following you all day, waiting for them to make their move. When they did, you caught me off guard. I didn't expect you to get away."

"Sorry to disappoint you," Colback said. "How about we start with the basics. Who exactly are *they*? The ones at the cop station said they were Homeland Security."

Eva opened a bag of chips, took a handful, and passed the rest to Colback. "That's a start," she said. "Would you recognize them if I showed you some mug shots?"

"Sure. One of them called himself Wills, if that helps."

"Probably an alias but I'll check it anyway."

She turned to face the laptop again, and Colback walked over to stand next to her. She brought up a new window and Colback recognized the Department of Homeland Security seal above a login box.

"You have access to their system?"

"Only some of it. If there are areas I can't get into, I phone a friend."

Her fingers danced over the keys and three images appeared on the screen. Two of them were female; Eva clicked on the photo of the male. "Is that him?"

"Not even close. The guy at the station was thirty years younger."

"Then we'll have to do it the hard way," she said. "Describe him."

"About six-three, mid to late thirties, very short hair, almost shaved. It could have been black or dark brown; it was hard to tell."

Eva entered the parameters and set the search running. "It might take a while to find all the matches," she told him.

"Great. That'll give you time to explain what this is all about."

CHAPTER 4

Anton West paced the control room, chewing ferociously on a flavorless piece of gum. Computer monitors surrounded him, encrypted radio networks chattered and all manner of staff were busy sifting through information feeds. What should have been a simple takedown had quickly turned into a clusterfuck, and his team of incompetents had compounded their stupidity by losing the target. The last reported sighting was outside the NYPD station on 51st Street, where the subject had been spotted getting on the back of a motorcycle. It had taken precious minutes to get that information and then to set his intelligence analysts to work on the problems. Hacking into the traffic management system was only the first of the issues they faced.

"Sir, we have the bike. We're looking to see where it went."

West ran a hand through his short, black hair. Silver had begun to show through in recent weeks and he had a feeling today was going to add even more gray. "Transfer the coverage to the main screen."

West watched the black street bike dodge traffic as it sped away from his men on the ground. The time stamp told him the footage was nine minutes old.

"Speed it up," he ordered, frustrated at the real-time view. The film began to run at double speed, and when the bike left the camera's field of view, the man at the keyboard quickly switched to the one in the adjoining street.

A minute later, West watched the motorcycle head into a parking garage underneath a shopping mall. "They're either switching vehicles or trying to make it on foot," he said to everyone and no one in particular. "Listen up." He slammed his fist onto the long planning table in the center of the room. "Pearson, get me coverage inside of that mall. Hughes, I want to know about every vehicle that leaves in the next thirty minutes, including registered owner and facial recognition on all occupants."

West looked down and toyed with the phone in his hand. Protocol dictated he update his superior on the latest development, but it wasn't a conversation he was looking forward to.

The previous three removals had gone like clockwork, but there'd been no congratulations or backslapping. He'd been given a task and been expected to complete it, period. He'd only held the position for three months, ever since his predecessor, a well-regarded man in the covert operations community, had inexplicably vanished. The fact that his disappearance hadn't been thoroughly investigated confirmed one thing: survival was based purely on results.

That was why they'd chosen him to head up the East Coast unit. Fifteen years in the field had seen him register nineteen confirmed kills, none of which had been officially government-sanctioned. As a black bag operative, he'd been given *carte blanche* when it came to the execution, as long as it was within certain parameters and time frames. He'd quickly become Homeland Security's number-one choice when it came to eliminating the country's enemies on its own soil. Whether journalists who got too close to an awkward truth, or a foreign national suspected of stealing military secrets, they all met with unfortunate accidents.

The same fate had befallen the first three people on his current hit list, but the fourth and last wasn't playing ball. That was due to sloppiness on his team's part, but West was under no illusions as to where the buck stopped.

"I've got a hit on a light brown Nissan," one of his men said.

"Who is it?"

"That's the thing. There's no registered owner for the vehicle, and facial recognition comes back as classified."

West stared at the screen as the operative zoomed in on the female driver. He had no idea who she was, but it was too much of a coincidence that someone with a sealed file should be leaving the garage so soon after the bike entered. "Tail her. I want to know everywhere she stops. And get a bird to track her. She has to be part of this."

West looked at his phone again. Despite all the resources at his disposal, certain things remained beyond his reach. He could access the tax returns of anyone up to and including active senators, read their emails, even comb through their bank accounts. A few thousand people at most were safe from his prying eyes, and for some reason this woman was one of them. To learn anything more about her, he had no choice: he'd have to pass the request up the chain.

West spat out his gum and replaced it with a fresh stick, then dialed his superior's number.

CHAPTER 5

"What's with the oversized shoe?" Eva asked.

Colback explained that it had happened during a firefight in Afghanistan. The round had shattered his femur, and after being medevacked back to the base near Zaranj on the Iranian border, he'd been flown to a Role 2 medical treatment facility in Germany to spend six months in plaster. As a result of the surgery, his right leg was half an inch shorter than the left, and if he walked on bare feet it felt as if he were wearing one shoe. The top brass, while sympathetic, had informed him that his time in Special Forces was effectively over and offered him three choices. Colback instantly rejected a return to his former unit, the 141st, and the prospect of sitting behind a desk held no particular appeal either.

"In the end, I accepted a medical discharge and a small pension."

"Bummer." Eva took a photograph from a backpack and handed it to Colback. "You'll recognize the faces."

Colback took the picture and immediately recalled the setting. The image showed him standing with Jeff Driscoll, Danny Bukowitz, and Ron Elphick outside a bar in Phuket, Thailand. Driscoll had a snake draped around his neck, some kind of harmless python.

"That was taken in . . . 2009?" he said. "We had two weeks' R & R and decided to go somewhere exotic. We'd been stationed in Afghanistan and after rotating back to Kuwait we went to Thailand. Danny had been to Phuket a few times and showed us his favorite haunts. That snake belonged to a woman who worked the bar. We paid a couple of bucks each for a copy of that photo. Mine's back in Okeechobee." He looked up at Eva. "How did you get this?"

"Jeff sent it to me."

The penny finally dropped. "You're *that* Eva? His sister?"

She nodded.

"But he told me you worked for the DMV. Do all state employees have secret underground hideouts?"

"I told him that because I couldn't tell him the truth." She stood and took a bottle of water from the refrigerator. "Jeff and I were always competitive as kids. We played on the same little league team, were both high school athletes, had the same karate instructor, you name it. Everything we did was like our own personal Olympics."

"I knew that much from Jeff, but what's this truth that you can't share with him?"

Eva looked less serious than she had done so far. Her shoulders seemed to relax, and a faint smile brushed her lips as she reminisced. "When the time came to go to college, Jeff dropped his bombshell. He was done with school. Instead, he enlisted in the Army. Our dad lost his mind. He even threatened to cut Jeff out of his will, but Jeff didn't care. We weren't exactly a rich family, and Jeff said he'd prefer to live his life without regrets than exist to please others."

"So he signed up for the Rangers." Colback knew that Driscoll had served with the Rangers for a few years before meeting him, Elphick, and Bukowitz in the Green Berets.

"That's right. And I wish I could have seen the look on his face when I sent him a photo of myself in uniform two months later. I got the same threats from our dad, of course, but my parents eventually realized that we weren't kids anymore. They were more worried about me, naturally, but I still had a thing or two to prove to my big brother. Back in those days, I couldn't join a combat regiment, but I sure as hell intended to get my first stripe before he did."

"And did you?"

"Yep," said Eva. "By two months. But then he one-upped me by joining Special Forces. Women still aren't allowed to serve, so no way could I follow him. I left the military soon after. Compared to what he was doing, I could have made general in Logistics and it wouldn't have been worth bragging about."

"So you quit and joined the DMV."

"Close. It was the CIA. I figured if Jeff could do something worthwhile for his country, then I could too."

"Which explains this place," Colback said, looking around the room. "So why couldn't you tell Jeff?"

"When I signed up, they took one look at my school and military records and offered me a role in clandestine services."

"Ah, I see. The first rule of spy club is you don't talk about spy club."

"Exactly. I told my family that I'd landed a job with the government, and the rest is history."

"Not quite," Colback said, helping himself to a bottle of water from the fridge. "What the hell is today about?"

"Jeff emailed me a couple of weeks ago that Danny Bukowitz had died in an accident. The official report was that he'd been speeding on a mountain road, lost control, and gone over the edge."

"I heard about that." The news had come as a shock, particularly as Bukowitz had been the squad's designated driver. He had completed all the unit's fast-driving courses, including high-speed tactical vehicle and close-protection driver training, so his manner of death had seemed horribly ironic, to say the least. You survive eight years in Special Forces, undertaking the most dangerous missions imaginable, only to die in a single-vehicle car wreck? "I only found out after the funeral, otherwise I would have attended."

"Jeff said the same thing. It was an aunt who was going through Danny's things. She found his contact book and called everyone in it."

Colback nodded. Danny's aunt had been close to tears when she'd told him the news. She'd raised Danny since he was five years old, so it must have felt like losing her own son.

"I was in California when Jeff contacted me," said Eva. "He asked me to lay some flowers at the site of the crash, and that's when I suspected something wasn't right."

"What do you mean?"

"The road he was traveling on had a mountain on one side and a sheer drop on the other. There was a ten-foot gap in the barrier, and that's where he went off. It was a straight piece of road, not a bend, and there were no skid marks anywhere."

"Could they have been washed away in the rain?" Colback suggested.

"There hadn't been any. If he'd lost control, he would have tried to brake when he left the road, but there was no indication that he did. He either drove over the cliff on purpose, or someone staged his death to make it look like an accident."

"You think Danny was murdered? Based on what? A *lack* of evidence?"

Eva crushed her empty water bottle and shrugged. "It's something I'm familiar with. Wet jobs, black bag ops, call it what you will. I introduce people to fatal accidents for a living."

Colback could hardly believe the person before him was capable of killing another human being. Front a gothic rock band? Maybe. But carry out murders for a living? Although it did begin to explain the day's events. "So, you think the people who killed Danny are the same ones who came after me?"

"Yes, I do."

Colback's mind raced. He tried to work out what other connections he'd had to Danny Bukowitz, but all he could think of was the time they'd spent together in the Green Berets. He looked again at the faded photograph of them in Phuket. Ron Elphick had succumbed to cancer a year ago. With Danny gone, that left only Driscoll and him.

"We need to warn Jeff," he said.

"I thought so too. That's why I went to see him two days ago."

"What did he say?"

"Nothing," Eva said, tossing the crushed bottle in the trash. "He was dead."

CHAPTER 6

West's phone buzzed in his hand and he took a deep breath before answering it. The earlier conversation with his superior hadn't gone well, but thankfully they'd made progress since. His team had managed to remotely erase the digital recordings of the botched attempts to apprehend Colback and—thanks to a dedicated satellite—gotten a live feed on the woman's vehicle.

"West," he said, after connecting the call.

"We sent her file over. What's the latest?"

"We tracked her along I-80 to a place an hour and a half outside New York. Thermal imaging from the satellite showed someone climbing out of her trunk. We're assuming it's Colback. I've got two teams converging on their position, ETA thirty-five minutes."

"Don't underestimate this woman. I want an update within the hour and it'd better be good news."

The call ended, and West used his terminal to look at the file that his superiors had managed to dig up. The logo on the front showed that it had come directly from the CIA.

The woman's face appeared on the screen, although her hair looked lighter and much shorter than in the photo they'd taken as she left the parking lot. Her name suggested the reason she'd become involved in the operation, and as he scrolled down to her bio, it confirmed she was Jeff Driscoll's sister. He hit print and produced a glossy image of the young woman.

It only got better from there.

He skipped over the nonessential stuff: born in Pittsburgh, Pennsylvania, thirty-one years old, high school grad before enlisting. It was the time after she'd left the military and joined the Agency that was most interesting. She had aced the entry tests and completed a long list of operations. Impressive stuff, by anyone's standards.

The last entry had been added eight minutes earlier:

Rogue. Terminate on sight.

It brought home the precariousness of his own position. Here was an operative—albeit from another agency—who had served her country with distinction, and she was being discarded like a used tissue. He looked again at her photo and noticed his own hand was shaking with the decision he had to make.

As with all assignments, he played the role of scalpel rather than surgeon. It wasn't his job to know the nature of the ailment; he had only to remove the offending tissue. In this case, the tumor was Rees Colback, and the moment Eva Driscoll had intervened, she'd sealed her fate.

"Sir, the closest team is twenty-six minutes out."

West studied the target house. It stood in a sparsely populated, rural area, which meant little chance of anyone witnessing Colback's demise.

And the woman's, of course.

"We've got confirmation that it's a CIA safe house," Hughes said, looking over the top of his bifocals.

"Get me everything you have on it. I want to know what security measures they have in place."

"Already checked, sir. Nothing listed."

That could mean there actually was nothing to prevent his men going in, or that the CIA documented things differently from his own organization. Either way, this takedown had to go smoothly.

"Contact both teams and tell them to exercise extreme caution. Colback and the woman are pros."

Twenty minutes later, the two teams, five men in each, radioed to say they were in position, half a mile from the house.

West switched from the satellite feed to drone footage and watched his teams split up, five men approaching each of the side and rear of the house, their heat signatures glowing bright orange through the drone's thermal-imaging camera.

'Nest, this is Eagle One, all teams in position, over.'

'Roger, Eagle One, on my command—wait one.' Anton West went through the plan one more time in his head and then re-opened communications to execute the assault.

"All call signs, this is Nest: READY, READY, READY! GO! GO! GO!"

CHAPTER 7

"Jeff too?" Colback's throat tightened as he absorbed the news. "I spoke to him three days ago . . . We were going to meet tomorrow."

"Well, that's not going to happen, is it?" Eva stood and retrieved another bottle of water.

"How did it happen?" Colback asked.

"It was made to look like an overdose. Combination of Wild Turkey and sleeping pills. I looked around his place and didn't find a single clue, but given Danny's death, then Jeff's, I had a strong feeling they'd come for you next."

"And you couldn't just pick up the phone and warn me?"

"They would have had a trace on your cell. That's probably how they found you in the city, and why I trashed it in the parking garage. I was watching you, waiting to see if they would strike, and they did."

"If you were watching me, you could have just come up and introduced yourself."

"I had to be sure," she said.

As Eva turned to face her laptop, Colback couldn't detect much visible sorrow over her brother's passing. A little anger, perhaps, but Eva didn't strike him as a woman in mourning. Then again, she'd known of

Jeff's death for a couple of days, whereas he was only coming to terms with it.

He'd known Jeff Driscoll for ten years. They'd first met at Fort Bragg while taking the Special Forces Assessment and Select course, the initial step to becoming a Green Beret. Colback had attempted to join after three years in 1st Battalion, 141st Infantry Regiment, while Driscoll's background included four years in the 75th Ranger Regiment. They'd both aced the grueling, three-week trial before moving on to the Q Course, or Special Forces Qualification Course. That had taken another eighteen months, with both men opting for the Military Free Fall Advanced Tactical Infiltration Course.

It all seemed so long ago now. In the eight years since, they'd worked many missions together, including the fateful day when a stray bullet had ended Colback's military career. Three months after getting his release papers, he'd begun to regret his decision. He'd applied for numerous positions within the private security sector, but despite his exemplary military record, the injury worked against him. Limping into an interview was never a good start, but it was unavoidable. Colback had purchased some custom-made shoes, one of which had a thicker sole, but that hadn't alleviated the problem. The first impressions went better, but once prospective employers saw his discharge papers, it was game over.

Jeff had put a word in with his employers and—despite knowing about the injury in advance—they'd offered Colback an interview. He'd been looking forward to the reunion, but someone, somewhere, had different plans.

"The results are in," Eva said. "Take a look at these faces and let me know if any of them are familiar."

She stood and let Colback take the chair. The first mug shot was already on the screen, and it was numbered one of more than three hundred. He started to scroll through the list. "If I find him, what next?"

"You can't defeat an enemy if you don't know who they are. The first step is to identify them."

"And the second step?"

"Figure out why they want you dead."

Colback flicked through, image after image. A couple of times he paused to study a face more closely, but after hitting the halfway mark he still hadn't found the one claiming to be Wills.

A beeping sound interrupted his search. Eva tapped him on the shoulder and told him to get up. She took the seat and hit a couple of keys to bring up a screen showing four views of the perimeter.

"We've got company," she said calmly as two figures stepped into the top-right screen, both carrying assault rifles.

"How'd they find us?"

"It doesn't matter—they're here."

Eva zoomed in on the intruders and hit a key to capture the image, then shut the laptop's lid and removed it from the docking station. She stuffed it into an already-bulging backpack, then went to her armory and selected three handguns. She checked the chamber on a Glock 17 and tossed it, together with two extra 17-round magazines, to Colback. The other two pistols went into her waistband and she slung a Heckler & Koch HK416 assault rifle over her shoulder, then crammed as much ammunition as she could into the bag.

"This way."

She led him to a corner of the room and grabbed a black leather jacket from the closet, then pulled the whole thing away from the wall to reveal a passageway. She shoved Colback through and then pulled the closet back into place.

Colback found himself in a tunnel. Light bulbs hung from the ceiling every few yards and he could see that the tunnel ran at least the length of a football field. The walls and ceiling were cut stone, contrasting with the dirt floor. It was tall enough to stand up in but only wide enough to walk single file.

Eva handed him the backpack. "Get moving. I'm gonna set up a surprise welcome."

He watched her hit buttons on a numeric keypad.

"*Go*," she growled.

Colback set off at a jog and, soon after, heard footsteps gaining on him.

"Pick up the pace, soldier."

Colback obliged, breaking into a sprint.

A minute and a half later, he came to an abrupt halt. They'd reached the end of the tunnel and a ladder secured to the wall looked to be the only way out. He stood at the bottom and looked up, but the last of the overhead lights hung seven yards behind him. He found himself gazing into a void.

"I'll go first." Eva pushed past him and scampered up the ladder.

Colback gave her a brief head start, then began the ascent.

It took three minutes to reach the top, and in the darkness, he could hear Eva pull a deadbolt aside.

"Wait here," she said, and Colback felt a welcome breeze brush past him as the chamber opened above them, the hatch moving silently on well-oiled hinges. Eva stuck her head out and looked around, then climbed out and told him to hurry.

Colback took his time, not wanting to make any noise that would attract unwanted attention. He emerged to find himself at the top of a hill, surrounded by bushes, as Eva dropped the well-camouflaged hatch silently back into place.

Eva pushed her way through the foliage and Colback followed, the half-moon barely penetrating the leafy canopy above. After a couple of minutes, she stopped at the foot of an ivy-covered rock face. Eva grabbed a handful of ivy and pulled leaves and tendrils aside like a curtain, revealing the entrance to a cave.

"Hold this," she said, and disappeared inside, while he kept the ivy to one side. She was back in seconds, walking a dirt bike out of the cave. Colback expected her to stop so they could mount up, but she wheeled it onto a track that led downhill. Smart move, not starting the motorcycle until they were farther away. It would buy them a little time but they'd have to hurry.

"What happens when they find the basement?" he whispered as Eva broke into a trot. "Should I expect an explosion?"

"No," she replied, electing not to elaborate.

Colback followed her for around half a mile until the trees gave way to a road. Eva unclipped a helmet from the side of the motorcycle and put it on, then climbed aboard and hit the electric ignition. She folded the stock on the assault rifle and shoved it inside her jacket before zipping it up. Colback got on behind her and wrapped his arms around her waist, and she eased out the clutch, careful not to over-rev the engine.

"Where to?" he asked, but got no reply. As with their earlier ride, he had no choice but to hold on tight and hope she had a plan.

CHAPTER 8

Matt Hannagan assumed charge of both assault teams, his service record and seniority implicitly outranking his counterpart in the second squad.

"Take your men to the rear," he told Eckman, "and give the place a wide berth. Once you're in position, we'll hit the front and back simultaneously."

Willard Eckman didn't question the orders. In fact, he looked relaxed, which was a good thing, but Hannagan didn't want it to lead to complacency.

"Remember," he warned, "we're dealing with someone who does the same shit we do, plus a Green Beret. On top of that, they know we're coming for them. Assume they're alert and heavily armed."

Eckman nodded. Hannagan looked at both teams, meeting each man's eyes until he was certain they understood the challenge. Once he was confident everyone knew their roles, both teams slipped into the darkness and Hannagan awaited Eckman's call.

It came seven minutes later. Hannagan and his team were stretched out in a line facing the front of the house, their bodies hidden by the tree line. The approach had been stealthy, no sign the occupants knew of their presence.

"I can see the back door," Eckman radioed. "No sign of anyone and we haven't detected any defenses."

"Roger," Hannagan replied. "Send two men in and watch for friendlies. We're coming in the front."

He ordered two of his team up and watched through night-vision glasses from the trees as they ran at a crouch toward the front porch. They bounded up the four steps and pressed themselves up against the wall, one either side of the door. One tried the handle, then shook his head. The pair exchanged hand signals, then one took two steps back and fired shots from his silenced rifle at the lock. He kicked the door in and both men disappeared inside. Hannagan waited for more shots to ring out, but all he heard was the all-clear in his earpiece three long minutes later.

"Where are you?" he whispered aloud. The subjects had to be nearby. The car remained outside the garage that abutted the house, and the eye in the sky would have told him if the pair had left the area.

He instructed two men to check the garage and told Eckman to look for any outbuildings that Colback and Driscoll might be hiding in.

Both came back negative.

"Nest, Eagle One," he said over the comms.

"Go ahead, Eagle One."

"No sign of them. Can you confirm they haven't left the scene?"

"That's affirmative. They entered the garage and there's been no movement since."

"Roger that."

It was time to take a look for himself. Hannagan approached the garage and let his colleagues know he was coming in, just in case they were edgy and mistook him for one of the targets. Inside, he looked down at the floor and saw faint footprints in the fine layer of dust. Two pairs were attributable to his own people, while the others led to the rusting engine in the corner, where they abruptly stopped. Using hand signals only, he told the pair to pull the pallet aside while he covered them.

Although it was a large engine block, he didn't expect it to pose them much of a challenge, but after a minute of grunting and heaving, they hadn't managed to move it more than a couple of millimeters. That in itself was telling, and Hannagan knew there had to be a mechanism holding it in place. The room had only one visible switch, but when flicked, it did nothing but illuminate the small space. He winced as the light flared in his NVGs, then turned it off again.

The pallet remained in place.

By combing each wall, he eventually found a switch in a hole in the drywall. He told his men to cover the engine, then pressed the button and quickly raised his own weapon. The pallet raised a couple of inches on near-silent hydraulics, then shifted to one side to reveal a brightly lit basement.

Hannagan pushed the NVGs up and waited for Colback and Driscoll to make their move, but the gunfire he'd expected failed to materialize. From his position, he could see much of the interior. While it appeared to be abandoned, he had no choice but to send one of his men down to investigate.

He watched his subordinate gingerly descend, rifle up and ready to unleash hell, but when he reached the bottom of the stairs and scanned the room, he called up the all-clear.

Hannagan quickly climbed down to take a look for himself. It was indeed deserted. He checked for signs that it had recently been occupied and soon found what he was looking for. A water bottle had a thin sheen of moisture on the outside, meaning it had recently come out of the fridge. He found two more in the trash.

That they'd been here was now beyond doubt, but where had they gone? Hannagan saw no obvious exits apart from the stairs leading back up to the garage. "There must be another way out," he said. "Search everywhere but watch out for booby traps."

Exactly 120 seconds after the first man had descended the stairs, the pallet swung back into place above with a resounding *thunk*. The lights went out, leaving the two men in darkness.

Hannagan put his night-vision glasses back into position and raised his rifle, expecting an attack. Instead, the sprinkler system overhead burst into life, drenching him and his companion to the skin.

CHAPTER 9

After fifty or so miles, Eva turned the motorcycle onto a dirt road and headed into the woods. *Good*, thought Colback. If they were stopping, it would give him the chance to ask some of the questions that had been bouncing around in his head for the last hour.

When they reached a small clearing, Eva stopped the bike and turned the engine off.

"We'll rest here until morning," she said, putting the helmet on the handlebars. She gestured for the backpack.

Colback shrugged it off and handed it to her. "Then what?"

"We're going to need help. They managed to track us to the cabin, possibly by satellite, or someone told them this was a CIA safe house. If we're going to evade them, we need to be in the loop."

Colback frowned. "I don't understand."

Eva put the bag on the ground. "I'll explain in the morning. Right now, we need to get some sleep."

"I don't know about you, but I'm not that tired."

"Great," Eva said, handing him the rifle and settling down, using the backpack as a pillow. "You can take first watch. Wake me in three hours."

She closed her eyes and within seconds was purring gently.

During his time in the Green Berets, Colback had come to appreciate the value of grabbing sleep whenever possible, but this was a new situation. Back then, the nature of his missions been simple: engage the bad guys and kill them. Now he didn't even know who the bad guys were, or why they wanted him dead. He only knew that they seemed to be US agents of some kind. He'd hoped Eva would shed light on the problem, but as her priority was getting rest, he'd have to be patient.

Colback studied her as she slept and saw little family resemblance. Jeff Driscoll had been quite a few inches taller, with ears that an elephant would have been proud of. His face was rounder too, whereas Eva's tapered from her eyes down to her slightly pointed chin. After the extended time they'd spent in the cabin basement, he'd come to realize that the Asian-seeming cast to her eyes was the result of makeup rather than genetics. He didn't know if she'd done it to evade the facial recognition system she'd mentioned, or simply to make herself look more attractive.

Not that she needed much help on that score.

Despite the circumstances, Colback felt something stir within him as he watched her snore gently. It wasn't merely a physical attraction. He'd never met a woman so cool and assured under pressure. Few men, either. He could hardly have asked for a smarter or more capable ally in the nightmare they were living.

Colback looked away from Eva and struggled to think of a reason why anyone would want to kill all the members of his squad. Nothing leaped out at him. The people after him appeared to have connections to the government, so it wasn't likely to be an act of revenge for one of the insurgents he'd killed in Afghanistan or Iraq during his numerous tours. What could have turned his friends and him into such a liability?

He spent the next few hours with various ideas going through his head, none of which made any sense at all. Finally, he shook her awake.

Eva was instantly alert. "Any sign of visitors?"

"None," Colback said. "I have a few questions though."

"You should rest. I have a feeling tomorrow's going to be a busy day."

"I will, but I want to know what you've got planned. You said something about satellites and being in the loop."

Eva took a bottle from her backpack, swallowed a big mouthful, and passed it to Colback. "The satellites operate 24/7 and the signals they send back can be seen by anyone with the proper equipment and clearance. I have a friend who has access to both. The only way we can avoid the eyes in the sky is if we know what they're looking at. First thing in the morning, I'll take the bike to the nearest town and swap it for a car, then we'll go see him."

"Where does he live?"

"New Lexington, Ohio."

"That's hundreds of miles away," Colback said.

"Three hundred and eighty-three from our current location, and that's as the crow flies. With a couple of stops for food and gas, we'll make it by sundown. Any earlier and we'll be sitting around waiting for night to fall."

"You think they'll be watching him, is that it?"

"Probably," Eva admitted. "By now they'll have a complete file on me, including known associates. All of my credit cards, bank accounts, passports, and anything else that leaves an electronic signature will be on their watch list. We have to go off-grid, which means giving you a crash course in spy shit 101."

"I know the basics," Colback countered.

"You know squat and that's putting it mildly. You're also hard-headed and that's not gonna fly."

Colback's nape bristled. He shot her a glare that normally sent tough men cowering, but Eva continued as calmly as before.

"You need to lose the attitude," she said. "I wouldn't dream of telling you how to take out a Taliban machine gun nest, but this is my domain. If I speak, you listen. If I give you an order, you obey without question. You got that?"

"I got it."

"I hope so, because so far I've had to tell you everything twice, and that could get me killed. If you slow me down, you're on your own. I want to find out who killed my brother, and you can be part of the solution or part of the problem."

"I said I got it."

"Good." Eva checked her watch. "Get your head down. I'll wake you at seven, then go get some new wheels."

"How do you plan to do that if your credit cards are being monitored?"

"Always with the questions." Eva sighed and dug into the backpack, then pulled out a bundle of hundred-dollar bills. "We pay cash from now on."

"How much have you got? We could be on the run for weeks."

"Fifteen grand," Eva told him. "But your guess is way off the mark. If we're careful, we might have four or five days at the most."

"Why don't you contact the CIA for help? Surely they'd send a team out to support you, or at least look into who's behind all this."

"Gee, why didn't I think of that?"

Despite her sarcasm, Colback felt his question deserved an answer. "Well?"

Eva shook her head slowly and stared at the ground, as if conflicted. Colback got the feeling she didn't want to go into it, but eventually she relented.

"Who runs this country?" she asked at last.

Colback frowned. "The president, of course. Well, the government."

"Wrong. You couldn't be further from the truth. It's a body that calls themselves the Executive Security Office. They've been the power behind the White House ever since the end of the Second World War. Back then, they were mere billionaires, but now they control everything.

The ESO decides which 'unsavory' acts are carried out and by whom. Need to destabilize the government of an African country in order to gain access to its oil? The ESO gives that task to the CIA. Got a reporter sniffing too close to a politically sensitive story? ESO tells us to make it look like an accident. All of my orders were given to me by my superiors, but I suspect they ultimately originated from the ESO."

"How come I've never heard of the ESO?" Colback asked.

"Few have. I first learned about them from my friend Farooq but dismissed it as conspiracy theory. It was only when Bill Sanders let it slip that I knew it really existed. You ever hear of a guy called Edward Perkins?"

Colback shook his head. "Doesn't sound familiar."

"It shouldn't be. His death barely made the local newspapers. Perkins claimed to have created an engine that ran on water."

"I've heard of those," Colback said.

"Well, they're all bogus. To extract hydrogen from water, you need to use more energy than the hydrogen will create when it's burned. It goes against the first and second laws of thermodynamics."

"I'll trust you on that."

Eva let the remark slide. "I did my own research when I first heard about it. Most inventions like it are scams designed to get people to invest in shell companies that fold after a few months. Typical boiler-room scams. Turns out, though, Perkins had actually done it. He'd created an engine that worked. It was still in its infancy, but once verified, panic set in. Oil is just about our single biggest reason for going to war, and the profits line the pockets of very influential people. Once they'd worked out the financial impact—and we're talking trillions of dollars—it was decided that Perkins had to go."

"They told you all this?" Colback asked.

"No, I worked it out. A substantial amount was deposited in Perkins's bank account the day the patent was signed over to a government body, though he wasn't able to spend a penny of it. His car mysteriously ended up in a lake, with him inside."

"Fascinating stuff," Colback said. "But why does this stop you from contacting the CIA?"

"For the ESO to know about the safe house, Langley must have handed over my file. They would only do that if ordered to, and the ESO are not going to allow them to hinder their mission by helping me. I'm as much a target as you are."

She must have known this would happen, Colback thought, *yet she still decided to help me*. That took a lot of guts, but he knew it wasn't really about him. Eva was clearly driven by the desire to get to the people behind her brother's death, and the only reason she'd saved him was because he might have information that would help her achieve her goal.

One thing was for certain: he wouldn't last long without her.

"Back to the satellites," he said. "I still don't see how knowing what they're looking at via the eye in the sky is going to help us. If we stay with your friend, we'll know if they zoom in on his place, but by then it'll be too late. We'd be trapped. Staying mobile would be better, but then how do you contact your guy if we can't use cells?"

"I have an app on my phone," she said.

"That's it? You download an app and want me to believe it's secure?"

"This one is. Farooq created it himself. It uses technology even I don't understand, but I know that if anyone manages to intercept the messages, it's impossible to decode them. As for using it to locate us, the digital package is bounced off servers all around the world. By the time they pin down a location it'll be too late to do anything about it."

Colback had to concede to her greater knowledge. His own experience with the latest gadgets was limited to the social media applications he had installed on his cell phone, and he had no idea what went on in the background. "That reminds me. You owe me a new cell. The one you smashed cost four hundred bucks."

"I'll buy you a top-of-the-range model when this is all over. Until then, steer clear of all electronic devices unless I say so."

Colback was no longer in the mood to argue. Weariness had snuck up on him, and as he let out a yawn, the prospect of getting his head down suddenly seemed the most important thing in the world.

"One last thing," he said as he made the backpack-cum-pillow as comfortable as possible. "What was the little surprise you had for the guys in the basement?"

"If they manage to get it open, anyone still inside after two minutes will be doused in a permanent blue dye. It's not toxic, but looking like a Smurf for the next couple of weeks should take them out of the game."

CHAPTER 10

"Open it, goddamn it!"

Hannagan pounded on the trapdoor as if his anger would speed up the process, but the hatch remained firmly in place.

"The switch isn't working," his subordinate said over the comms unit, and Hannagan cursed once more at his own stupidity. He should have known the place would be rigged, but the subject had been smart enough to use a timer to suck more people in. This wasn't a mistake he'd make again.

With the stairs to the garage cut off, his only hope of seeing daylight again was to find the exit Colback and the woman had used for their own escape. The sprinklers had stopped, which was one small crumb of comfort, but the lights remained off, meaning he would have to conduct the search through the dim green tinge of the night-vision glasses.

It only took a minute to find the passageway hidden behind the closet and, as Hannagan stepped into the illuminated tunnel, he saw for the first time what he had been soaked in. His hands were stained dark blue, and when he ushered the other team member into the tunnel he could see the man was covered from head to toe with the same dye.

"I gotta feeling this ain't gonna wash off," Hannagan heard, but he was already contemplating his own future. There was no way he could be seen like this in daylight, which meant he had until dawn to find the pair.

The consequences of failing didn't bear thinking about.

Hannagan radioed the other team leader to let him know about the discovery of the escape route. He didn't explain his own personal predicament, as he knew it would take his teams' minds off the job. "Looks like they got out through a tunnel. It leads east from the rear of the garage and it's at least a hundred yards long. Send some men out that way."

Hannagan switched frequencies, then took a deep breath before updating West on the situation. "Nest, Eagle One. We just missed them. She had an escape tunnel. Expand the satellite image and check the woods for thermals. Set the focus a hundred yards east of the building and expand from there. They can't be too far away."

"They'd better not be," West warned, and Hannagan waited while the pencil-pushers adjusted the bird's field of view. He tried wiping his hand on the wall to get rid of the dye, but he only succeeded in leaving a navy streak on the stone. Driscoll wouldn't have gone to the trouble if it were something that would rinse off in the shower. He'd be wearing it for days, he knew, if not weeks.

"Eagle One, we have two heat signatures moving away from you."

Hannagan entered the coordinates into his GPS as they came over the air. "Can you confirm it's them?"

"Negative. We can't see through the treetops."

"Roger, Nest. We'll check it out."

There was little to gain from telling West about his impromptu blue shower. Plenty of time to explain once he'd completed the mission.

"Eagle Two," he said, addressing Eckman. "What's your position?"

"Seventy yards from the house, heading east."

Hannagan gave him the coordinates he'd received from West, then ran to the end of the tunnel. He scampered up the ladder and caught his breath when he reached the top, wary of his quarry and her tricks. He stepped down a couple of rungs, then used the muzzle of his rifle to ease the hatch open a couple of inches. There was no explosion, and no one tried to pepper his face with bullets. He pushed the hatch all the way open, then climbed out and put his NVGs back into position.

He saw footprints in the dirt and broke through the foliage to follow them. The trail led in the direction of the recent sighting, and he checked in with the rest of the men to synchronize the takedown.

"Nest, Eagle One. What's the current location of the targets?"

"Two hundred yards to your east, moving away slowly."

"Roger that."

Hannagan had no idea if Driscoll had access to NVGs but decided to proceed as if she did. He ordered the men to close slowly, staying silent imperative. A few minutes later, he saw the figures in the distance. He could make out their movements between the trees, and they didn't appear to be in any particular hurry. "Hold up," he whispered into his mic. "I have them."

Three others also reported that they had eyes on.

Hannagan moved to his left to get a better view, and as he did so, he saw one of the targets raise a rifle. Now that he had a better view, judging by the figures' build and dress, they seemed to be ordinary poachers using the cover of night to take illegal game.

Before he could alert the team to his discovery, a single shot rang out as one of the hunters got a deer in his sights.

The response from Hannagan's men was ferocious.

Hannagan saw the first poacher's body shudder as bullets pummeled it, the *thwack-thwack-thwack* of their silenced rifles sounding like twigs breaking underfoot.

"Cease fire!"

In the time it took for Hannagan to rein his men in, at least forty rounds had been loosed. He jogged to the fallen pair, one of the bodies still twitching as it tried in vain to endure more than a dozen puncture wounds.

"Great!" Hannagan said, kicking the base of a nearby tree. Not only had he lost Colback and Driscoll, but he now had two innocents to dispose of. Any hopes he had of rejoining the mission once he'd dealt with the blue dye were well and truly over.

"Eckman," he said into his throat mic. "Bury these two and make sure the men account for every shell casing. I'm calling it in."

Hannagan stalked away, as if putting distance between himself and this debacle would soften the blow he was about to receive.

CHAPTER 11

Anton West resisted the urge to throw his coffee cup at the nearest screen. Instead, he slammed it down on the desk, splashing the cold liquid over his wrist. He shook the drops away and wiped his hand on his pants, loosing yet another curse.

Hannagan had screwed up big time. What should have been a simple task had seen his hit teams' capabilities reduced by a third. The three men Rees Colback had taken down in New York wouldn't be available for days, and now Hannagan and one of his men had fallen prey to a simple trick that meant he wouldn't be able to show his face for weeks. That left West with only ten men. Given that Colback and Driscoll's whereabouts remained unknown, the teams were going to be spread pretty thin.

"Bring up Eva Driscoll's known associates and pinpoint their addresses on the map."

Her involvement complicated matters. Although he didn't know the big picture and how the three kills he'd orchestrated fit together, West surmised that Driscoll had seen a connection between her brother's death and Rees Colback. She'd clearly seen through the staged murder of Jeff Driscoll, but he could only guess her intentions. Was she simply hoping to protect Colback, or did she have something more proactive in mind?

An analyst worked furiously to transpose the data onto the main screen, and West digested the result. Many of the flags were concentrated in and around Washington, D.C., which was what he'd expected, but West thought it unlikely she'd show her face there. No, she'd head off-grid to regroup and plan some kind of counterattack. That's what he would do.

He looked further afield and chose the nearest four locations to the safe house, then returned Hannagan's phone call. "Put Eckman on."

"Eckman here."

"Divide the remaining men into four teams of two. You'll be checking out some of the target's contacts. I'll send you the names and addresses in the next minute."

"Yes, sir. And . . . what about Hannagan?"

"He can make his own way home. You worry about finishing this mission."

West ended the call, then told an analyst which details to send to Eckman's phone. He then dialed the number for Saul Bennett, one of the two remaining operatives from the New York mess. "I want you in Knoxville, Tennessee. Immediately. I've got four teams watching the woman's nearest contacts outside D.C., and they're all in the general area. From Knoxville you provide assistance once she turns up."

"You don't want us to pay Colback's sister a visit?" Bennett asked.

"Not yet. There's no point holding her as leverage unless Colback knows about it, and we can't exactly pick up the phone and call him."

"We could plant something and have her arrested," Bennett said. "Plaster her face all over the media . . . that might draw him out. We could name Colback as an accomplice and offer a reward. We'd have 300 million people looking for him. He couldn't hide long."

"The media works both ways," West said. "If we make Colback public enemy number one, what's to stop him giving his side of the story? Worse is Driscoll. She knows where lots of bodies are buried. If she starts talking, heads will roll. No, we do this quietly. Get to Knoxville and await further instructions."

West looked up at the screen once more. Apart from the four addresses dotted around Knoxville, there were three others, all much farther west. One was in New Mexico and the other two were in California.

He thought about what he'd do if he were in Driscoll's shoes. He'd want answers, and fast. Air travel was out of the question, so she'd have to drive. That meant her contacts in San Diego and Fresno could be scrubbed, because she wouldn't waste days on the road when she had closer options. He discarded Albuquerque for the same reason.

"I want you to start logging all voice and data in and out of those addresses immediately," he ordered. "Also, tell her contacts that she's a wanted felon. Anyone found helping her will spend the rest of their lives behind bars, but there's a huge reward for information leading to her capture."

"I'm on it," Pearson said, his fingers a blur, his bespectacled eyes never leaving the screen in front of him.

Now that he was confident of her next move, West wondered if he had enough men in place to deal with her. He'd dipped back into her file earlier, and it was clear that she warranted some respect. When she turned up at one of these places, he would only have two people on site, with Bennett at least an hour away. It wouldn't be enough.

Reluctantly, he dialed the number for his superior.

CHAPTER 12

"That didn't sound good," Simon "Sonny" Baines said as Len Smart put the phone down.

"How very perceptive," Smart deadpanned. "Naylor Resources is pulling the plug."

"Don't tell me, they're going with Stormont . . ."

"Who else?"

It had been the same story over the last few months. For ten years, Minotaur Logistics had provided security personnel to corporations and governments throughout the world, but as contracts came up for renewal, Stormont International was jumping in and undercutting them.

Minotaur, the brainchild of former SAS sergeant Tom Gray, had once been the go-to security firm, with an unparalleled reputation. That was until Gray flipped, following the deaths of his wife and son. He'd sold the business—which had been called Viking Security Services at the time—to fund his campaign to highlight what he perceived to be inadequacies in the British justice system.

It hadn't ended well.

Gravely injured, Gray had spent a year recuperating in the Philippines under an assumed identity before the British government reneged on a deal and tried to silence him once and for all. Len and Sonny had gone to his rescue, and after a long, hard fight they'd finally made it home and exposed the rogue wet-ops department.

Following that episode, Minotaur Logistics had risen from the ashes. All had gone well until a nosy reporter revealed Gray's role with the company. Up to that point, he'd had someone else do the face-to-face meetings, and the major shareholder was listed as a shell company out of the Cayman Islands. Clients had begun leaving Minotaur until Gray chose to step aside, leaving Len Smart to run the business. That move had stemmed the flow, leaving Stormont—not Gray's reputation—the latest threat to the company.

"I'll let you break the news to Tom," Sonny said.

Although no longer officially connected to Minotaur Logistics, Gray still drew a monthly salary through a different Caribbean shell company and had a say in the day-to-day running of the business.

"Nice try," Smart replied, "but I'll wait until we go see him tomorrow. That'll give me time to work on some financial projections. I'll tell you now, it won't be good. Naylor Resources was just about keeping us afloat."

"Leave it for now," Sonny suggested. "It's lunchtime. Let's grab a sandwich."

"I'm going to need something a little stronger. Let's eat at the Pig and Whistle."

When Len stood, the contrast between them became immediately apparent. Blond-haired Sonny, who stood a foot shorter than Smart, had earned his nickname during the SAS selection process. He'd been a fresh-faced twenty-one-year-old but had looked no older than fifteen. Even now, eighteen years later, he could easily pass for thirty.

Smart, also ex-22 regiment, looked as if he belonged in the boardroom, not behind a rifle. His hair had begun receding a few years earlier and his bushy black mustache and spreading waistline meant few people would have guessed his former profession.

As they walked to the pub, Smart was his usual quiet self, but Sonny couldn't contain his concern about the company's future. "Do you think we'll fold?" he asked.

"That's up to Tom. The contract with Naylor's mining division in Afghanistan was covering the cost of the office, staff, and the training facility. With them gone, we're running on fumes. Unless we land a similar contract, I reckon we've got enough in the bank to survive another six months. Tom might want to sell up while he can, or just wind the business down. Either way, it's time to update your résumé."

"Really? Six months?"

"If we're lucky."

When they reached the pub in London's East End, they ordered a pint of bitter for Smart and lager for Sonny. Both opted for the steak pie.

"What are the chances of us landing another Naylor?" asked Sonny.

"Slim to none. Stormont's business model seems to be built on the idea of cheaper contracts, and lots of them. Even blue-chip companies need to tighten their belts these days. We simply can't compete with them, no matter how good our setup or personnel."

"Well, at least we've got a few months to prepare for the worst. I've got a little put away and I could always find a contract with someone else."

"The way things are going, the only one left in a couple of years will be Stormont," Smart said. "I've made inquiries and the pay isn't that great. Expect a forty percent pay cut at the very least."

Sonny drained half of his drink and licked his lips. "Sobering thought. What about you? Started making plans?"

"I might get out of the game altogether," Smart told him. "I always wanted to run my own business and I've got enough money put aside to do it. I might even take a year off to write a novel."

"Seriously?"

"Why not? It worked for others. I could base it loosely around my own exploits. It's not as if I'm short of material."

"Material is one thing. Talent's another. If you do go through with it though and base a character around me, don't forget to mention that I'm six foot three and built like a Viking god."

"It'll be an action thriller, not fantasy."

Their meals arrived, and they dived in.

"My concern is Tom," Smart said. "If he can't offload the business, he'll have to find work. It's not cheap raising a child, and he doesn't take much of a salary as it is."

"This couldn't have come at a worse time," Sonny agreed. "Hopefully he's managed to put some money aside. I guess we'll know more when we tell him about Naylor jumping ship."

They finished their meal in silence, both aware that a memorable chapter in their lives was about to draw to a close.

CHAPTER 13

Bill Sanders passed through security with barely a nod to the guards, then took the stairs to his office on the second floor. At this early hour, the usually bustling building felt eerily quiet.

Sanders normally arrived shortly after eight each morning, but his sleep the night before had been fitful at best. At three in the morning he'd given up hope of any shuteye and had taken a shower before dressing for work. He'd spent the next hour flicking through the latest report while consuming a morning's worth of coffee.

The journey in had taken only forty minutes—half the time of his normal commute—and he'd spent every moment thinking about one thing. It was the same thing that had kept him up most of the night.

Eva Driscoll.

When she'd first joined the CIA a decade earlier, Sanders had been the director of clandestine services, and like almost every other male—and a couple of females in the department—he'd been captivated by her. At the time, Sanders had been married for fifteen years, and his hair had been nowhere near as gray as it was now. He'd been forty-three years old, in excellent shape and with movie star looks. It was clear from their first meeting that the physical attraction was mutual.

Over the next few months, Sanders had made as many excuses as possible to visit the training facility, all in the hope of catching a glimpse of Driscoll. Her reports had been outstanding, her scores off the charts, and he'd found himself thinking about her every day. Eventually, he found the opportunity to get her alone, and her eyes had danced at his suggestion that she join him at his lake cabin. What followed had been two glorious days and nights in her arms.

Days later, she'd dropped the bombshell.

Using the CIA's own equipment, Driscoll had recorded their love-making. A disk of the footage had been couriered to his office, along with a note, the contents of which remained burned into his memory.

I know how things work. Sometimes assets become expendable, but this one plans on living a long life. Within three months of my death, copies will be sent not only to the mainstream media, but also to several antigovernment bloggers. I only have to fail to check in once each quarter and your hairy ass will be all over the internet. It is in your best interests to keep me alive.

Love,

Eva

Downright fury had eventually been replaced by a grudging respect. Driscoll was sharper than even he'd realized, but her private insurance policy made doing his job almost impossible. When the time had come for Driscoll to cut her teeth, Sanders had made sure she was assigned an easy kill; but as the years wore on, the assignments came with an increasing level of danger. She was soon their number-one resource, their first choice for the riskiest missions. Finding excuses not to send her into the field became progressively more difficult. Every time she left on a new mission, Sanders became a bag of nerves. It was only when she reported in with kill confirmations that he could relax . . .

Until the next termination order hit his desk.

Sanders walked into his office, the lettering on the door advising the unfamiliar that it belonged to the director of the CIA. He powered up his PC and, once through the security protocols, opened her file. At the bottom were the four words he'd been instructed to add the night before, and they affected him as much as Driscoll. Once the sex video hit the Internet, his marriage and career would be over.

A phone chimed and vibrated inside his jacket pocket, and Sanders fished it out and stabbed the connect button. No need to check caller ID; only one person knew the number. "Sanders."

"We need some of your assets to help in finding Driscoll."

The words were like a punch in the gut. To compound his misery, he was now being asked—no, ordered—to help facilitate his own downfall.

"I'm not sure we have anyone available," he said, trying to keep his voice steady. "I'll look into it and get back."

"Make it quick. If you must, postpone other assignments. She's our number-one priority, so I want your best people on this."

"I'll need everything you have on her latest movements," Sanders said.

"They'll be with you in the next few minutes."

The phone went dead in his hand. Sanders slowly replaced it in his pocket, then used a handkerchief to wipe a layer of sweat from his brow. After taking a moment to compose himself, he closed Driscoll's file and opened a list of the assets in his charge. Two agents were waiting their next assignment.

Sanders opened the file on the first, a man who went by the name of Dennis Hacker. Not his real name, but one he used to blend in with the rest of society. His cover was that of freelance writer, which enabled him to work from home, a three-story brownstone in Manhattan.

Sanders had never met him, having moved on from his role in clandestine services before Hacker joined the CIA. Because of this, he ruled him out.

The other name was more familiar. Carl Huff had gone through basic training shortly after Eva Driscoll. His evaluation scores were good—almost as good as Driscoll's. That wasn't surprising, as they'd spent a lot of time in each other's company—so much so that rumors had begun to surface that they were more than just classmates. Thankfully, the gossip was never substantiated, because relationships between assets were strictly forbidden. Any breach would result in immediate expulsion from the program, and it would have been a huge waste to lose two outstanding candidates over a simple case of lust.

The irony of his own actions wasn't lost on Sanders as he tapped his pen on the walnut desk and considered Carl Huff. Given the man's affinity with Driscoll, could he carry out the orders that Sanders would issue? The clock had already started ticking. The ESO would want a response in minutes rather than hours. Given the lack of other options, Sanders looked up Huff's number and dialed.

"Westguard Consultants," the voice said. "Ned Evans speaking."

"Hi, I'm looking for advice regarding pensions for my asset management company."

There was a brief pause as the man digested the coded phrase and fashioned a suitable response. "I'm sorry, that's not something we deal with. I can give you the name of two other companies that might be able to help."

"That won't be necessary. Thank you for your time."

Sanders ended the call. In two hours, Carl Huff would be waiting on the bank of the Potomac just off George Washington Memorial Parkway in Lady Bird Johnson Park. It was only an eight-mile journey from Langley, which gave Bill Sanders plenty of time to respond to his superiors and prepare a file for the man who would deal with Eva Driscoll.

CHAPTER 14

Colback woke with a start as the events of the previous day gatecrashed his dream. He sat up and shielded his eyes from the sun that had crept over the horizon.

Eva was gone and so was her bike. She had even taken the backpack he'd been using as a pillow, which proved how tired he must have been the night before. He got up and relieved himself, all the while reflecting on how things had turned upside down so abruptly. One minute he'd been heading for a steak dinner; now here he was with his dick in his hand, waiting for some shadowy organization to track him down and kill him.

A twig snapped, and Colback spun to face the danger.

"Thanks for the offer," Eva said, looking at his crotch while holding out a disposable cup, "but I prefer coffee first thing in the morning."

Colback turned away and put his dick back in his pants, annoyed at having let her sneak up on him.

"I hope you take it black with no sugar," Eva said.

Colback avoided eye contact as he took the cup. "That's fine."

The coffee was barely warm, but he drank greedily, grateful for the caffeine hit.

"Time to go," she said, heading back down the trail without checking to see if he was following.

Colback followed in her wake and a minute later saw their new transport. "You think that's going to make it to Ohio?"

The Chevy Impala was at least ten years old, judging by the rust patches on the doors and wheel wells and the fading paint job.

"It'll have to do. I wasn't going to blow the entire budget on something we might have to abandon. It runs well enough, so quit moaning."

Eva got behind the wheel. Her backpack was on the seat beside her, and she took a blonde wig from it and used the rearview mirror to ensure it sat properly.

Colback got in beside her and put on his seatbelt.

"There's a cap in the bag," she said. "Put it on. There's also a new T-shirt."

"This one's fine," Colback told her.

"You might think so, soldier, but I have to live with the smell. Besides, it's about changing your appearance. There are cameras all along the highway, and the agencies can feed footage into facial recognition software, so get changed, pull the cap over your eyes, and keep your head down."

"And your wig is going to defeat the software, is it?"

"No," she said, "but this is."

She pulled a pair of joke glasses from her pocket, complete with a large false nose and black mustache.

"You're kidding. Please tell me you're kidding."

"Billions of dollars' worth of technology defeated by a couple of bucks' worth of plastic." Eva smiled. "It's not the perfect solution, but they must have spotted me when we left the underground garage in New York. The makeover didn't work, so hopefully this will."

She started the engine, which caught first time. Within a few minutes they were on the highway heading west, the road and sky both clear.

"This guy we're going to see, Farooq. How do you know you can trust him?"

"He owes me," Eva replied. "He had a family issue and I helped straighten it out."

"That's it?"

"That's the version you're getting," she said, her eyes never leaving the road.

Colback knew Eva well enough by now to realize there was no point in pushing the topic. If she wanted to share details, she would. She'd told him plenty about being Jeff's sibling, but now she was keeping things close to her vest. *A little consistency would be nice . . .*

"We're going to need help," she said a few minutes later. "Our first task is finding out why they want you dead. Once we've done that, we need to get to them before they get to you. Neither of us will be able to get close enough, so we need fresh faces. I'm talking people who are not on any watch lists."

"Any ideas?"

"One," Eva said. "A guy I met ten years ago. If he's still in the business, he'd be a good place to start."

"Still in what business?"

"The British security services. MI5."

Colback laughed. "Seriously? You're going to turn this into an international incident?"

"That's not the plan. I just need him to put me in touch with the right people."

"People like you?" Colback asked.

"If possible. Failing that, anyone with a military background in covert ops."

"I could give you a couple dozen names off the top of my head."

"Nope," Eva said. "Anyone you've ever worked with will be under surveillance. The moment you contact them, they'll be all over us. No, it has to be someone neither of us has any association with. Hopefully my old contact will be able to find the right people."

"Do you want to stop and give him a call?"

"No, we have to get to Farooq first and then we'll see if Andrew is still with MI5."

"Again, pardon the paranoia, but what makes you feel you can trust this Andrew character?"

Eva considered the question momentarily. "As you're never going to meet him, I guess I can tell you. When I was doing my training, one of the assignments was to create a legend. It's basically a fabricated background. I had to pretend to be someone else and see if I could get away with it. The thing is, we're not just talking about using a fake license to buy liquor. My task was to get close to a foreign national who was working for the security services. The harder the assignment, the better the score, so I chose London. MI5 and MI6 are meticulous when it comes to vetting their staff's potential partners. I contacted the local station at the US embassy and got a list of possible candidates, and I went for Andrew Harvey. A few days later, after watching his movements, I met him in a bar. I bumped into him and spilled his drink, bought him another one, and we got talking."

"It was that easy?"

"Hell, no!" Eva chuckled. "I said I needed to use the restroom and left my handbag with him. It contained my driver's license, including an address in London. That was all he needed to start researching me. When he dropped me back at my place, I tried to talk him into coming up for a coffee, but he asked for a raincheck."

Colback's eyes narrowed. "Seriously? He turned you down?"

"Yep. I'd plied him with drink and flirted enough to make a eunuch amorous but he was a professional. We met up three days later, by which time he would have gone through my personal history with a fine-tooth comb. The fact that we were allowed to spend a couple of weeks in bed together meant my legend had held up to the finest scrutiny."

"So you dumped him and came home, is that it?"

"No. Having cultivated a bond, I thought it best to part on friendly terms. I told him my employer was bringing me back to the States for a promotion. I said I didn't want to leave London but that I wouldn't get this opportunity again. I wrote to him a few times and got a few replies, then eventually I told him about a man I'd met, and the letters stopped coming."

Colback could sense regret in her tone, a subtle softening of her persona. "You think he'll help you after all this time?"

Eva shrugged. "As I said, he might not even be with MI5 anymore. People move on. All I can do is try."

"If he is, won't he be listed as one of your contacts?" Colback asked. "I thought you were trying to avoid known associates."

"They would expect me to contact people here in the States, but not someone in England. They'll have the airports screwed down tight and think they have me confined, but there are ways . . ." When she fell silent, Colback guessed it was the end of that conversation.

A couple of hours later, they stopped for gas. Eva—minus her comedy disguise—filled the tank while Colback went into the store to get coffee and Danish to go.

"You drive," Eva said when he returned with their sustenance. "Just follow the highway and keep it under the speed limit. Wake me when we're just outside Akron. I'll take it from there. If you see anything suspicious, give me a shout."

Colback pulled back onto the highway, while Eva donned her Groucho glasses and closed her eyes. She was asleep within minutes.

CHAPTER 15

Tom Gray glanced at his watch as the buildings on the outskirts of San Giovanni in Fiore came into view. He was outside of his best time for the three-mile run, but that had been set two years earlier when the uphill climb hadn't taken such a toll on his aging body. At forty-eight, he remained in great shape, but he would be the first to admit that he was well past his prime.

His pace slackened as he reached the first of the multicolored four-story buildings, and he slowed to a walk as he approached the small *panetteria*, a bakery he frequented each morning.

"*Buongiorno, Tom. Il solito?*"

Every morning the baker's wife asked if he wanted the usual, and his reply was always the same.

"*Buongiorno, signora. Si, per favore—il mio solito.*" He took a seat at one of three tables set up outside the little store, and a minute later, a small espresso was placed in front of him. "Another beautiful day," he said.

"*Come sempre.*"

Not quite always, Gray thought. The weather was much like England. Cold in winter, nice in summer, although here it felt a little more predictable.

It was also quiet.

Gray had always imagined he'd miss the bustle of London, but he was settling into the rural lifestyle nicely. Living a few miles from the small Italian town gave him the perfect excuse to exercise each morning, and the air was the cleanest he'd known.

There were drawbacks though, and Melissa's school fees were the biggest. His daughter had just turned five, and with no English-speaking schools in the area, he'd chosen to pay for private tuition rather than place her in a local Italian-language school. That was eating up a healthy chunk of his income, and with the state of his company's finances, he wasn't in a position to award himself a pay raise. He hoped that when Sonny and Len arrived for their bi-monthly meeting later that day, they'd have a new contract or two to tell him about.

He certainly needed some good news.

Stormont International, the Walmart of the security world, could afford to charge lower rates due to the sheer volume of clients on its books. It seemed that every week he heard of another small operator folding, and Gray feared his own firm would be next.

Perhaps now really was the time to sell up. He'd revisited the option countless times in recent weeks, and the longer he delayed it, the less Minotaur Logistics would be worth. If he could sell it as a going concern, then at least the men working for him might have an income for a few more years, as opposed to nothing if he were forced to dissolve the company.

The trouble was, finding a buyer wouldn't be easy. He'd had to cut his rates to counter Stormont's tactics, so his current contracts barely brought in a million a year. With personnel costs accounting for over 70 percent of that, there was just about enough left to cover office rent, insurance, upkeep of the training facility, and his own salary. Anyone performing due diligence would immediately see the perilous state of the company's finances and walk away.

Gray downed his espresso and resolved to discuss it with Len and Sonny. After all, it would affect them too.

He took his empty cup inside and collected his bag of *cornetti*—similar to croissants but filled with fresh whipped cream.

"Same time tomorrow," he said, and began the brisk walk home. As it was mostly downhill, he made good time, and when he arrived back at the cottage he saw his daughter playing on the swing he'd hung from the branch of an olive tree in the garden.

"Daddy!"

"Good morning, darling. I've got breakfast."

He knelt down and held up the bag, and Melissa ran over to him, snatching it from his grasp before reaching up to deliver a peck on his cheek and disappearing into the house. He followed her inside and found Mina Hatcher preparing the table.

"Can I have orange juice please, Nana?"

"Of course you may, sweetheart," Mina told Melissa.

Mina and her husband Ken were in fact the aunt and uncle of Gray's late wife Vick, but to Melissa they were the grandma and grand-dad she would otherwise have never had. The couple were delighted to take on the role and had jumped at the chance to have Tom and Melissa share their home. In their sixties, the Hatchers seemed to enjoy some young blood around the house.

"Do I smell bacon?" Gray asked.

"If you're ever going to finish that annex, you'll need to build your strength."

The annex had been Gray's idea and had seemed a good one at the time. The three-bedroom cottage, its white plaster walls and terracotta roof typical of the region, seemed to get smaller as Melissa grew. Gray had offered to build an extension onto the side of the house, comprising a bedroom with an en-suite bathroom, a playroom, and a small kitchen area. That would free up one of the upstairs bedrooms for Mina to pursue her cross-stitch hobby.

The problem was, Gray was no builder. Laying bricks one on top of the other was a doddle, but the plumbing and electrical requirements were beyond him. He'd had to hire professionals to complete those aspects of the work.

Yet more expense.

"I'll have the south and east walls finished by the end of the week," Gray promised.

Then it's just two more walls, the roof, final-fit electrics, plastering, windows, doors . . .

Next time, Gray, keep your big mouth shut.

He ate his fill of bacon, eggs, and toast, then supervised Melissa as she brushed her teeth and combed her hair in preparation for another day in school. Gray usually cycled to the private lessons with his daughter, but as Mina was heading into town, she offered to give Melissa a lift.

Once the girls had left, Ken went out to tend to his garden while Gray donned a sun hat and began mixing mortar.

"You didn't have to get dressed up, especially for us." Sonny Baines grinned as he stepped out of the rental car. "Still not finished, I see. What has it been, three years?"

"Six months," Gray said, removing his gloves and shaking hands.

Len Smart, Gray noticed, didn't seem so jovial.

"I'm guessing you're not here to bring me good news."

"We lost Naylor Resources."

A knot grew in Gray's stomach. Instead of landing some new fish, he'd lost his whale. "Do I need to ask why?"

"Not really," Smart said.

Gray led them indoors and they took a seat at the kitchen table while he sought refreshments. He returned from the refrigerator with a six-pack of beer. "I was hoping to use these for a celebration, but we might as well drown our sorrows. How bad is it?"

Smart took some papers from his leather briefcase and laid them before Gray. "As of next month, when the Naylor contract ends, we'll be running at a loss. Unless we manage to land a replacement, the money in the bank will run out at the start of next year. That's the rose-tinted version. If we lose another client, we've probably got until November, and two more contracts are coming up for renewal."

Gray opened a can of Peroni and took a long drink. "Thanks for not sugarcoating it."

"I'm afraid that's the ultra-sweet version," Smart said. "I spoke to the two companies whose contracts are about to expire. The Oman job is ours for another year, but the telecoms outfit in Iraq received a Stormont prospectus and they're considering their options."

It wasn't as if he could lay people off to stave off the inevitable. Apart from the three men around the table, the only other full-time employee was Gill, their receptionist. All the men doing the security work were freelance, hired on when contracts came in.

Gray stood and walked over to the sink, staring out of the kitchen window as if inspiration lay in the grounds of the smallholding.

It didn't.

The moment he'd been dreading had arrived, and it was time to face facts. "I've no choice. I have to sell up," he said, his eyes still on the olive trees outside.

"We expected as much," Sonny said. "Want us to put the word out when we get back to London?"

Gray returned to his seat. "If you could, that would be great. I guessed this day might eventually come, so I asked my accountant to put the feelers out. I haven't heard from him, but I'll follow up later today."

"No worries," Smart said. "I'll get in touch with Hereford and see if anyone is interested. Private security is the natural progression after leaving Two-Two, and hopefully someone coming to the end of their stint will want to take it on."

"Thanks," Gray said. "Be honest with them though. Let them know it's not going to be easy. The last thing I want to do is screw over one of our own."

"Of course."

"So, what about you guys?" Len and Sonny had been uppermost in Gray's mind over the last few weeks, and leaving them without an income was the main reason he'd delayed the inevitable.

"Len here reckons he's the new Mickey Spillane. He's gonna be a rich and famous author."

"Spillane wrote American crime thrillers, you philistine. Besides, I haven't decided if I'm going to write anything yet."

"You should," Gray said, finishing off his beer. "Better you than Sonny, anyway."

Laughter broke the tension, and the men chatted about which of their exploits should be included in Smart's upcoming masterpiece, but the conversation inevitably returned to the subject of finances.

"I can't remember the last time I had to worry about money," Gray told them, swigging his beer. "It isn't a nice feeling."

"You should have written your autobiography when it was fresh in people's minds," Len said. "That would have set you up for life."

They were interrupted by Mina, who stuck her head into the kitchen. "I'm going to pick Melissa up. Want anything from town while I'm there?"

Gray looked at his friends and knew there was only one thing they needed. "A few more beers wouldn't go amiss."

CHAPTER 16

A pair of sea birds flitted across the water before arcing away toward the Washington Monument that dominated the far shore of the Potomac. Bill Sanders watched their flight until they were dots on the horizon, then turned his attention to the foot traffic on Mount Vernon Trail. From his bench near the Merchant Marine Memorial, he scanned the joggers and walkers for signs of the operative. He was looking for someone a shade under six feet tall, with short black hair and Latino features.

Carl Huff arrived a minute early. He was wearing beige chinos and a shirt with the top two buttons undone, revealing a tanned chest. He took a seat next to Sanders, who was pretending to read a newspaper.

"Since when does the director personally issue new assignments?" the agent asked, adjusting his Ray-Bans.

"Since it became necessary. I trust you remember Eva Driscoll."

A smile crept onto Huff's face. "She's not the type you forget. Let me guess. She's botched a job and you need me to pick up the pieces."

"Hardly. I've been instructed to put a kill order on her."

Huff's face changed immediately. Sanders had trouble reading the new expression, which was one of the reasons why Huff was so good at his job. One minute he could be radiating ambivalence, then a second later he was sticking a knife through your eye socket.

"It's a shame," Huff said finally. "She was good."

"She's the best, so don't underestimate her."

Sanders was still unsure as to whether or not Huff would follow the instructions in the envelope nestled inside his jacket pocket, but he had to get the ball rolling or the next name on the kill list could be his own. The trouble was, he was still unsure about Huff's feelings for Driscoll. A lot depended on whether the rumors about the pair that had circulated a decade earlier were true or not.

"Is this the first time you've had to take out one of your own?" Huff asked.

"Not personally, no, but I've given the order before." *Which probably explains why Driscoll took out her insurance policy*, Sanders thought. "Twelve years ago, an operative was tasked with taking out a woman. He was waiting for her outside her home in the boondocks when she came out with her daughter. The kid was just a few years old. Blonde hair in a ponytail, waddling to the car with her schoolbag. The operative couldn't do it. He was supposed to follow her and run her car off the mountain road, but instead he got out and told her that she'd been marked for elimination. He said he'd help her to escape and start a new life. Of course, the woman didn't believe him. Who would?"

"So what happened to them?"

"The woman went straight to the police and told them about the crazy man who'd turned up at her home. The moment the complaint was recorded on the police computer, we knew about it. That night, her house mysteriously burned down, killing everyone inside."

"And the operative?"

"After we got his side of the story—which I believe took several painful hours—he was buried at sea."

"He must have been new to the job."

"He was. It was his third and last assignment."

Huff nodded ruefully. "And Driscoll? I take it she knows she's being hunted."

"She does."

"That makes it tricky. She's going to be on her guard, especially when she sees a familiar face."

"That's what I was saying. If you're not up to the job, tell me now and I'll find someone else."

"I can handle it," Huff said. "I don't suppose you're going to tell me why she's marked for termination?"

Sanders hoped his silence answered the question. In the majority of cases, he himself had no idea why a person had to be eliminated. The orders came down from the ESO and his job was to provide the assets, period. A couple of times he'd been shown the bigger picture, but that had been some time ago, before the new chairman had been selected. These days, the most he was given was a name and a photograph.

A small sailboat passed by, a father taking his son out and teaching him the ropes. Sanders himself had never had children, one of the few regrets in his life. They'd tried, but his wife's body was an inhospitable environment, according to the specialists they'd seen. The idea of adoption had never sat well with him or his wife, so they'd spent their lives alone. Christmas and Thanksgiving became particularly tough times. Sanders wondered if the lack of children had been one of the reasons for his dalliance with Driscoll. She hadn't been the first, but she was certainly the last.

"Is anyone else involved in the hunt?" Huff asked.

Sanders took the envelope from his jacket and handed it over. "The details are in there. Your contact is Anton West over at Homeland Security. They got first bite at the apple but blew it, which is why you're here. West will update you on the situation as it stands."

"Am I expected to follow his orders?"

"No, you're expected to follow mine. Everything you need to know is in there, including my direct line. Keep me updated on your progress."

Sanders stood as Huff tucked the envelope in his pocket. His future was now in the hands of a killer, and there was no turning back.

CHAPTER 17

Colback nudged Eva awake as they hit the outskirts of Akron, Ohio. She had been sleeping soundly since the last pit stop, leaving him alone with his thoughts, which had mostly been about his tours in Afghanistan with Jeff Driscoll, Danny Bukowitz, and Ron Elphick.

His team had spent a total of twenty-six months in-country, with Colback serving as an 18 Bravo, the designation for a weapons specialist within an Operational Detachment Alpha. They had served in the 3rd Battalion, 3rd Group, tasked with various unconventional warfare missions in the Middle East area of operations.

Colback could recall every assignment they'd taken part in. Most were routine, but there had been plenty of fierce engagements too. They'd captured two Taliban warlords and killed four others, and there had been a few rescue missions, one of which hadn't been successful. Could that be the reason someone high up in the political hierarchy wanted to take them out? Was the dead soldier somehow related to one of these mysterious figures, and they were now seeking revenge?

It was a tenuous link at best. Colback and his team had risked their lives to pull out the infantryman, but he'd been dead for at least an hour before they arrived. After-action reports had laid no blame at their feet. Still, it was all he could think of.

"Take the next exit," Eva said, stretching in her seat. "Find a diner. I'm famished."

"I may have the reason they're after me," Colback told her. "It's not much, but it's all I've got."

"Let's hear it."

"It was a rescue mission. A unit from the 1st Battalion, 32nd Infantry Regiment had been caught in an ambush and lost contact with one of their men, a Private Leo Hurwitz. They sent up a drone that tracked the Taliban to a nearby village and we went in just after nightfall. We found Hurwitz, but he was already dead. Could someone close to the kid blame us for not bringing him home alive?"

Eva considered it, her face impassive. "Nothing else you can think of?"

"That's the only thing that makes sense. The rest of the time was spent killing Taliban or guarding villages. Nothing to create enemies stateside."

"I'll get Farooq to dig up what he can on Hurwitz."

Colback looked over at her. "Is this where you share your brilliant plan, or are you going to keep me in the dark?"

"Pull in here and get some gas," she said, effectively answering his question.

Colback turned into the gas station and filled the tank while Eva remained in the car. Once he'd paid cash, he got back in but didn't start the engine.

"If we're going to work together, you're going to have to start trusting me," he said, gripping the steering wheel.

"Likewise," she replied.

Colback gave her a look that said they weren't moving until she opened up.

"Okay, here's what we're going to do. We'll find somewhere to eat, then I'll drive us to New Lexington, where we'll hole up until late. I'll send him a message and we'll go see him. Is that okay with you?"

"You're just going to drive up to his house while they're watching?"

"No, that would be plain dumb. My plan is subtler and involves a pizza delivery."

Driscoll expanded, and a couple of minutes later, Colback was smiling as he cruised the streets in search of a suitable place to eat.

They settled on an old-style diner. Colback parked around the back with the car's nose pointing toward the exit, just in case they needed to leave in a hurry. Inside the diner, they took a seat in a booth near the restroom. Colback saw no CCTV but decided against removing his cap.

A waitress sporting a beehive and a mouth full of chewing gum stood at their table and reeled off the specials with all the enthusiasm she could muster, which wasn't a great deal.

"I'll have coffee, a burger—hold the pickle—extra fries, and a slice of apple pie."

"Just coffee and pie for me," Colback said.

"You should eat more," Eva said once the waitress had retreated to the kitchen. "Things are going to move quickly from here on in."

"I filled up with potato chips while you were sleeping."

"Still, you never know when we'll get another chance. I'm hoping for a clean getaway tonight, but things don't always go as planned."

She took out her phone and opened a browser window. After a couple of minutes tapping at the virtual keyboard, she put it back in her pocket. "The message is ready to go. I'm not going to send it now because I don't want to give the bad guys too much notice, otherwise New Lexington will be crawling with 'em."

"Don't make that face of yours, but I have another question. If that's a burner phone, how can you send an encoded message to Farooq?"

Eva couldn't help herself and her frustration showed. "The app can be downloaded from a Web server he manages. The encryption is built in, so all I have to do is type in the Web address and enter my password and it downloads automatically."

"But what if someone else goes to the website and downloads it?"

Alan McDermott

"They won't," Driscoll said. "It's not your typical Web address like Google.com. This is a subdomain of an IP address. You won't find it in any search engine, and the chances of anyone typing the correct sequence of numbers and letters into a browser are infinitesimally small."

"But let's say someone did trip across it," Colback persisted.

"They'll just see a page that says the site is under development. One of the letters in the word is a clickable link to the login page, but once you get there you've only got thirty seconds to enter a valid password. If you don't, a worm is installed on your device, be it a phone or computer. That gives Farooq complete access, and if it's on a network, the whole thing is compromised."

"Sounds like he's got it all thought out. I'm guessing he's not a janitor with the CIA."

"He's no longer with them. They kicked him out a couple of years ago. Biggest mistake they ever made, but it's our gain."

"Why get rid of him if he's so good?"

"Because his supervisor was a useless prick," Eva said. "Whenever Farooq came up with a brilliant idea, his boss kicked it upstairs with his name all over it. Farooq had enough and went over the guy's head, but then got shit-canned on a trumped-up charge of drinking at work. Sure, he might have turned up hungover a few times, but it never affected his performance. They did a random inspection one day and found half a bottle of whiskey in his desk drawer. He was breathalyzed and tossed out of the building that same day."

"Is he still on the sauce?" Colback asked. "That could be a problem."

"He's been sober for two years. I helped clean him up and now he's working freelance as a security analyst."

"If he's out of the CIA, how does that help us?"

Eva smiled. "Because, like me, he realized that his usefulness had a finite shelf life. He'd been thinking of going solo for some time, and nothing would give him an edge in an ultracompetitive field than access to the CIA mainframe, so he created a back door."

"Can't they trace those?"

"Not this one," Eva assured him. "Farooq wrote all the trace protocols years ago, and it would be a huge task to update them all. If you're going to navigate a minefield, it helps if you're the one who laid the mines."

The waitress brought their order, and Eva tucked into a burger loaded with two juicy patties.

Colback picked at his pie as he watched her devour her food. Even with a mouth full of meat, she was the most captivating creature he'd ever seen. In another lifetime, he might have made a move on her . . .

"I've seen that look before, mister," she said. "Don't even think about it."

Colback blushed and turned away, staring out of the window in an effort to hide his embarrassment.

Eva wiped her hands and handed him her phone. "If you're not going to eat, make yourself useful. Look for pizza delivery joints in New Lexington."

Colback took the phone and began his search. He soon had a long list to choose from and passed it back to her. "There're dozens. Take your pick."

Eva zoomed in on the area around Farooq's house. "Three within a couple of miles of his home, all open late. Hopefully one of them will be suitable."

Twenty minutes later, they paid cash and left the standard tip, so as to remain nondescript in the waitress's memory. Eva took the wheel as the sun headed for the horizon. It would be dark within the hour.

~

"He looks ideal," Colback said, pointing to the delivery guy who had just left the pizzeria laden with boxes. "He's the right height and shape."

"It's about time," Eva replied. This was the third outlet they'd visited in the hope of finding someone who was enough of a match to one of them in physique. The previous two pizza joints employed young white males as delivery drivers, likely college kids supplementing their tuition. Now, they finally had an athletic-looking African American who could be mistaken for Colback from a distance. She would have preferred to use a white female, but this would have to do.

"I'll be right back," Eva said, and got out of the car, which was parked thirty yards from Joe's Pizza Emporium. She jogged over to Colback's doppelgänger as he loaded his deliveries onto a rack on the back of his moped.

"Hey."

The man turned, and his face lit up at the sight before him. "Hey to you too."

She smiled. "I was wondering, are they looking for help here . . . ?"

He stuck out a hand. "I'm Orlando, but my friends call me Lanny."

"I'm Sue," Eva said, shaking his hand. "So, are they hiring?"

"Nah, sorry. Joe just took on a new waitress and he's already got three delivery guys. It's a shame. If I got to look at something as fine as you all day, it'd make coming to work worthwhile."

Eva gave him a pout, then shrugged. "Some you win. Hope to see you around, Lanny."

She walked back down the street, knowing Lanny's eyes would be on her swaying hips every step of the way. She didn't stop at the car, in case he took note of the plates. Instead, she walked around the corner and disappeared out of sight.

Two minutes later, Orlando rode past on the way to his first delivery. Eva waited until he was out of sight, then ran back to the store and went inside.

A man in his fifties stood behind the counter and gave her a practiced smile. "Welcome to Joe's. What can I get you?"

"I'd like to place an order for delivery."

"If you care to wait, we can have a pizza ready in fifteen minutes."

"Delivery would be better. My friends and I are having a party and don't need it until later." She chose three varieties from the menu and asked if they could be delivered at midnight.

"Sure. That'll be forty-five bucks."

Eva handed over a fifty. "Can you please ask Lanny to bring them?"

"Sorry, he clocks off at eleven."

She gave him a wink and another twenty. "Tell him it's for Sue and this is part of his tip. He'll get more when he turns up."

Joe gave her a knowing look as he took the money. "What's the address?"

She gave him Farooq's home details, then took her phone from her pocket as she walked back to the car. She opened the messaging app and hit Send on the missive she'd composed earlier.

"We're all set," she told Colback as she got in and started the engine. "Let's just hope it plays out the way it's supposed to."

CHAPTER 18

Farooq Naser was about to turn in for the night when the cell phone on his desk chirped. The screen lit up and he immediately recognized the Taurus logo. It was the messaging app he'd created a few years earlier, and only a handful of people knew of its existence.

He knew it had to be Eva Driscoll before he looked at the message. The phone call he'd received from the CIA earlier in the day had warned him that she might be in touch, and they'd also spelled out the consequences of not reporting any contact.

Throughout the day, he'd wondered what she could possibly have done to incur the CIA's wrath. As far as he was concerned, Eva was as patriotic as they came. Her job was her life and she wouldn't jeopardize it for anything.

Farooq picked up the phone and walked to the window, easing the curtain aside and peering out through the one-inch gap. The car he'd spotted at lunchtime was still there, with both men still sitting inside. They were obviously waiting for Eva to turn up. Her and Rees Colback—the one they'd called a terrorist.

After hours of deliberation, Farooq had decided that Eva at least deserved to have him hear her side of the story before he called the CIA. He opened the notification window on his phone and read her message.

It consisted of three paragraphs. The first explained why the CIA had turned on her. The second told him what she required of him. The last confirmed that she was on her way and gave him instructions to follow.

He read the message twice. It didn't ask for a reply, so he didn't send one. Instead, he sat back and stared at the landline. He knew the CIA protocols well. They would have detected the data package hitting his phone and would probably be trying to decrypt the message at that very moment. That they would fail was a given, but they'd suspect it came from Eva and would be expecting a call from him.

It all boiled down to one simple question: Who was he going to betray? Eva, who had risked her career to help his sister, or the CIA, who had enough assets to hunt him down and kill him a hundred times over?

Farooq took a deep breath, held it for a few seconds, then let it out slowly. He picked up the landline and dialed the number he'd been given.

"West."

"It's Farooq Naser. Eva Driscoll has been in touch. She'll be here in an hour."

"Stay where you are. I'll route my men into position."

"No. If she walks into a trap, she'll know I turned her in. I'll be the first person she kills. Even if she doesn't, there's bound to be shooting. I don't want to be caught in the crossfire. I'm clearing out. You can tell me when it's all over."

Silence greeted his outburst and Farooq worried that his request would be denied. The last thing he wanted was to be there when West's men turned up.

"Okay," West said at last. "But stay close. We want to debrief you on the method of contact."

As Farooq had expected, they'd intercepted Eva's message but were unable to crack the built-in algorithm.

"Just tell your men not to destroy my place. And please let the goons in the car outside my house know that I'm leaving. I don't want them getting trigger-happy."

"I'll warn them," West promised. "Is Driscoll coming alone?"

"I've got no idea. She just said I should expect a pizza delivery. I'd assume she knows your men are here waiting for her."

"You've done the right thing, Farooq. The Agency won't forget it. Just remember to leave the lights on when you go. I want her to think you're still home."

Farooq put the phone down, disgusted by West's false reassurances. If the CIA were so caring, they wouldn't have canned him two years earlier. No, any employer worth their salt would have helped him battle his alcohol addiction rather than tossing him aside after years of loyal service.

Eva hadn't forsaken him.

She'd helped fund his stay in the recovery clinic and visited every couple of days for three months. When he finally got clean, his debt to her had doubled.

This had been his chance to repay her.

With a heavy heart, Farooq began packing a go bag: in went his laptop, an address book written in a code only he could understand, a change of clothes, and several flash drives containing the tools of his trade.

Three minutes later, he wheeled his bicycle out the front door. The occupants of the SUV across the street watched him leave, but he was pleased to see them remain inside.

With one last look back at his house, he threw a leg over the bike's frame and began pedaling.

～

"I want all assets rerouted to New Lexington immediately!"

The operatives sprang into action the moment they heard West bark his command. All of the teams in the region were given their new orders and the geostationary satellite was instructed to adjust its camera to focus on Farooq Naser's home.

West called Sanders's man Carl Huff personally to update him on the situation. He knew Huff's kind, and they rarely liked to work as part of a team. West wasn't one to pander to others, but having Huff on his side was a huge bonus. It wouldn't hurt to give him free rein, especially since he knew how Driscoll operated. Teaming Huff up with his own men would only be counterproductive.

"Sir, Eagle Four reports movement."

West turned to the screen and saw Naser mounting his bicycle. "Let him go. Stay on the house."

"Yes, sir. Eagle Three reports ETA two hours. Eagle One and Eagle Two are three hours out."

"Tell them to haul ass." He needed the extra bodies. Although it would have been nice to have the Ohio State Police set up a five-mile cordon around Naser's home, keeping the operation covert took precedence. Besides, he had two armed men on the scene and more on the way.

It should be enough.

"We've found her," West told Huff when the call connected. "She's in New Lexington, Ohio. We expect her to be at Farooq Naser's home within the hour. How close are you?"

"Two hours out. How'd you find her?"

West explained how Naser had called in the contact and had fled the house in advance of her arrival. "We're expecting her to masquerade as a pizza delivery person."

It took Huff some time to respond to that. "Tell your men to be on their guard. She's good."

"Yeah, I keep hearing that. Don't worry, we can handle her."

"Try not to kill anyone before I get there. The director would like to take her in alive."

"That's up to her," West replied. "My orders come from another source."

"I appreciate that, but there's no harm in making a friend of Sanders."

The call ended, leaving West to contemplate the options. It didn't take long. Compared to the ESO, Sanders was merely another grunt destined to carry out the bidding of others. Earning his friendship would do squat for West's career prospects.

West walked over to the nearest operative. "Open a channel to Eagle Four."

"Done."

"Eagle Four, this is Nest. We need both of them, understood?"

"Roger that, Nest."

"When you have positive IDs, take 'em out."

CHAPTER 19

"Are you sure he's going to come?"

"He'll be here," Eva told Colback, although as the minutes ticked by, she was beginning to wonder if her faith in Farooq had been well placed.

Of course it is, she told herself, but it hadn't stopped her taking precautions. From where she sat, she could see down the street to the gas station. If any suspicious vehicles pulled up nearby, she would know that Farooq had betrayed her.

"Wait! That could be him."

Eva saw the tall, slender man arrive on the bicycle.

"It's him," she confirmed.

"Aren't you going to pick him up?"

"Soon. First I want to see if he was followed."

They waited for five minutes before Eva started the car. If anyone were tailing Farooq, she'd have seen them by now.

She drove to the gas station and stopped just long enough for Farooq to climb into the back seat. A CCTV camera was pointing at the car, but she'd expected as much. By the time their pursuers realized Farooq had tricked them, and tracked him to this location, running the license plates would be futile.

"You never mentioned having company," a nervous Farooq said as he eyed Colback in the front passenger seat.

"Farooq, meet Rees. Rees, Farooq."

The men shook hands but Farooq remained wary. "So, now that I've thrown my life away, what do you need?"

"Aren't you going to ask what we're supposed to have done?" Colback asked, as Eva pulled away.

"It'd probably be a lie," Farooq said. "I know how these people work." He looked at Eva. "So, what do you need?"

"A few things. First, everything you can find on a soldier named Leo Hurwitz. Rees will fill you in. And by the way: I'm really sorry I dragged you into this."

"It's the business we work in. Plus, I owe you."

He left it at that as he took the laptop from his bag and connected it to his phone. Colback gave him details of Hurwitz's unit and the date of his death. "Specifically, we're looking for a connection to anyone in high office."

After a few minutes, Farooq shook his head. "I checked the CIA, FBI, Homeland Security, and Pentagon databases. Hurwitz was the only child of Edwin and Mary Hurwitz, from Brady, Texas. Edwin died earlier this year; Mary is a retired waitress."

Colback slapped the dashboard. "Damnit."

"If you tell me what this is about, I might be able to help," Farooq offered.

It took Eva twenty minutes to recap the events of the last few days, during which time Farooq's eyes seldom left his laptop screen.

"In addition to finding out why someone wants to kill Colback and the rest of his team, I need you to be our eyes and ears. If their satellite is watching us, I need to know about it. I'd have done it myself, but my access will have been locked down by now."

"I can do better than that," Farooq said. "How does access to their command center sound?"

"You're shitting me."

"Nope. Each bureau has its own self-contained network, but in order to share data and interrogate each other's databases they created bridges. Linked information highways. All I need to do is find out which terminals are monitoring the satellite data feed over New Lexington and gain access to the LAN. Once I'm in, I can deploy Sonia."

"Sonia?" Colback asked.

"He gives all of his worms women's names," Eva explained. "Tell us what she does."

"All of the agencies use digital signals to communicate with people in the field. The person's voice feeds into a computer and gets scrambled before being sent over the air. This prevents anyone listening in. What Sonia does is copy the voice message before encryption and convert it to text. She also intercepts incoming transmissions. We'll know everything they say to each other."

"We can stay one step ahead of them forever," said Colback, smiling for the first time in days, it seemed.

"Not really," said Eva. "If we evade them enough times, they'll realize their comms are compromised. Once they start digging, they'll find Sonia. Besides, running isn't the answer. We have to make them call off the chase."

"How do you plan to do that?" Farooq asked.

"We find out who ordered the hits on Rees's team and take them out. Unfortunately, that's not the kind of thing they record on their systems."

"We have a starting point," Farooq told her. "The man I spoke to was called West. He must have received orders from someone. Give me a minute to check the NSA database for all calls to and from his cell phone."

It took longer than promised but Farooq soon had a list of numbers on his screen. "I've got a couple of phones registered to Homeland Security, one unregistered cell, and one blocked number from West's cell phone."

"Blocked?"

"The number wasn't recorded on the NSA database. Trust me, they record everything, so it must take some serious pull to have your number withheld. It must be the ESO."

"That doesn't do us much good," said Colback.

"Maybe it does," said Eva. "Can you pinpoint West's location?" she asked Farooq.

"Sure, though I'm telling you now, it's Henry Langton. He's the head of the ESO."

"You've been saying that for the last few years and I keep telling you, you read too many conspiracy theory blogs. Langton is a rich recluse, nothing more. No one bent on sucking the population dry would donate hundreds of millions to charitable causes like he does."

"A smoke screen, nothing more."

Eva was bored with the conversation. "Just pull West's record in the personnel files. We need to know what he looks like."

"Sounds like you plan to get up close and personal with him."

"Unless you can hack into his phone, it might be our only option. The NSA didn't record the blocked number but it'll be in his cell's log."

Farooq's fingers went to work, but he ended up shaking his head. "No way in. You'll need the handset."

"Then find out where he is. Once you've done that, check the CIA database for an Andrew Harvey."

They were now on US-22, with a full tank and clear roads ahead. As Farooq worked his magic, Colback asked Eva what her immediate plans were.

"If Harvey's still with MI5, I'll need a new look and fake passport. If not, we'll need to recruit some people locally. Fortunately, I can find both in Tennessee."

"Why do you need a new look to call this Harvey guy?"

"I don't. I'm going to meet him."

Colback shifted in his seat to face her. "You're going to fly to England? The most wanted fugitive in the United States is going to walk into an airport and get on a plane? Are you crazy?"

"A little, but that's another story. Don't worry, I've done this before."

Colback was markedly uncomfortable with the idea. "What about us?" he asked, flicking a hand between himself and Farooq. "What if you don't make it?"

"I'll be back. In the meantime, just lie low. I'll be gone a couple of days at the most. Anyway, it's all moot if Andrew's no longer with MI5."

"He is," Farooq announced. "I got into the station account at the US embassy in London. Andrew Harvey, age forty-one, engaged to Sarah Louise Thompson, also with MI5. They have a daughter, Alana, four months old. Their wedding is planned for next May. I've got an address for the place they rent in Notting Hill."

"Then I'm heading to London," Eva said. "The fact that they have a child together gives me an edge."

"You're not going to threaten her, are you?"

Eva looked at Farooq in the rearview mirror. "I'm hurt that you'd suggest such a thing. No, just a little emotional blackmail."

"Good," said Farooq. "You can save the torture for Anton West. He's currently in Homeland Security's Bethesda office. Or you could take him at his home in Olney."

"You're sure that's the West who contacted you?"

"One hundred percent. I checked a log of his calls and matched the voice to the one I spoke to. It's him."

Driscoll checked her mirror but the road behind was clear. "I was going to ask you to run some mug shots of the people who attacked my place, but there's no need now. Rees, keep thinking about why you and your teammates needed killing. Farooq, start by pulling their files and checking for recent entries."

"Already got them open," Farooq said. "The only entry in the last few weeks was on Ron Elphick's record. It mentions the death of Adrian Holmes. Just going to cross-reference the files . . ."

"And?" Colback asked.

"Holmes is a journalist. Or was. Worked for the *Washington Post* until three years ago, then quit to set up his own website. Apparently, the *Post* wasn't keen to run his stories as they got a little close to the truth. His forte was exposing illegal activities within the government. Looks like he chased one story too many. He fell asleep in his bathtub and drowned."

"He didn't fall asleep," Eva said. "He was forced to ingest a muscle relaxant that made it impossible to move. That's why there were no signs of a struggle."

"How could you possibly know that?"

"Because I made him swallow it. He was my most recent hit."

"Oh, that's just great," groaned Colback. "We finally get a lead and *you* killed him?"

"It's what I do," Eva said. "I had no way of knowing he'd end up being connected to Jeff's murder."

"Then please tell me you got information out of him first."

"That wasn't part of the mission," she told him as she tried to control her anger. It was one thing to kill her brother, but to use her to obfuscate the trail was beyond contempt. Her last shreds of loyalty to the CIA evaporated as she gripped the wheel tightly. "Find the connection between Elphick and Holmes. And we're going to need money. Lots of it."

"Cash isn't a problem. Just tell me how much you need."

"More than you've managed to save over the years," Eva said. "I'm thinking half a million if we're to recruit quality help."

"I can get you ten times as much in the next few minutes. Just tell me where to send it."

"What're you gonna do," Colback said, "cash in your 401(k)?"

"Not quite," Farooq answered, without a trace of humor. "You ever heard of Air America?"

"The movie?"

"Well, yeah, that was based loosely on true events. Actually, it was an airline set up by the US government in 1950 as a dummy corporation for CIA operations in China, but it's mostly remembered for transporting opium from Laos. The Hmong population needed the hard currency the poppy harvest brought in, but some in the CIA wanted their own slice of the action. More and more of the drug made its way stateside, and once the hierarchy saw the profits to be made, it soon became their number-one source of income. They created a network of front companies to hold the cash."

"Those things still exist today?" asked Colback.

"Not only the companies, but the money. I have a list of every bank account linked to the front organizations and I've been working on a program that will siphon off a couple of hundred dollars a week from each company—and there are over a hundred of them—but I'm months away from finishing it. The plan was to fund my retirement and I needed to make the money untraceable. Obviously, we don't have time for stealth now. Let me know how much you need and it'll be in your account in minutes."

"How much are we talking about?" Colback asked.

"If you want it all, about seven billion dollars, but big withdrawals will trigger alarms. I could take fifty grand from each account and no one would know until they got their bank statements."

"Then do it." Eva gave him the number for the Cayman account that she'd committed to memory. "I've got a feeling we'll be on the run for the rest of our lives, so get as much as you can."

Farooq worked in silence for a few minutes, then hit the Enter key with a flourish. "I've set it on a loop. It'll request a transfer of fifty grand from every company, and once it's done that it'll start again. Let's see . . . okay, three of them requested further verification . . . make that four."

He watched the screen as the results came in, and it didn't take long for the program to finish running its first iteration. "Okay, seventeen refused the request, but we managed to net $4.6 million. It's going back to try them all again."

"And you're sure it can't be traced?" Colback asked.

"Not a chance. I set up a string of bank accounts all around the world, with instructions to forward the money as soon as it arrives. The money passes through half a dozen countries that have no disclosure agreement with the United States and then on to Eva's bank."

"How are we doing now?" she asked a few minutes later.

"One sec . . . almost done . . . $50.3 million. They've all refused further withdrawals, so that's all we're gonna get."

"It's enough for now. Rees, get some sleep. I need Farooq to dig up what he can on Holmes. I'm sure he's the connection we've been looking for."

CHAPTER 20

"I spy, with my little eye, something beginning with D."

"Knock it off, Burke. They'll be here any minute."

Danny Castleton couldn't believe he'd been teamed up with Paul Burke. Of all the men in the unit, he'd got the one with the immature sense of humor, and Burke's shtick had begun grating on his nerves.

"Lighten up, Cass."

"Who the fuck shortens Castleton to Cass? Cass is a fucking girl's name."

"Jeez, someone hasn't gotten laid in a while."

Castleton felt the Glock nestled in his shoulder holster. The temptation to whip it out and shoot his companion between the eyes was almost too much to resist.

"Hey! That's gotta be him."

Castleton looked to where Burke was pointing and saw the large figure pull up outside Naser's house on a moped.

"Nest, this is Eagle Four. We have eyes on Colback. No sign of Driscoll."

"Copy. Do not move in until you see her."

"Roger that."

Burke was suddenly all business. "She's not gonna show," he said. "I bet you a hundred bucks she's waiting for Colback to take Farooq to her."

"Of course she is, you moron."

Both men watched as Colback got off the bike and carried the pizzas to the house. He rang the bell. After a few moments, he moved to a window and peered in, then shook his head and took out his cell phone.

"He's got to be calling her," Castleton said. "Let Nest know. They might be able to intercept the call."

Before Burke could get on the radio, Colback put the pizza boxes on the porch and returned to his bike.

"Too late. We'll have to follow him."

Castleton waited until the moped had rounded the corner, then fired up the engine and set off in pursuit.

The lack of late-night traffic on the road made it difficult to get close to the subject. Castleton was forced to hang back and let the rider open up a lead while Burke kept West updated. "We're heading north on South Main Street, just crossed the railway tracks. We're a hundred yards behind the motorcycle."

A burst of static preceded West's reply. "Stay on him. Other units are closing in. ETA . . . twenty minutes."

They followed the bike through the center of town. Colback seemed to be in no particular hurry, sticking to the speed limit and even obeying stop signs at this hour.

A few minutes later, they found themselves in a residential area off Carroll Street. The bike passed several one-story buildings before pulling up next to one of the white dwellings.

Castleton stopped the car and killed the lights. He and Burke watched the suspect walk into the house and turn the light on in the living area.

"She must be in there," Burke said. "I say we go in."

"No, we wait for backup."

"You're such a pussy. There's two of them and two of us."

Castleton ignored him and got on the radio. "Nest, Eagle Four. We followed the suspect to an address north of town. He's inside the house. We suspect Driscoll's in there too."

He gave West the address, then waited for instructions.

"One of you go around the back in case they try to leave, but do not enter the house until the other teams arrive. Is that understood?"

"Copy."

"I'll cover the rear," Burke said, getting out of the car before Castleton could object.

There were no fences marking out the plots, so Burke was able to walk between two houses and make his way to the back of the building. He'd been out of sight for just a few seconds when West came on the radio.

"Did you get a good visual on Colback?" the boss asked Castleton.

"No, not up close, but who else could it be?"

"The registered owner of that property is one Orlando Simmons. African-American, age twenty-six, weighs 220. Sound like the guy you saw?"

"Affirmative," Castleton replied, not liking where the conversation was going.

"He works as a delivery driver at a pizza joint. Get in there and get a confirmed visual—now!"

Castleton sent acknowledgment and sprang out of the car. He raced to the front of the house, drawing his weapon as he ran. At the front door, he radioed Burke and told him to go in hard on the count of three.

Castleton took a deep breath, then kicked in the door and rushed into the room, his weapon searching for a target. Simmons was on the couch holding a bag of potato chips while a movie played on the TV mounted on the opposite wall. The deliveryman dropped the bag and raised his hands. "Hey, man, I ain't got nothing worth stealing. There's just a few bucks in my wallet over there on the table. Take it."

Castleton was joined by Burke, who had come through the kitchen door.

"It's not him," Castleton said. He'd studied Colback's picture enough times that day to know he was looking at the wrong man.

"Why were you delivering pizza to the place on Fowler?" Burke asked.

"It's my job. I deliver pizza."

"Yeah, but who requested it?"

"Some girl called Sue. Paid the boss in advance and said to deliver it for a party, only no one was there. I just left the pizzas and came home. Is that what this is about? The pizza?"

"What did Sue look like?"

"Kinda hot, if you know what I mean. Small, tight body, about twenty-eight."

Castleton dug out his phone and flicked to the photo gallery. He handed it to Simmons. "Is this her?"

"Yeah, that's her. The hair's different, but the same sweet face."

Castleton holstered his Glock and took his phone back, then indicated for Burke to follow him outside.

With weapons no longer on show, the pizza guy seemed to gain confidence. "Who are you guys, anyway?" he asked as he stood, puffing out his chest. "And who's gonna pay for my door?"

Castleton pulled a money clip from his pocket and peeled off a couple of hundred-dollar bills. He put the cash on a small table by the door on his way out.

Unsurprisingly, Driscoll had set them up. All Castleton could do now was call it in.

"Nest," he said into his radio once clear of Simmons's house, "Eagle Four. No sign of Colback or Driscoll. My guess is that Naser's plan was to join Driscoll, not avoid her. They've got over an hour's head start."

Having followed instructions to the letter, he couldn't be blamed for the fuck-up. At least, that's what he hoped. The wait for a reply was almost unbearable.

"Get back to Naser's house and turn the place over. We need some clue as to where they're going."

Castleton acknowledged the order and got behind the wheel of the car. He was sure it would do no good, but after the pizza fiasco, it was best to just do as he was told.

At least there would be free pizza while they worked.

CHAPTER 21

Carl Huff's laptop was already logged into the Homeland Security network via a socket they'd opened for him. Using his phone as a Wi-Fi hotspot, he brought up the satellite image of Naser's home, a simple row house on a residential street devoid of any character.

With one eye on the road as he drove, he used two fingers to expand the view on the laptop's touchscreen. Two streets from the target house, he saw a figure on a bicycle heading into town.

Where are you going, Farooq?

Naser's story about fleeing to avoid bloodshed might have fooled West, but Huff knew Eva Driscoll all too well. She wouldn't try anything as amateurish as posing as a pizza delivery person. Walking into traps was not one of the observed protocols in their business.

Red taillights loomed in front of him, and Huff overtook the slower vehicle before returning his attention to the laptop screen. Naser was now on the main street that bisected the town, and Huff watched him pull into a gas station before disappearing under the canopy that sheltered customers from rain and snow.

Is this where you're meeting her?

Huff made the decision to pull off the highway onto the shoulder and concentrate on Naser's movements. It was a toss-up between missing Naser leaving the station and getting into the area before Driscoll had a chance to leave. His priority was knowing her exit plan. Once she met Naser, she wasn't going to hang around.

Cars flashed past his window as he concentrated on the laptop. Traffic on the screen was sparse, and no one seemed to need gas at such a late hour.

After what seemed an age, Huff saw the glow of headlights illuminate the image on his screen. They came from a car parked on the opposite side of the road from the gas station, around a hundred yards down the street. He hadn't seen anyone approach the vehicle, so the occupants must have been inside all along.

Waiting for someone.

Naser.

Huff watched the car pull out and drive quickly up to the gas station. It passed under the canopy and emerged a few seconds later, joining the light traffic heading north.

It looked like she'd stopped just long enough to pick up Naser, but he had to be sure. It took a minute to tap into the street camera network, and he had to wind the coverage back a couple of minutes. Soon enough, a Chevy Impala filled the screen, and he could see a woman behind the wheel with an African-American male in the front passenger seat.

The recording wasn't of sufficient quality to zoom in for a positive ID, but it was too much of a coincidence not to be Driscoll.

Huff entered the vehicle's plate number into the nationwide alert database, requesting a notification every time the car was spotted by traffic cameras on the network.

He could now follow at his leisure and pounce at the optimum moment.

Huff started the car and rejoined the highway, sticking to the speed limit. A few miles down the road, his laptop beeped to inform him that

Driscoll was now heading west on US-22. He checked the map for a course to intercept her.

Anton West would be pissed that he hadn't shared his discovery with the team, but Huff didn't care. They'd soon realize that Farooq had double-crossed them, by which time Huff would be on Driscoll's tail while everyone else chased shadows. The less time spent dealing with West and his amateurs, the better. He was happy to accept any information they cared to feed him, but it was a one-way street. Carl Huff worked alone. End of story.

The next update showed the target car on I-70, approaching Columbus. Huff's only concern was that with three people in the car, Driscoll and her cohorts could keep moving all night as they took turns driving, while he would have to stop and sleep at some point. All he could do was pray that Colback or Naser demanded a comfortable bed; otherwise they'd eventually open a big lead on him.

It was half past midnight when West phoned him to say that Farooq had disappeared, presumed to be with Driscoll and Colback.

"Keep your men in the area," Huff said. "I'll head west to check out her known associates out there."

"I'd prefer it if you remained in the area to help close the net."

"Sure," Huff replied. "What's she driving?"

"Unknown."

"And her last known heading?"

"We're working on that," West said.

"Which means you have no idea, and as they've got a good head start, my guess is that they've put New Lexington far behind them. I'm going to Fresno. I'll contact you once I get there."

He ended the call before West could argue, now more astounded than amused by the DHS man's incompetence. Only an idiot would have failed to put a tail on Naser.

By three in the morning, after many more updates from the traffic cameras, it was obvious Driscoll wasn't stopping. He'd closed to within fifty miles of them, but fatigue was hammering at the door.

A road sign gave him an idea. It was showing the turnoff for Dayton International, and he decided to kill some time at the airport hotel and see where Driscoll was when he woke up. She wouldn't be more than a few hours away by plane, and he could even overfly her position and lie in wait for her.

Five minutes later, Huff was being admired by the young woman behind the hotel's reception desk. Normally he would have flirted and perhaps even had a little fun, but business came first. He took his key and found his room, which was functional at best. After plugging his laptop in to charge, he took a quick shower and settled naked on the bed.

The laptop was still running, and the latest report was that Driscoll was still driving west. Huff closed his eyes and pictured her as she'd looked a decade earlier, until sleep came and robbed him of the vision.

CHAPTER 22

The black limousine pulled up outside the Calico Club just off Park Avenue in Washington, D.C. The driver got out to open the door for the sole passenger and offered his hand, but the old man in the back seat waved him off.

Henry Langton gingerly climbed out. He straightened his cashmere Burberry overcoat and adjusted his fedora, then made his way slowly to the front door of America's most exclusive private club. The attendant had the door open before he'd left the vehicle, and he closed it just as quickly behind the great-grandson of the club's founding member.

The Calico Club was more than 170 years old and its decor had changed little in that time. The original oak panels still lined the walls, although the carpets and furniture had been replaced over the years.

For the last sixty years, it had been the meeting place of the ESO.

Langton handed an attendant his hat, coat, and scarf. "I'll take breakfast in thirty minutes."

The man responded with a simple bow of the head, and Langton continued down the wide corridor lined with portraits of former members, his great-grandfather Isaiah among them.

The Langtons were old money—a line of bankers that few people had even heard of before the advent of the Internet. These days, the name was synonymous with extreme wealth and secrecy. The mainstream press portrayed them as philanthropists, and as long as Langton controlled the major newspapers and networks, that would continue.

For more than a century, the Langton dynasty had owned most of the central banks of the world, including the US Federal Reserve. The family's net worth was estimated by some to be a shade over a trillion dollars, a figure that always made Henry Langton laugh. Their true wealth was beyond the comprehension of most people, and he went to great pains to ensure the exact amount remained a closely guarded secret. That was one of the reasons the Langtons never made the *Forbes* list, even though their capital reserves were enough to match that of the largest governments in the world.

The alternative press did its best to warn people about the Langton empire, but to no real effect. When their allegations were quoted in mainstream media interviews, the rumors were said to be baseless lies. On the odd occasion when someone got hold of information that could prove Langton's involvement in unpatriotic behavior, the matter was dealt with swiftly and permanently.

Those irksome websites aside, Langton had the population of the United States exactly where he wanted it. Decades of dumbing down the education system had produced a couple of generations largely incapable of free thought. They believed what they were told because that's all they knew growing up. Listen, repeat, accept as true. When the news outlets spun a story the way Langton wanted it to be told, few people doubted the veracity. Those that did were blasted as conspiracy theorists, ironically labeled too dumb to know the truth when they heard it.

Even the three most popular social media sites were pawns of Langton and his associates in the ESO. They'd recognized the potential at an early stage and had invested heavily in making them yet another tool in the misinformation game.

Langton reached the room at the end of the hallway. He opened the door and walked in, glad to see everyone else was already in attendance.

Judging by the smoky atmosphere, they'd been there for some time, all keenly aware that he didn't like to be kept waiting.

"Gentlemen," he said, as he took his seat at the head of the ornate oak table, "what's the latest on Colback?"

The six other men in the room looked at Langton as he lit a cigarette and exhaled his own contribution to the haze in the room. Smoking laws were for normal folk, not the men who ran the country.

"The latest update said he'd managed to evade our men in Ohio. He and Driscoll met up with one Farooq Naser, a former IT specialist with the CIA."

The man who had delivered the report was Langton's eldest son Edward. At forty-six, he was the youngest in the room by fifteen years, and next in line for the unofficial throne. His status and bloodline did not prevent him from receiving his father's ire.

"How the hell did they slip through the net? I thought West had this all covered."

"He's working with limited resources," Edward said. "And it's a big country. We need to throw more people at the problem."

"I've already set the CIA's best after them," Langton said. "It'll have to be enough. The chance of this going public is too great to involve the police or other agencies, and we all know what happens when news leaks."

None of the men in the room needed reminding. Almost two years earlier, the presidential candidate they'd chosen to be their mouthpiece, Ryan Appleton, had aced the primaries and caucuses and had commanded a seventeen-point lead in the polls heading for the November elections. That's when disaster had struck. In late October, only twelve days before the nation went to cast their vote, a series of emails had been uploaded to the WikiLeaks website and soon brought the campaign to a crushing halt.

It emerged that the former Texas governor had a few skeletons that even the ESO hadn't known about, one of them being the fact that he'd slept with a prostitute many years earlier. That in itself would not have been a terribly serious matter, but it turned out that she'd recorded the sordid encounter and tried to blackmail Appleton. WikiLeaks's incriminating emails centered around Appleton's attempts to silence the woman. Her death at the time had barely rated a couple of column inches in the local newspaper, but with less than two weeks before the election, the FBI had launched a full investigation. George Carson, head of media relations, had done his best to keep the news off the air and out of the papers but the damage had already been done.

The result had been immediate and catastrophic.

The ESO had thrown their weight behind Appleton, using the media to spin the allegations as lies and falsehoods concocted by the opposition, but it had proved a futile exercise. Their opponent had won by a landslide, and once in the White House had begun to work with Congress on the liberal agenda that had made him such a weak adversary.

Many of the corporations that Langton and his cronies had interests in were immediately wounded by the new legislation that followed. The pharmaceutical companies were ordered to rein in their prices or face huge fines, and marijuana was due to be legalized in the coming months, adding another nail to their coffin. It was widely known within the industry that weed was a safer and more powerful painkiller than anything they manufactured, but they'd paid enough people to keep that a secret. Why use a cheap, natural product when you can charge five hundred bucks for a synthetic alternative?

The military budget also suffered. It was cut by almost 30 percent after the new president announced the complete withdrawal of all troops in the Middle East within the next five years. Private prisons were being renationalized, and the vast majority incarcerated for nonviolent crimes were having their sentences cut drastically, ending decades of profiteering.

In all, the new administration had already cost Langton more than a trillion dollars, and he wasn't about to face another six years of abuse.

"I said at the time that we should have gone with someone else, but you insisted on Hank Monroe," Edward said, referring to the candidate Langton and the ESO had chosen to back in the coming presidential election.

The remark drew a look of utter disdain from his father. "Monroe's had a distinguished career in the CIA and as the governor of Nebraska. From the public's perspective, he's the perfect choice."

"I agree on your assessment of Monroe, but I think we should at least have had a contingency, in case the worst happened."

"The worst is happening and I don't see you offering up any solutions." Langton glared at his son. "Saying 'I told you so' doesn't help our cause. We've spent years pitting black against white, rich against poor, left against right, all so that we could carry on with business as usual while they fight among themselves. Now this liberal jerkoff is reuniting the country!" Langton slapped a bony hand on the table. "He's undone twenty years of hard work and cost us a fortune."

"It isn't as though we have an unlimited supply of people we can call on," one of the others said. Joel Harmer was the member in charge of security, but he'd seen fit to let the younger Langton take the lead so far. A billionaire many times over and a man of enormous power in his own right, he owed his fortune and position to Langton, much like the others gathered around the table. "There are only around a hundred operatives trained to carry out this type of task. When you subtract the ones Driscoll and Colback eliminated and those already on overseas missions, we only have around twenty to call upon. Eleven of those are already on their trail, which leaves us only nine more."

"Then throw them in," Langton said, stubbing out his cigarette and lighting another. He looked at the faces around the table and suddenly sensed that he hadn't been told the whole story. "Whatever it is, spit it out."

Harmer, the only nonsmoker in the room, cleared his throat. "Someone managed to get into our CIA black-book bank accounts this morning. They took a shade over fifty million before protocols kicked them out. We suspect it was Farooq Naser but we have no proof yet."

The amount was nothing, pocket change to a man like Langton, but if Naser was behind it, then Driscoll now had a sizable war chest.

"Are you telling me that after he skipped with Driscoll, Naser was able to access his old CIA account? Why wasn't that closed off, as a priority?"

"His access was shut down the moment he left the CIA a couple of years ago. We think he created back doors during his time there."

"You *think*?"

"We've got the best people working on every line of code he wrote while he was employed with them," the younger Langton said. "If we find his way in, we can shut it down."

"Close the stable door after the horse has bolted, you mean."

Edward looked at the other faces for support. "It wasn't as if we could foresee this happening. We only learned of Naser's involvement a few hours ago."

Langton stared at the ashtray next to him, idly making patterns in the gray embers with the end of his lit cigarette. "Once we find these back doors, can we trace anyone using them?"

"We should be able to," Harmer said. "But there's no telling what damage he might do if we let him into our systems again."

"If he was going to wipe the hard drives, he would have done it by now. No, let him have access. It might be our best chance of finding them."

Harmer took out his phone to update the CIA on the new orders while Langton addressed the rest of the room. "It's imperative that Monroe's campaign remains on track. I appreciate that we still have more than two years until the election, but we must ensure nothing tarnishes Monroe's image. George, remind the editors that they can't publish a story about him without running it by me first. Alexander, I want someone monitoring state and local police communications in the region. If any of them stumble onto Colback's trail, shut their investigations down."

Langton stubbed out his cigarette and rose. "I'm going to have breakfast. Before we meet again tomorrow, I want this thing put to bed."

CHAPTER 23

Carl Huff woke a couple of minutes before the alarm was due to go off at eight in the morning. It was a habit, his body somehow knowing when to exit deep sleep, and he felt perfectly refreshed despite only four hours in bed.

On the desk, his laptop had gone into hibernation mode, so he woke it and checked on Driscoll's progress. As he'd expected, they'd continued traveling through the night. Their course had been west by southwest, the latest data showing them entering Louisville thirty minutes earlier. Huff quickly considered a course to head them off. According to her file, Driscoll had no known associates in the immediate area, so she would probably continue on a westerly heading. Then again, aware that she was being hunted, she would most likely try to throw people off her scent. That's what Huff would have done in her shoes.

But where would she head?

Mexico would have been Huff's first choice. US intel and law enforcement agencies had little reach over the border and would not easily gain the help of the Mexican authorities in capturing Driscoll and her companions. Going south of the border would give her time to evaluate the situation and formulate a response, or simply disappear.

If that was indeed her destination, he had plenty of time to intercept her. Buying a ticket for a scheduled flight would be too risky for her, as would chartering a plane. She knew as well as he that passenger manifests would be watched closely, which meant she would have to drive to the frontier.

It was roughly eleven hundred miles to San Antonio, Texas, which she and her compatriots could probably drive in sixteen hours under the right conditions. That gave him plenty of time.

Huff opened a new browser window and booked an American Airlines ticket to San Antonio via Charlotte, North Carolina. It would get him to Texas at five in the evening, and he could reevaluate his plan once on the ground.

He took another quick shower, then dressed. His bag contained enough clothes to last him three days.

He was confident he wouldn't need that long.

~

Colback was awake and alert the moment Eva touched his shoulder. "What is it?"

"We're approaching Louisville. Hitting the outskirts in ten minutes."

Colback looked in the back and saw Farooq fast asleep, his laptop still open and resting on his chest.

It looked like another glorious day, weather-wise at least. The trees flashing past his window were in full bloom, and he might have taken a moment to enjoy the lush landscape under different circumstances.

The clock on the dash told him it was half past seven.

"How about we find some chow?" he said. "I'm starving. Get me some breakfast and I can take over driving."

Eva sighed theatrically. "I did warn you to fill up when you had the chance but you thought you knew better."

"You always this grumpy first thing in the morning?"

She ignored him and handed over her burner cell. "Look for a diner, ideally near a gas station."

Colback typed in a search and was rewarded with the name and address of a franchise restaurant in the center of town. "Farooq, wake up. It's time to eat."

Inside the diner, they ordered coffee and pancakes. They'd been unable to find a quiet booth where they could discuss their situation, so they ate in silence. Colback, lesson learned, ordered a burger and fries after finishing his first course, and all three welcomed their coffee refills.

After a visit to the toilets, Eva ordered Colback and Farooq into the gas station next door, where they purchased toiletries, water, and snacks to see them through the next few days.

Colback took the wheel and followed Eva's directions as she read them off the phone. Farooq was back on his laptop, still trying to dig up what he could on Adrian Holmes, the journalist-turned-blogger Eva had killed.

Her directions led them to a location that looked like little more than a parking lot with a small prefabricated cabin that served as the office.

"What's this place?" As he pulled in, Colback saw a sign outside that read QUALITY DRIVEAWAY.

"Watch and learn," said Eva as she exited the car.

Colback accompanied her inside the small building, where Eva spoke to a middle-aged man behind a cheap plastic counter.

"Hi. I'd like someone to drive my car to San Diego," she said, giving the guy a dazzling smile.

"Sure thing," the clerk replied. "I'll need to take a few details."

Eva handed over the fake ID she'd used to register the car, then gave him an address.

"San Diego, huh?" said the clerk. "When do you need it to arrive?"

"As soon as possible. Do you think someone could take it today?"

The man began biting his upper lip as he checked his computer. "I've got one couple waiting for a ride to Los Angeles, but nothing for San Diego, I'm afraid."

Eva nodded and maintained the smile. "Maybe you could ask them if they'll take mine to San Diego and I'll give them an extra three hundred bucks to get to LA."

The clerk shrugged. "I can try." He picked up the phone and dialed the number on the screen, then told the woman who answered that he had an offer for her. A minute later, he hung up with a smile. "They'll be here to pick it up at lunchtime."

Eva handed over the keys and the fee, plus the bonus for the drivers and another for the clerk.

"San Diego, huh?" said Colback when they reached their car. "Where are you sending it?" he whispered. "CIA safe house?"

Eva simply winked, took her backpack from him, and collected Farooq from the vehicle. Together, they walked down the street toward a coffee shop.

"You guys wait here," she told them. "I'm going to find an Internet café and transfer some funds to a local account, then get some new wheels. If I'm not back in an hour, find somewhere to lie low. I'll message you," she told Farooq.

"And if you don't get in touch . . . ?"

"It means I'm dead, and they'll be coming for you next."

Eva walked away before Colback could prolong the conversation.

"She's a regular fun factory," he said, watching her stroll down the street.

"You get used to her," Farooq assured him. "You certainly couldn't wish for a better friend in your current situation."

Farooq held the door open and both men walked inside. They ordered coffees, then found a quiet table, the pre-work crowd long gone.

"So, what's wrong with your foot?" Farooq asked as he took out his laptop and plugged it into a wall outlet.

"War wound."

Colback told Farooq about his ill-fated visit to Jeff Driscoll and his employer in New York City. "I had no way of knowing he was dead before I even got there."

Farooq nodded as he hooked up to the café's Wi-Fi.

"I've only known Eva since New York," said Colback, taking a sip of his coffee. "She kinda comes across as a loner, but she didn't hesitate to contact you. What makes her trust you so much?"

Farooq shrugged. "I owe her, and she knew she could count on my help."

"I got that, but what exactly did she do for you?"

Farooq sighed as he looked up from his screen. "My sister Sana lives in a small town called Bottle Creek, Arkansas. That's where I'm originally from. I went to visit her for her twenty-first birthday, but she wasn't her normal happy self. It took a while to get it out of her, but she eventually told me that her boss had sexually assaulted her.

"Her boss—his name's Mike Herron—is a big man, late forties, and Sana had zero interest in him, which she made perfectly clear. One day, he told her to stay behind after work to help prepare some paper-work for an upcoming business trip, but once everyone else was gone, he attacked her. He grabbed her breasts and tried to kiss her, and when she tried to fight him off, he hit her in the face. She fell to the floor, and before she knew it, he was on top of her. Now, Sana's only five feet tall, and Herron goes at least 250. There was nothing she could do."

Colback didn't need all the sordid details to imagine what had happened next. "Did she report it to the police?"

"Not at first," Farooq told him. "I saw her a week after it happened, and we went to see the sheriff together. She filed a complaint, but when she went back two days later to follow it up, she was told that no further action would be taken."

"Why not?"

"Because the sheriff was Herron's brother-in-law. Of course, that wasn't the official reason, but they said there wasn't sufficient evidence to pursue the case. Don't forget, this is small-town America we're talking about. Bottle Creek has a population of just over two thousand, ninety-eight percent of whom are white, and the sheriff had held the post for twenty years."

"So how did Eva get involved?"

"I'd known her for some time. Toward the end of her training, I was her assigned IT instructor. My job was to get her up to speed on the latest surveillance tech, and she soaked up the information like a sponge. After the course finished, she'd come by every month to keep current. I guess during one of those visits, I mentioned Sana's problem. Eva could see I was troubled and made me tell her everything.

"By that time, Sana had found a new job as a waitress, but when Herron found out, he went in every day and kept harassing her. He knew he could get away with it, and that made him bolder. I told Sana she should leave the area for good, but she refused to be bullied out of her hometown."

Farooq sipped his coffee, staring at the dark brew for a few moments.

"So, what did Eva do?"

"She told me she got an office job at Herron Construction. She created an impressive résumé, but Herron barely glanced at it. He only had eyes for her. She started the next day, and he didn't waste any time. The touching started immediately, but instead of being pissed, Eva laughed it off and even started flirting with him. On her third day, Herron asked her to stay late, and she happily agreed. Once everyone else went home, Herron pulled out a bottle of bourbon and two glasses and invited her to join him on the sofa in his office. She refused, saying she'd changed her mind after noticing the wedding ring and the picture of his wife on the desk. Well, he reacted just as she'd expected he would. He definitely didn't expect much resistance from someone so small. At first, she played the weak victim, allowing him to rip her blouse open and fondle her, all the while begging him to stop. He just carried on, pushing her onto the couch and forcing his hand up her skirt. At that point, while he was trying to kiss her neck, she bit off half his ear."

"Whoa! He must've freaked."

"You have no idea. Eva said it was just the reaction she'd been hoping for. She let him slap her across the face, then she cowered on the sofa as he hit her some more. He then reached up her skirt again and pulled her panties off. She let him do it until he started unzipping his fly. Then she pretended to try to escape but let him catch her by his desk. He bent her over the desk and used his weight to pin her down. The second he had his dick out and tried to force himself inside her, she stomped a foot and swung a hard elbow back into his temple. When he staggered back, she grabbed a letter opener from his desk and sliced his cock open lengthwise."

Colback was stunned. "And she told you all this, in detail?"

"Better than that, she narrated the video for me."

"She recorded it?"

"Every second. She put three cameras in his office the first day she was there. Once it was over, she removed them and made several copies of the recordings. She took the first one to the sheriff's department and after filing her complaint, she asked for a receipt. As expected, the following day the video had been mysteriously lost and they said there was nothing they could do."

"What did she do then?"

"She mailed copies to the local judge, newspaper, and Herron's wife. Not only that, she sent copies to all of Herron Construction's clients, along with a note saying the case wasn't being pursued by the sheriff. You can imagine the shitstorm that kicked up."

"Wait. Wasn't she worried that she'd be recognized if the video got onto the Internet? She doesn't seem the kind of person to make a rookie mistake like that."

"No, she'd altered her appearance enough that even I didn't recognize her from the video."

"So, what happened to Herron?"

Farooq smiled. "I followed events for a few months and it wasn't pretty. He went to the hospital, obviously, but he must have had a fabulous excuse because his wife was quoted as saying she was devastated by the result of the 'industrial accident.' It wasn't until a week later, when Eva posted the recordings, that he was arrested. His wife filed for divorce the next day and Herron Construction folded within two months. The last I heard, Mike Herron was doing fifteen to twenty-five in prison, even though the victim had disappeared off the face of the earth."

Colback sat back in his chair and smiled. Eva had taken action he would never have dreamed of. While he would have simply beaten Herron to a pulp, she'd seen the bigger picture, played a slightly longer game, and ruined him for life. His admiration for her cranked up another couple of notches.

They spent the next half hour trying to find reasons why the ESO would want Colback and his squad dead, but nothing made sense.

"We need Eva's analytical brain working on this," Farooq said.

As if she'd been summoned, Eva walked through the café door and made a beeline for their table.

"Time to go."

Colback smiled. "Yes, ma'am."

The men followed her outside, where a nondescript Ford was waiting by the curb. Eva took the wheel and drove them through town, heading east until they came to an industrialized area that looked long-abandoned. The landscape was gray and lifeless, like the set of a zombie-apocalypse movie.

She pulled up outside a two-story building that had a metal grille over the window and a door that looked like it hadn't seen a paintbrush in a couple of decades.

"Wait here," she said. "I'll be back in a few minutes."

Colback had no intention of going anywhere. Thirty yards away, on the corner of the street, a couple of gangbangers had noticed their arrival and were taking an interest in the cheap Ford rental. As they started walking toward the car, Colback took the Glock from the small of his back and chambered a round in full view of the approaching punks. The young men stopped, conferred for a few moments, then sauntered back to their spot on the corner, all prospects of a simple carjack gone.

One situation averted. What would come next? Farooq remained silent in the rear, while Colback kept his eyes on the mirrors. No one else approached by the time Eva emerged.

"Get what you came for?" he asked her.

"Not yet. I have to come back in a couple of hours. In the meantime, let's get you guys a room."

Ten minutes later she pulled up outside a seedy hotel in what was clearly Louisville's red-light district. A couple of hookers were already out in the hope of attracting some daytime trade, but apart from them, the streets seemed quiet.

Eva reached into her bag and pulled out a wad of notes, handing it to Colback. "There's five grand. If I'm not back in three days, take off. That should keep you going for a while. Farooq, you've got my bank account number. If things don't work out, transfer the money to your own bank and spend it wisely."

"You don't sound too confident," Colback said. "Maybe the England trip isn't a good idea."

"That part will be a walk in the park," Eva told him. "But planes crash, and people get killed just crossing the road. Go book yourselves in for three nights and stay in the room. You've got enough supplies to last you until I get back, so there's no need to go anywhere. Oh, and Rees, stay away from the local women."

"Not my scene," Colback assured her as he pulled a few notes off the bundle and put the rest in the bag he'd bought at the gas station.

Farooq and he exited the car and watched Eva drive away.

CHAPTER 24

Eva Driscoll's first stop was a department store in a mall, where she bought a tweed skirt and woolen top that were a couple of sizes too large. She topped off her new ensemble with a wide-brimmed hat and a pair of frumpy boots. Happy with her wardrobe for the flight, she also bought two separate changes of clothes to put in a suitcase she planned to buy. Minor details counted, and she didn't want to attract attention by flying across the Atlantic without any luggage.

After completing her shopping, she still had an hour to kill, so she got a coffee and sandwich and ate them in the car.

At one in the afternoon, she drove back to the shuttered building and rapped on the door. As before, a panel slid open and a pair of eyes looked her over before a deadbolt was pulled aside and she was allowed into the drab room.

The guard was still alone. A cigarette burned in an ashtray on the small table that sat between an ancient leather chair and a television. The room was otherwise empty, with only a wooden door to break up the monotony of the nicotine-stained walls.

The man frisked Eva again, then searched her shopping bag. He inspected her cash and every other item she carried. Satisfied she was unarmed, the guard gave a thumbs-up to a camera hidden in a wall vent. The internal door clicked open, and Driscoll walked through.

"Watch the car," she said, tossing the keys to him, then climbed the stairs. At the top, another door clicked open and she once again stood before DeBron Harris. In his late forties, the 280 pounds of muscle he'd once carried as a high school linebacker had long since turned to fat.

"Welcome back," DeBron said from behind his desk. On the wall to his right hung a bank of CCTV monitors; on the other side of the room, a woman sat on a sofa. "This is Nolene. She'll be doing your makeover."

The woman stood and held open a door, and Eva walked into what looked like a stage actor's dressing room. Eva put her bag of clothes on the table and sat in a swivel chair facing a huge mirror.

"DeBron said you wanted to add thirty years and forty pounds," Nolene said.

"That's right. I also want the nose a little bigger."

"No problem."

Nolene worked nonstop for more than three hours, barely speaking a dozen words except to ask what Eva thought as the work progressed. When she'd finished, the transformation was stunning.

Eva looked at the unrecognizable senior citizen in the mirror. The extra weight did wonders, as did the wrinkles and liver spots that Nolene had added to her hands.

"Let's try the bodywork," Nolene suggested.

Eva stripped down to her underwear, then pulled the padded vest over her head and fastened the Velcro straps. She then stepped into the leggings that added another inch or two to her waist. After putting on the woolen top and skirt, the result was impressive.

"Are you going to be traveling in those clothes?" Nolene asked.

"Yes, later today."

"Then wear this shirt instead." She handed Eva a flowered blouse. "It's not a good idea to have your passport photo taken in the clothes you'll be flying in."

Such professionalism was the reason Driscoll had driven so far to avail of DeBron's services. While the CIA had their own department that handled alternate identities, she'd thought it prudent to seek out someone who worked outside of official channels. This was the third time she'd been here, and she'd never walked away disappointed.

After having her picture taken, she put the woolen top back on. Nolene gave her a touch-up kit and instructions on how to use it. With that in hand, Eva went to sit with DeBron while he created her new documents.

"Your name will be Adele Bennett," he said, his tone suggesting it wasn't up for discussion. Others in her profession might have asked for the new name to have the same initials as their own, making it easier to remember, but it wasn't a technique Eva cared for.

The first thing DeBron handed over was a prepaid credit card in her new name.

"It's loaded with two grand," he told her.

That was more than enough for Driscoll, who only intended to use it to purchase her plane ticket.

She watched DeBron as he skillfully crafted a driver's license, followed by a passport with an issue date of three years earlier. A smattering of stamps showed the holder to be an infrequent traveler.

Nolene provided refreshments while Eva waited, and it was almost six in the evening by the time DeBron was done.

Eva scanned her new passport and found it impeccable.

"A pleasure doing business with you," she said as she handed over two bundles of hundred-dollar bills that she'd withdrawn from the bank earlier that morning.

Back out in the street, having collected her car keys from the guard downstairs, she saw that the Ford thankfully remained in one piece. The locals had clearly been warned not to mess with DeBron's clients.

Eva got in and used her phone to look up a flight. The earliest available flight to Heathrow had a brief stopover in Paris, but it would get her to London by two in the afternoon, leaving plenty of time to get into the capital and intercept Andrew Harvey on his way home from work.

Her ticket booked, Driscoll found a gas station and filled the tank, then began the seven-hour drive to Atlanta.

CHAPTER 25

The encounter with the TSA agents at Atlanta Airport couldn't have gone more smoothly. They barely paid Eva any attention as she walked through the metal detector, and the contents of her handbag gave them no cause for concern.

The flight to Charles de Gaulle was wonderfully mundane, and after switching planes in Paris, she was soon jetting over the English Channel. Eva guessed that getting through Heathrow would be a completely different challenge, but she felt confident that she wouldn't be seen as a threat to the nation's security.

At the immigration desk, she was asked the standard questions regarding length of stay, purpose of visit, and funds available during her stay. She had already prepared her story, and after explaining that it was a fleeting visit to get fitted out for her niece's upcoming wedding, she was allowed to pass through and collect her suitcase before exiting through the Nothing to Declare lane. She changed five hundred dollars for the local currency at a miserly exchange rate, then walked out of the terminal. The weather was as glorious as it had been back home, slightly warmer if anything.

With only two hours until five o'clock, Driscoll decided to take a taxi into London rather than rely on public transport. She wanted to be outside Andrew Harvey's house when he arrived home from work, otherwise it could be awkward. The last thing she intended to do was involve anyone else, and that included Harvey's fiancée Sarah.

His home turned out to be a three-story townhouse in a crescent off the main road. Eva asked the driver to drop her at the corner, then walked back past the building and continued to the other end of the street, getting a feel for the area. She saw no off-road parking, so Harvey would either have to pull up to the building in his car or walk to it. With that in mind, she decided to wait for him in the park opposite.

As the clock edged toward six in the evening, Driscoll feared that Harvey might pull an all-nighter. She'd known some men with newborns who had spent as much time away from the family home as possible, but most couldn't wait to get home to see their baby. She wondered which category Harvey fell into.

It had been a decade since she'd last seen him, and during their two weeks together there had been no talk of kids or settling down. Harvey, unable to admit to his role in the security services, had told her he was in finance. She'd taken great pleasure in watching him squirm as she pressed for details, but he'd worked hard on his legend and had been able to hold his own as their brief time together progressed.

Eva looked back fondly on the time they'd spent together. Andrew Harvey had been a considerate—not to mention gifted—lover, and she'd always regretted the day she'd walked away without a word. She'd completed her mission, earned top credits for her course, and it had been time to move on, but that hadn't stopped her thinking of him from time to time.

While reflecting, she almost missed Harvey's arrival. He was striding toward the house with his jacket over his shoulder, a spring in his step despite having just spent nine hours at the office. He looked much as she remembered: six feet tall, same slim build. If anything, his brown hair appeared a little longer than he'd worn it back then, but the face was unmistakable.

Driscoll sent the text message she'd prepared, then sat back in her seat to await his reaction.

~

Andrew Harvey bounced up the stairs to his front door, the keys already in his hand and a smile on his face. The weekend was approaching, and the fabulous weather they'd enjoyed for the last few days looked set to continue. It was the perfect opportunity to get away for the weekend, and he planned to raise the idea with Sarah. A couple of days at the beach, soaking up the sunshine—

His phone chirped and he dug it out of his pocket. A new text message from an unknown number . . . and its first line made him frown.

Walk across to the park and . . .

Harvey unlocked the phone and read the entire message.

Walk across to the park and sit on the bench facing your house.

Harvey looked around to see who could possibly have sent the message, but the street seemed empty. Whoever it was, they had to be in the park, waiting for him.

His first thought was to ignore the message and go inside, but something stopped him. Few people had his number, apart from his colleagues at MI5, and their name would have been displayed if it had come from one of them. Could someone have typed his number by mistake? It was possible, but the reference to the bench opposite his house was too much of a coincidence.

Harvey slowly descended the stairs and peered through the trees into the park. The bench was occupied, by an elderly woman from the look of it.

Something wasn't right. Warning bells were going off inside his head, and he knew that going into the park alone would be foolish. The least he should do was let a colleague know where he was going. Or tell

Sarah . . . But he didn't want to worry her needlessly, especially when she was looking after Alana.

He opened his phone and selected Hamad Farsi, his most trusted friend in the office. He'd just pressed the Call button when a new message came in from the unknown number.

There's no danger. I just want to talk. Emilie.

Despite the years that had passed since he'd last seen her, Harvey instantly recognized the name. In fact, a crystal-clear image of her popped into his mind's eye.

Harvey disconnected before Farsi could answer. He looked again at the woman on the bench, who appeared to be reading a paperback. He put his phone back in his pocket and crossed the road, then walked through the entrance to the park. As he strode through the gates, he scanned the area, looking for someone of similar height and build to the Emilie he remembered.

No matches.

He continued his search as he made his way for the bench, his head aiming straight ahead but his eyes darting from side to side. The message said there was no danger, but Harvey remained wary.

As he approached the seat, the old woman glanced up, then returned her attention to the novel in her hands. Harvey sat down at the other end of the bench and took his phone out. He opened Farsi's contact page once more and started typing out a quick message. That way, he only had to press Send if things turned ugly.

"It's been a long time."

Harvey's head snapped up as he looked for the owner of the voice, but he saw only the elderly woman sitting next to him. She looked up and winked as he stared at her, and he recognized the smile from a decade earlier.

"Emilie?"

She looked down at her book once more. "You're looking good, Andrew. The years have been kind to you."

"I wish I could say the same for you."

She chuckled, a sound that pulled at his heartstrings. "It's makeup and you know it. I also know you work for MI5, which is why I chose you all those years ago."

Harvey's mind was racing, a thousand questions battling to be asked.

"I know you want to get home to Sarah and Alana, so I'll be brief. My name isn't Emilie."

"So what is it?"

"That doesn't matter. When we met, I was training with the CIA. Clandestine services. My task was to create a legend and have it scrutinized by the best. I picked your name from the CIA station list at the US Embassy, and I passed my assignment."

"Wait. You used me to get extra credits? That's it?"

"Essentially, yes, but it doesn't change how I felt about you. Now, please, save any other questions until the end, or Sarah will start worrying where you are."

She was right about that. Harvey had sent a text to say he would be home within thirty minutes, and that time was almost up.

"I'm sorry, this is all just a shock."

"I'm sure it is. Let me be frank. I'm here to seek your help. For reasons unknown, agents of the US government killed my brother, and now they're after me. I need you to put me in touch with some of your ex-colleagues who can help me get to the bottom of it."

Harvey couldn't help laughing. "You know I can't give you any names. It would cost me my job."

"They wouldn't have to know it came from you. Just point me in their direction."

Harvey shook his head. "You turn up after all these years, tell me you're a CIA agent, and expect me to forget all the lies, forget how you broke my heart by disappearing suddenly, and now you want me to put my career on the line to help you? Are you crazy?"

"Maybe, but you're still here. If you won't do it for me, do it for our daughter."

She handed the stunned British agent a photograph of herself with a girl who looked to be about nine years old. "Her name's Maria. That was taken a couple of months ago."

Harvey felt like he'd been hit by a bus. The photo showed Emilie just as he'd remembered her, and the young girl was the spitting image of her.

"But . . . how?"

"No contraceptive is one hundred percent effective," she told him. "She's safe, for now, but if they catch up with me, she won't last long."

He searched the smiling face but couldn't see any of himself in Maria. That wasn't unusual though. He'd read enough parenting books to know that one parent often had a dominant gene, and Alana took after her mother.

"If you want, we can go inside and ask what Sarah thinks."

"No!" Harvey shot back, a little too harshly. Then, "I'm sorry. Let's leave her out of it."

"Okay, but I need names of good people you know. I'm willing to pay well."

"Why can't you use your own contacts?"

"Because they're all compromised, and I can't use mercenaries because I need people I can trust."

That was understandable. "What would they have to do? Is it just surveillance, or would they have to get their hands dirty?"

She held back her response until a passing jogger ran out of earshot. "I'd prefer someone with a little tradecraft, but it's essential that they know how to handle weapons. If they've ever been in a firefight, then all the better."

That ruled out anyone Harvey had ever worked with at MI5, but three other names leaped to mind.

"I know some people. They're ex-SAS, British Special Forces."

"Ex-forces are a dime a dozen. I could find a hundred to choose from on the Internet. Most of them are just in it for the money, and they'd run at the first sign of trouble. No, I need someone more reliable."

"I trust these guys with my life. In fact, I have. They risked their own necks to break me out of a Russian prison, and they did it out of loyalty, nothing more."

She considered it momentarily. "Okay, give them a call."

"It won't be that easy," Harvey told her. "One of them has a daughter of his own, and it'll take a lot to get him on board. If he's going to risk his life, it had better be worth it."

"How much?"

"How much are you offering?"

"I'm not price-sensitive," she replied. "Within reason."

You'd better not be. Harvey knew all about Tom Gray's financial situation. If anyone could do with a serious cash injection right now, it was Tom, Len, and Sonny.

"When do you need an answer?"

"I need them on a plane to the States by tomorrow lunchtime, preferably with new identities. I don't want them setting off alarm bells before we even get started."

"That's short notice, but I'll see what they say."

"No time like the present."

"It's not something I can discuss over the phone," Harvey told her. "I'll call you after I've spoken to them in person."

"There's no point. I'll have a new phone fifteen minutes after you leave. Not that I don't trust you, but you understand."

Harvey nodded. "Then how do I get in touch with you?"

"There's a Starbucks a couple of blocks away. Meet me there at eight tomorrow morning."

"And if they want to negotiate?"

"Do you have any alternates in mind?"

"No," Harvey admitted.

"Then there's nothing to discuss. They're either in or out. If they don't want the job, I've wasted my time. I hope that's not the case, for everyone's sake."

The inference that it would affect his newly discovered daughter wasn't lost on Harvey, and he could imagine the effect it would have on his relationship with Sarah if she found out about Emilie and Maria.

"I understand. I'll see you tomorrow."

He looked at her one last time, but still could only see the barest hint of the woman he'd fallen for all those years earlier. He walked away wondering what it would take to get Tom Gray to part with his daughter and take on such a mission to save Harvey's own.

He prayed it wouldn't be too much.

CHAPTER 26

Harvey pulled into the parking lot of Minotaur Logistics a few minutes after seven. He'd thought long and hard about how to explain his reason for going back out and had decided to keep it as close to the truth as possible. After all, Sarah had been with him when Len Smart called. That followed a text message he'd sent Len from the toilet after getting home—a message he had deleted immediately after. He doubted Sarah would search through his phone, as Len was a longtime friend, but he was taking no chances. He'd have to concoct a story about their meeting by the time he got home.

Sonny Baines held the door open as Harvey approached the building.

"Howdy, stranger." Sonny smiled. "Please tell me this is business, not pleasure."

"You're in luck," Harvey replied, although in truth he had no idea what he was about to ask his friends to sign up for.

Sonny led him into the manager's office, and Len Smart walked around the desk to shake his hand.

"I'm intrigued," Smart said. "You text me to call you, then you say, 'Yeah, I can be there at seven.' What gives?"

"I've got a job offer, but it's not for Minotaur. It's for you two, plus Tom."

"He's unlikely to be interested," Smart said. "He's got a lot on his plate at the moment."

"I know, but this could be a huge payday for all of you."

"Now *I'm* intrigued," said Sonny. "Who do we have to kill?"

"Joking apart," Harvey said, "that might be necessary. I haven't got all the details, but I'll tell you what I know. The client is being hunted by agents of the US government. They killed her brother and now they're after her."

He omitted the fact that Emilie had a daughter, saving it as leverage in case they had misgivings.

"So, you want us to take on the might of the US government, is that it?" Smart asked. "CIA, FBI, et cetera?"

"It sounds more like a rogue section of it, but basically, yes, you'll be up against the lot."

Smart and Sonny looked at each other, then burst out laughing.

"What have you been smoking?" Sonny asked.

"Guys, I'm serious."

"Sorry," Smart said, trying to adopt a straight face. "It's just . . . they're friendlies, right? If it was the North Koreans, or the Russians, then we'd probably be interested. But the Americans?"

"You mentioned a woman," Sonny said. "What did she do to piss them off?"

"She doesn't know, only that they want her dead."

"What's she to you?" Smart asked. "You wouldn't come to us with something this big if you didn't have a stake in her well-being."

Perceptive, as always.

Harvey had hoped it wouldn't come to this, but he'd known them too long to lie now. These men had saved his life and they deserved to know the truth.

"She has a daughter," he said. When that didn't prompt a reaction, he added, "I'm the father."

Both men looked shocked, with Sonny the first to grin. "You kept that quiet."

"I only found out an hour ago," Harvey said. He told them about the meeting with Emilie, down to the last detail.

"And you're positive the child's yours?" Smart probed.

"She didn't show me a birth certificate with my name on it, if that's what you're asking, but the timeline makes sense."

Silence descended while Smart and Sonny considered the offer.

"When do you need a response?" Smart asked.

"Ideally, now, but definitely before eight tomorrow morning."

"Then we'd better get Tom on the phone. How much did she say she was offering?"

"She didn't," Harvey said as Smart dialed Gray's number, "but she gave me the impression you can name your price."

"That should help."

Smart put Gray on speaker. "Tom, it's Len. I'm here with Sonny and Andrew. Andrew has a job offer for you. I'll let him explain."

Harvey exchanged quick pleasantries, then got down to business. He told Gray exactly what he'd shared with the other two, with Gray remaining silent throughout. It was only when Harvey asked what he thought of the offer that he finally spoke.

"I'm sorry, Andrew, but I can't go. I appreciate this might involve a daughter you didn't know about, but Emilie might just have said that to get you on board. Any schoolkid with Photoshop could have put that picture together. I've got to think of Melissa, and I need to be here to sort out my business."

Harvey had been hoping for a positive response, but he could hardly blame Gray. Tom had already saved Andrew's life once, and the idea that Emilie might have lied to him about Maria did make sense. It was something he planned to revisit with her later.

"I understand. I guess it was wishful thinking on my part." Harvey looked at the two men in the room. "What about you?"

"It's up to Tom," Sonny said. "We still work for him."

"Go for it, if you want," Gray said. "We all know how tight things are going to be in the next few months, so you might as well make some money while you can. I'll fly over in a couple of days and speak to Gill, get her to take charge for a few weeks. Anything she can't handle, she can pass on to me."

"In that case," Sonny said, "count me in."

"Len?"

Smart glanced over at Sonny. "Someone's got to keep an eye on this reprobate."

Although he was sending his friends into the unknown, Harvey was relieved that they were willing to take part. He had no idea how Emilie would react if he turned up empty-handed in the morning. At the very least she might call Sarah and tell her about Maria, and that was the last thing he wanted.

"What about your fee?"

The two ex-soldiers looked at each other for a moment.

"Two grand a day," Len said.

"But try for three," Sonny added.

"Plus expenses," said Len.

That seemed reasonable to Harvey. All that remained for him to do was to get false travel documents for each of them. That could prove to be a monumental task, given that it would require a written request from Veronica Ellis, and he had a feeling Emilie wouldn't be happy involving MI5's director general. On top of that, it usually took a couple of days to work up passports, and time was not on his side.

"Something wrong?" Smart asked, and Harvey realized his facial expression had mirrored his inner turmoil.

"Emilie wants you to use false passports, but we don't have time to organize it from my end."

"She's probably just being overly cautious," Sonny said. "We've been to the States a couple of times on our current passports and there were no problems at immigration. It's not as though we know the woman or hang around with her every weekend. I'm also guessing she used false papers to get over here, considering the US government is after her. I wouldn't sweat it."

"I agree," Gray said over the phone. "There's nothing to link her to the guys."

Given the logistical challenges at his office, Harvey had to concur. "Okay. I suggest you two get packing. I'll meet her tomorrow morning and let her know your terms."

"I'd be there if I could," Gray said. "I hope you understand."

"Of course. It was a bit much to ask you to go to bat for me again. Hopefully, once this is over, we can all get together and catch up."

"Deal."

Gray said his goodbyes and hung up, and Harvey turned to Len and Sonny, thanking them. The next words he spoke were unnecessary, but he said them anyway.

"We never had this conversation."

CHAPTER 27

Eva sat in an independent coffee shop across the street from the Starbucks. She had no reason to believe Harvey would report her visit to the CIA, especially as he believed the fictitious Maria could come to harm, but Eva didn't intend to take unnecessary chances.

Harvey arrived seven minutes early. She watched him walk into the coffeehouse, but her attention was on the street traffic. No sinister-looking SUVs had pulled up in the last half hour, and after another five minutes she saw nothing to cause her any concern.

Eva walked across the street and went inside, spotting Harvey sitting at a table, a disposable cup in front of him.

She took the seat opposite him. "Good morning," she smiled, trying to create as normal a scene as possible.

"Morning," Harvey replied.

"How did the house-hunting go?" The area they were sitting in was quiet, most of the customers queuing for coffee to go, but she didn't want to risk anyone listening in on their conversation.

It took Harvey a moment to realize what she meant, but his tradecraft quickly kicked in.

"Not bad. I saw three places but only two are available and they're not cheap. They're asking three grand."

Relief washed through her, despite the fact that only two of the three men would be taking part.

"That's each, obviously."

"Obviously," she echoed. The price was fine, a tad low even, if they were as good as Andrew said. "And you're sure there's nothing else on the market?"

"Nothing of this quality. I've got a personal stake in this, and I would only want the best of the best."

Eva would have preferred a few more capable fighters who could be trusted when the shit started flying, but she wasn't in a position to choose. Taking on the ESO with just Farooq and Colback by her side would make for an extremely short battle. Though another two probably wouldn't make it any easier. She considered doubling the asking rate if he could get others on board. But, once again, there simply wasn't time.

"Okay," she said, "go with those two."

"Will do," Harvey replied, handing over a piece of paper.

Eva took it and noted the bank account details, along with the instructions to wire the first five days' pay before noon. She would have demanded the same, so didn't complain.

"Is all their paperwork in order?" she asked.

"I was unable to arrange it without approval from above. I didn't think it prudent to involve the director at this early stage."

Not good. Traveling under their real identities was far from ideal. The weaker the potential link back to her, the better. But, once again, she had to accept what she couldn't change.

"Okay," she said. "I've written down the names of a few other areas you might want to check out."

Eva handed him a piece of paper with instructions for the new recruits. They were to rent a car when they landed at Atlanta's international airport, then meet her at the Hard Rock Café downtown at eight that evening. She would be wearing a red beret so that they'd recognize her.

"Thanks," he said, handing the paper back to her. "I'll check them out this afternoon."

Eva smiled and took Harvey's hand. "Thank *you*. For everything."

CHAPTER 28

Carl Huff sat behind the wheel of the Lexus, chewing on a sandwich as the latest traffic camera pinpointed Driscoll's car. He was in the parking lot of a roadside diner on I-40, and the target was still heading his way.

After arriving in San Antonio, he'd expected to see that she'd turned south, heading his way, but instead she'd continued due west. It seemed she was either aiming for the Mexican border in California or paying one of her western US contacts a visit. Fortunately, he'd been far enough ahead of her to position himself in her path, and now she was closing in.

Once she passed, he would pull out behind her, trailing her by at least half a mile and preferably with a few cars between them so she wouldn't notice his presence. They would have to stop at some point, if only to change drivers, and that would be his moment to reacquaint himself with her.

It was a moment he'd been looking forward to ever since Sanders had handed him the envelope.

During their CIA training, a rumor had surfaced that Driscoll and he had become intimately involved. Both had denied the charge but had been subjected to polygraph tests, which they'd passed with flying colors. Their lovemaking that evening had had an extra intensity about it.

Sadly—at least, as far as Huff was concerned—it had been the final time.

Driscoll was a driven woman, and the challenge posed by the clandestine-ops course added a new dimension to her competitive streak. In the early days, Huff had bested her in a couple of disciplines, and she hadn't taken it well. Those minor defeats had spurred her on to greater efforts, soon putting her in a class of her own.

Their relationship had started by accident. After an intense, week-long survival course, the class had been given the weekend to recover. While most had gone back to their apartments to shower and sleep, Huff had headed for the nearest bar and ordered the tallest, coldest beer they had. Ten minutes later, halfway through his second drink, Driscoll had climbed onto the stool next to him and ordered the same.

Alcohol had blurred his memory of the time in the bar, but the latter part of the evening would stay with him forever.

After that night, they'd gotten together every few days, their liaison lasting a few weeks before they'd been called before Sanders to respond to the accusations leveled at them. Both had vigorously denied the charges, but Sanders had been nothing if not thorough. The polygraph had been easy to fool, as they'd already been trained on defeating it. Forcing them to take it had been Sanders's way of showing how seriously he took the matter.

They'd decided that night—or rather, Driscoll had insisted and Huff had reluctantly agreed—that they would stop seeing each other until training was over. He'd assured her that he could wait a few more weeks, but by the time the course had ended, something in her had changed. After the graduation ceremony—attended only by Sanders, the instructors, and the three students who had made the grade—Driscoll had turned down his offer to join him for dinner and drinks. She'd made an excuse about her brother being in town for a couple of days and promised to catch up later.

That was the last time Huff had seen her.

Driscoll's disappearance hadn't been a complete surprise. Looking back, their relationship had been mostly physical: two people with strong sex drives, satisfying their mutual pleasures. They'd never spoken of love or commitment, only had sex with a raw intensity he hadn't known the likes of before or since.

Another update appeared on his screen. The car was only five miles away, still on the same road.

Not long now.

He'd provided Sanders with regular updates over the last couple of days, the most recent only an hour earlier. Anton West was another matter. The calls and text messages demanding to know Huff's whereabouts and plans had been nearly constant. Huff had answered in broad terms, saying that he was checking out some possibilities, to which West had demanded details.

He didn't get them.

When his phone rang again, Huff knew who was calling before he even checked the screen.

"Why the hell didn't you tell me you had her plate number?" West screamed through the phone. "Don't try to deny it. I knew you were holding out on me, so I had my guys check your account activity. You knew her location two days ago!"

West's tendency to turn apoplectic was one of the reasons Huff had no time for him. Managing a team wasn't about barking orders and ruling through fear—a fact lost on West.

"How many men do you have under your command?"

"What? Why is that relevant?"

"How many?" Huff asked again.

"Including here, twenty-two."

"Twenty-two men, and they've managed to lose her at least twice. That's why I didn't tell you. Your people are inept. Give them a weapon and a stationary target and they're probably world-beaters, but they're definitely not thinkers. If you want to catch Driscoll, you need brains, not brawn."

"You arrogant little shit. While you're under my command, you'll do as I say. Otherwise I'll assume you're out to derail my mission and help Driscoll, and that'll make you a viable target."

Huff almost laughed at the threat. He had more to fear from the Keystone Cops.

"We're on the same team," he said calmly. "I just don't need your amateurs getting in the way."

"Well, my *amateurs* are en route to intercept them as we speak. If you hang around, I'll show you how we take down a target."

The call ended and, seconds later, Huff's laptop beeped. He checked the screen and saw the login prompt for the Agency's network.

That was strange. It had never timed out before.

He entered his password and was rewarded with a message he hadn't seen before.

Access Denied.

West was clearly flexing his muscles, but denying Huff access to the network was simply childish and ultimately futile. Driscoll would be passing by within moments, and he would engage her before West's men got within a hundred miles.

CHAPTER 29

"I've got it!" Farooq declared, making Colback jump.

"Got what?"

"The reason they're after you."

Colback switched off the television and went to stand behind Farooq so he could see the screen of the laptop. Farooq seemed to be reading a blog post.

"What did you find?"

Farooq stood and offered Colback the wooden chair. "Read that."

Colback took a seat and scrolled to the top of the page. On the right-hand side was a photograph of the blogger Adrian Holmes. The title of the piece was "CIA Rakes in Billions from Afghan Opium." Colback absorbed the first couple of paragraphs, which reiterated what Farooq had told him when they'd first met: that the CIA had been in the heroin business for decades, and Afghanistan had provided the vast majority of the Agency's income over the last ten years. As he scrolled to the third paragraph, things got interesting.

He instantly recognized the photo to the left of the text. It showed his team relaxing at the base in Kandahar.

*Corporal Ron Elphick of the Green Berets didn't simply wit-
ness the drug trade in Afghanistan, he was actually tasked
with protecting the crop until it was ready for harvest.*

Colback remembered that assignment well. The team had been
based in a village for six weeks, and one of their tasks had been to
provide protection for the crop. The Taliban was fiercely opposed to
the cultivation of poppies for opium and had destroyed many harvests
over the years, killing the farmers in the process.

Until now, that mission had been memorable only for its tedium.
But it seemed that his superiors had either been duped themselves or
hadn't been entirely honest with Colback and his men. They'd been told
that the harvest was for one of the major pharmaceutical companies in
the US, which would use the opium to produce morphine. Some of it
would be earmarked for the US Armed Forces medical services, with
the rest benefiting patients back home.

Reading on, Colback realized that it had all been a lie. Holmes's
reporting had uncovered the true source of medical-grade opium.

It wasn't Afghanistan.

New Zealand and Australia produced more than enough opi-
ate alkaloid for both the medical and military industries combined.
Together, the two countries were considered the most efficient and
cost-effective opiate-producing states in the world, which made it
strange that the CIA would source it from the cottage industry setup
in Afghanistan. He'd been there when the crop had been refined. It
had taken place in a windowless building on wooden benches, not in
a sanitized laboratory.

"So they lied about what the drugs would be used for," he said.
"That doesn't sound like a good enough reason to kill us all."

"Read on," said Farooq.

Colback did and learned something new. In the time he'd spent in
the village, the team had been visited three times by a pharmaceutical

Alan McDermott

company representative. He'd given the name Lance Cook, but Holmes claimed that the man was in fact Hank Monroe.

"I still don't get it," Colback said.

"Click on the other tab in the browser," Farooq told him.

When Colback clicked on it, Monroe's face filled half of the screen.

"He worked for the CIA before becoming governor of Nebraska," Farooq said. "This is a press release announcing his candidature for the next presidential election. According to the pundits, he's the party's preferred candidate by a country mile."

Colback's interest in politics was minimal. As far as he was concerned, left wing and right wing were both parts of the same bird. "You're telling me that even politicians have skeletons in their closets?"

Farooq sighed. "Do you at least remember the election a couple of years ago?"

"Vaguely. I remember Ryan Appleton was leading in the polls until they did that exposé on him, and the other guy won."

"That's right. Appleton was a shoo-in, a party guy who'd do what he was told. When he lost, it was a huge blow to the 0.1 percent."

"You mean the one percent? The big corporate people?"

"No, they're paupers compared to the 0.1 percent. We're talking about a group of individuals who effectively run the civilized world."

"The ESO," Colback muttered.

Farooq was taken aback. "You know about them?"

"Eva told me."

"Oh. Okay. Then, yes, the ESO. The current president's policies are hurting them financially, and I'm talking hundreds of billions. That's personal wealth, not corporate losses."

"You're kidding."

Farooq shook his head. "With that much money involved, people will do anything to stem the flow. Don't get me wrong—they've adapted and are diversifying and investing wisely—but it still doesn't fit their long-term strategy."

"Which is?"

"World domination," Farooq told him with a straight face. "They control all of the world banks, with few exceptions. North Korea was next on their list until they lost the election. If Appleton had won, our warships would be parked off Pyongyang and they'd use one of Kim Jong-un's missile tests as a reason to go to war. This time around, they won't make the same mistake, which is why they're removing all negative references to Hank Monroe from the Internet and killing anyone who knows about his past indiscretions."

Colback was still confused. "Then why is this article by Adrian Holmes still available online?"

"It isn't. I found that on the Dark Web version of Web Archive. It's a site that caches all other websites so that pages are still available for viewing years after the original website disappears. So far, at least, the ESO's reach doesn't extend to the Dark Web. It's the lair of anarchists, activists, and the less morally guided, and takedown requests don't work in the underworld. Even if the ESO could get access, they couldn't do anything about the content."

"But why take the chance that someone might take that content back to the real Internet?" Colback asked. "Why not just choose a different candidate, one that's squeaky clean?"

"Time, money, commitment to the cause—take your pick. Whatever the reason, Hank Monroe's their man, and god help anyone who gets in the way."

He should have been relieved to finally know the truth, but Colback felt nothing but anger. Three of his friends were dead, two of them murdered, just so that trillionaires could add a few more billions to the bank balance. Jeff and Danny had spent their adult lives serving their country valiantly, and for that they had been sent to an early grave.

"How do we let Eva know?"

"We wait until she returns."

"And if she doesn't?"

Farooq pointed to the image of Hank Monroe on the screen. "Then you need to do something about him."

~

Carl Huff had his car positioned near the exit of the truck stop, ready to pull out the moment Driscoll passed by. He could see half a mile down the road, and with his phone's camera on maximum zoom he would be able to identify her vehicle before she got close enough to recognize him.

When the Chevy Impala came into view, Huff immediately sensed something amiss. He could see a male and female in the front seats but both appeared to be African-American. As the vehicle drew closer, he could tell that neither was Driscoll. This was confirmed when the driver hit the turn signal, pulled up to the diner, and both people left the car. The male passenger wasn't even a close match for Colback.

Huff wasn't overly surprised. He'd considered the likelihood that Driscoll might have switched cars but with nothing else to go on, he'd had no choice but to follow the Chevy. Now he had no leads and his access to the network had been terminated.

Sanders wasn't going to like it, but he had to call it in.

"Your account access will be reinstated in a few minutes," Sanders promised after Huff had updated him on the situation. "From now on, you might want to throw West the occasional bone to keep him happy. That aside, what do you think she's really up to?"

Second-guessing Driscoll was proving to be difficult, but Huff already knew what he would do in her position. Whether she would do the same was open to debate.

"If it were me, I'd eliminate the threat," he told Sanders.

Sanders grunted his assent.

"So," said Huff, "I need to know who issued the kill order so I can head her off."

"I think we both know where it came from, and it would take an army to get to the persons in question. Driscoll wouldn't risk it."

"Why not? What does she have to lose? Their reach is global. She's got nowhere to hide."

The phone went silent for a few moments, giving Huff time to contemplate the task facing Driscoll. He was aware of the ESO, as were a few hundred others, but few on the planet knew who made up their number or what they really did. Discovering who they were would be a monumental task on its own; getting to them would be damned near impossible.

"I'll pass that observation along," Sanders said after a moment. "In the meantime, if she's actually planning a strike, she'll need help. I'll send you a list of all private security firms. That's her best chance of finding the right personnel. I'd start with those in the eastern United States. Something tells me she's still out here somewhere."

Huff thought it highly unlikely that Driscoll would expose herself by making such an obvious move, and he couldn't afford to waste days making hundreds or thousands of phone calls simply to see if Sanders's hunch panned out.

"It'd be more efficient if you could send out an alert to all of them. Tell them to report all new contracts over the last few days, plus any that come in. Send all responses to me and I'll filter them myself, but you'll get more cooperation if your name's on the request."

"Okay, I'll work that up, but we need to start seeing results."

The call ended, and Huff started the car. Like Sanders, he believed Driscoll had remained back east, all the closer to the ESO's seat of power.

Time to book a ticket to Washington, D.C.

The phone rang, and he smiled as he hit the Connect button.

"It seems someone mistakenly cut off your network access," West said without apology. "It's now been restored."

"Thanks."

Huff considered letting West continue his wild goose chase, but now that he knew how petty the man was, he decided against it. The last thing he wanted was another accidental network malfunction at a critical moment.

He logged back into the network. "I'm uploading a video of the car's occupants," he told West. "They're not our targets. Driscoll must have switched vehicles at some point. You might as well call your men off."

The short recording was sent, and Huff gave him a couple of minutes to verify the contents.

"Okay, they're standing down. What's your next move?"

"I'm heading back to D.C.," Huff said truthfully. "I'll be in touch."

CHAPTER 30

Anton West poured his sixth coffee of the day and noticed a slight tremor in his hand as he picked up the mug. It wasn't a result of his caffeine intake. His superiors were not happy, and West was the focus of their ire. His only surprise was that he was still in charge of the mission, but for how much longer was anyone's guess.

For four days, Driscoll had given him the runaround, and now the best lead they had—the car she'd used to pick up Naser—had turned out to be yet another misdirection. Driscoll was good. Better than he'd expected. She was also human, and that meant she would eventually slip up. Perhaps not a mistake, as such, but after her recent gains, she would begin to underestimate him.

West needed it to happen sooner rather than later. Few in his position retired or went on to better things unless they were successful.

Failure came with the ultimate price tag.

Pearson suddenly dashed through the doorway of the small kitchen, causing West to spill his coffee. "Sir, we've found them!"

West abandoned his cup and followed Pearson back to the control room. "Where are they?"

"Louisville. A tech over at CIA found one of Naser's back doors and traced the data packages. He's using a cell as a Wi-Fi hotspot."

"Get the tech on the phone immediately," West ordered.

A few moments later he was patched through to the head of the CIA's cyber division.

"Can Naser detect your traces?" West asked.

"Negative."

"You're sure?"

"One hundred percent. Naser is good—very good—but I'm better."

West prayed the woman's confidence was well placed. "What's his exact location?"

"A hotel on 7th Street Road. The Beechwood. That's not all. Naser's been monitoring your communications. I found a worm that converts speech to text and he's been opening the file every ten minutes. He knows every move you're going to make."

Sneaky bastard. Well, two could play at that game.

"Give me the number of Naser's cell and keep looking. If he planted one worm, there may be more."

Once he had Naser's cell number, West passed it to Pearson. "Run a trace on that." He then dialed Eckman's cell phone. "From now on, you'll accept all commands via cell," he said. "They've managed to compromise our comms network, so we're going to use it against them. You can use closed comms to communicate with each other in the field, but I want you to ignore any commands I send over the net, do you understand?"

"All orders will come by phone. Understood."

"Good. Now haul ass to Louisville. They're staying at a hotel. I'll have the details sent to your tablet."

West turned to Pearson. "Bring up the locations of all teams and pinpoint Naser's phone."

The tech worked his magic and the main screen showed eight pulsing green dots and one static red marker in Kentucky. "The closest unit is two hundred and fifty miles away. They should be there in three hours if the local cops don't get in the way."

"Run the usual interference," West ordered.

In situations that required a high-speed response, his men would report any police tailing them, and Pearson would contact the local sheriff and order the squad cars to back off.

It would be midnight before all the assets were in place, and West had a decision to make. Should he send the two closest agents in once they arrived, or wait until all his men were in position? Naturally, he wanted it over as soon as possible, but Driscoll was proving to be a slippery fish. She'd outplayed him up to this point, and his superiors were not blessed with infinite patience.

No, best to wait and hit her with everything at his disposal.

Well, almost everything.

"What's Huff's position?"

Pearson pinpointed the location of the operative's cell phone. "He's currently over Baton Rouge, Louisiana."

Perfect. By the time he landed in D.C., Driscoll and her cohorts would be nothing but bad memories, and West would have done it without the aid of the arrogant Huff.

"Find out what flight he's on and the scheduled arrival time. I'll call him when he lands."

He was tempted to call Huff at that moment and let him know that he was heading in the wrong direction. West could imagine him sitting impotently in cattle class while the action unfolded thirty thousand feet below him.

West decided to stick to the plan and update Huff once he was on the ground. The lunatic might hijack the flight, or do something equally crazy, and it would be ultimately more satisfying to be able to call and say the mission was complete, thanks anyway.

A smile cracked West's face for the first time in days, but it was short-lived. One person in particular wouldn't appreciate being kept in the dark, and that was the man he answered to. West left the control center and made the call.

"What's your plan to deal with them?" the voice asked after West had briefed him.

"I've got sixteen men converging on their location. We should be ready to take them down just after midnight."

"Fine, but be discreet. I won't be happy if I have to fight to keep a pitched battle out of the news."

The call was over, but the thinly veiled threat lingered.

How the hell do you take down a highly trained killer and a combat veteran without causing a scene? Plead with them in a hushed voice to surrender?

What had seemed a straightforward task was now growing increasingly complex. The strike would have to be surgical, which required detailed preparation.

West walked back into the control room. "I want schematics of the Beechwood Hotel and everything in the local area."

Knowing the layout of the building would be a good start. His team would be able to cover all the exits and determine the best entry points. They carried suppressed weapons, and if they could get a jump on the targets it should play out quietly.

There was little else he could do to mitigate the risk of an all-out battle.

"Sir, it appears the Beechwood is in the heart of the red-light district. Midnight will probably be their busiest period."

"Well, that's just great . . ."

Another obstacle thrown in his path. West was beginning to wonder if the gods had something against him.

"We'll have to keep the teams in position and hit Driscoll once the area's quiet," he replied. "Let's plan for a four a.m. insertion."

All he could do now was hope the situation remained stable for the next ten hours. If Driscoll and the others were still in the hotel by the time his teams were in position, it would be a simple matter of waiting for the right moment.

Something told him he wasn't going to be that lucky.

CHAPTER 31

The Hard Rock Café was jumping.

Eva fought her way to the bar as Guns N' Roses exploded from the speakers, and when she caught the bartender's eye she ordered a loaded burger and a mineral water. His look told her she was out of place among the predominantly young crowd, and Eva felt the same way.

After landing at Atlanta Airport, she'd taken a taxi straight to the venue, touching up her old-woman makeup on the way. She'd have to continue wearing the disguise until she had a chance to buy some new clothes, but first things first. The British operatives she'd hired would be here within a couple of hours, and as soon as they arrived they'd all set off for Louisville to pick up Colback and Farooq.

After that, she expected things to get interesting.

Anton West was her first target. If he'd been in touch with the ESO, he would have a contact number. That should be enough for Farooq to trace the owner.

Hopefully.

If the ESO had the power to prevent their numbers being recorded in government databases, they would probably have other security measures in place. But then again, she'd never expected it to be easy. Taking on an entity that had unlimited resources at its disposal was suicidal at best, but the alternative—sitting around waiting for someone to put a bullet in her brain—was even less appealing.

Eva found a booth and used the maps app on her phone to look up the town Anton West called home. She'd already ruled out a strike on his place of work: it was bound to be guarded, and she didn't want to announce herself with a vicious firefight. She wanted West alive—if only initially—so it made most sense to hit him at home or in transit.

The township of Olney was in Montgomery County, Maryland, twenty miles north of D.C. West's house was one of just eight on a quiet leafy road near the country club. The surrounding houses were set back from the road, all of them with trees out front, which would help shield her and the team from nosy neighbors. The next step would be to set up reconnaissance on the place and determine the best time to strike.

Her food arrived and Eva tucked in, her eyes on the exits. She'd scoped out the place before flying to the UK, to know her options in case anyone suspicious entered the bar.

Eva managed to finish her meal without being accosted, then took her phone out again and pretended to be interested in it while waiting for her hired help to arrive.

About forty minutes early, two men entered the bar. They didn't seem the Special Forces type. One was small with short blond hair; the other was much taller and carried a little too much around the waist. She turned her attention back to the door as the newcomers disappeared into the crowd, hoping her new recruits would get there without any issues. There was no reason to think they would be stopped at the airports, but flights often got delayed or canceled. With no contingency plan in place, she would be forced to contact Harvey and get him to pass on revised instructions, but that would be a last resort. The CIA staff at the US embassy in London could easily intercept a call to his cell phone, so she'd have to come up with an alternate means of reaching him.

Eva almost jumped when the blond-haired man she'd seen earlier plopped down in the seat opposite her.

"Emilie." He smiled.

Eva slowly put her phone back in the purse on her lap and wrapped her fingers around the grip of her pistol. The second man came over and stood next to her, blocking her escape.

She saw two possibilities. They were her new assault force, or West had somehow tailed her and sent them to kill her.

Part of her wished it were the latter.

"Andrew sent us," said the smaller, younger one. Up close, he looked a little older than he'd first appeared. Laughter lines creased his eyes and forehead, and he had the air of someone who'd been around the block a few times.

"My name's Sonny," he said, holding out his hand. "This is Len."

Eva was tempted to walk away and write off the money, but that would only leave her at square one. Still, that might be a better choice than going into battle with this pair.

She ignored Sonny's handshake and pushed herself to the edge of the seat, waiting for the big one to get out the way. He duly obliged, and they followed her out to the parking lot.

"Which one's yours?" Eva asked.

Sonny pressed a button on his key and the lights on a nondescript Ford Sedan flashed twice. She claimed the front passenger seat and Sonny got in beside her.

"Put these on," Eva said, and handed them each a baseball cap. "Not the perfect disguise, but enough to obscure your features if we run past any traffic cameras. The longer we can go without them identifying you, the better."

Sonny put the cap on and pulled it down over his eyes. "Where to?" he asked.

"Louisville," she told him. "Head north and follow the signs for I-75."

Sonny started the engine and pulled onto the street. "Is something wrong?" he asked. "You don't seem pleased to see us."

That's an understatement.

"I was expecting . . . someone fresh out of the army. When did you serve?"

"Let me see now," Sonny said in a quavering voice. "Twenty-five, thirty years ago? It's hard to recall when you get to my age."

"Ignore him," Len said. "He always gets cranky around naptime."

Great . . . Harvey sent me a pair of comedians.

"We left the SAS eleven years ago," Len continued. "A friend started his own security company and we've been working for him since."

"A decade doing BG work?" Eva asked.

"Some of the men contract as bodyguards, yes, but Sonny and I are part of the management team. We have a facility outside London where we put new recruits through their paces. It has an assault course, shooting range—you name it—and we only accept the best."

"So, you've been behind a desk for ten years?" *What was Andrew thinking?*

"Not exactly," Len said. "We've been in the field too."

Probably grazing in it, you fat fuck. "Tell me about Russia. Andrew said you pulled him from prison."

"It was Tagrilistan and he was being held by Russian separatists. We went in and extracted him."

"So I heard, but I want details. How did you—"

She stopped herself as Tagrilistan suddenly registered with her. She kept up with the goings-on in the former Soviet states, as next to the Middle East they'd been her most frequent deployment destinations. She'd carried out a mission in Ukraine a couple of years earlier, and Tagrilistan was in much the same situation. "When was this?"

"About eighteen months ago," Len said.

The timeline fit. In January the previous year, she'd read a report about sixty-plus Russian soldiers being killed by unknown forces.

Western leaders had denied any involvement, suggesting the local Tagrilistan army had been responsible. The identity of the aggressors had never been established.

"That was you?"

"Us and three others," Len confirmed.

"What? Five of you took on the Russians?"

"Four of us, actually," Sonny said. "Mac was just there to fly the chopper."

Eva was willing to admit she'd misjudged them. Anyone with the balls to take on a Russian battalion wouldn't think twice about facing the ESO's hired guns. Perhaps Andrew had picked the right men after all.

Sonny looked over at Eva. "Now that you know a little about us, would you mind telling us what this mission involves?"

With a seven-hour drive ahead of them, Eva decided to start at the beginning.

CHAPTER 32

The Beechwood appeared to be the only building with more than two stories for a dozen miles in all directions. A sign with the hotel's name in neon lights stretched from the fifth floor down to the first, and a couple of letters looked to have burned out years earlier.

Willard Eckman, designated Eagle Two, drove past the building a couple of hundred yards, then made a right and parked up in the lot of a body shop. The cars of Eagles One and Four were already there, as were a couple of others. Eckman got out to introduce himself to the newcomers.

"I'm Eagle Two. I'll be coordinating the takedown."

The eight new men had traveled in four SUVs, and when the two men of Eagle Three arrived, they'd be sixteen strong. Eckman warned them against contacting Nest on open comms, then designated them Rook One through Rook Four.

It was two in the morning, two hours before the planned strike. Eckman intended to use the time productively.

"Has anyone done a walk-around?" he asked.

"I have," Danny Castleton of Eagle Four said. "There's a strip club seventy yards to the left of the hotel and a car dealership a hundred away to the right. Even if things get noisy, it shouldn't attract too much attention."

Eckman had been thinking the same thing, but it was the aftermath that concerned him. West had ordered him not to leave a pile of bodies in his wake.

"What about the hotel itself?"

"Five floors, two main exits. The front door, another at the rear, and there's a fire exit feeding each floor. The area behind the hotel's secured by a chain-link fence topped with razor wire. Just one external CCTV camera covering the back entrance."

Eckman produced a tablet computer and placed it on the hood of his car. On the screen were the building's blueprints, rendered in 3-D. "As you enter the building, the stairs are on the left. There's an elevator facing you, and between them is the reception desk, behind which is an office and toilet. On each of the top four floors there are twelve rooms, six facing the front and six at the rear. The fire exits are here, halfway down each hallway, all leading to the same external fire escape."

"Any idea which room they're in?" a member of Rook Two asked. "Or do we just clear each room until we find them?"

"I plan to find out," Eckman said. "Parker, if anyone looks like they need to get laid, it's you. I want you to go to the strip joint, pick up a girl, and take her to the hotel. Tell the receptionist your friends said they'd be staying there and find out which room they're in."

"Roger that." Parker grinned and began jogging in the direction of the Diamond Pussycat Club.

Eckman saw him emerge ten minutes later with a woman on his arm, and the pair walked into the Beechwood. Twenty minutes passed, and Eckman was growing worried, when Parker appeared at the door and trotted over to them.

"What took you so long?"

"Didn't want to seem suspicious. If I took her to the hotel, asked about Driscoll, and then left, it would have looked strange. So I took her to a room."

"Are you fucking serious? We're here to take down a highly trained killer and you bump uglies with a ten-dollar whore?"

"It was more like fifty dollars, and another thirty for the room. You think I can expense it?"

Eckman was tempted to put a bullet between Parker's eyes, but Castleton stepped in.

"He's got a point, Will. Who's gonna remember another john?"

Eckman calmed down a little, but vowed to deal with Parker once the mission was over.

"I wore a rubber, if that makes a difference."

Castleton slapped Parker on the side of the head before he could dig himself any deeper.

"At least tell me you got the room number," growled Eckman.

"Room 411, far end of the corridor on the right, facing the street. Only, it's just Colback and Naser. The guy said they arrived alone."

That was an unexpected development.

Eckman dialed West. "It's me."

"What is it?"

"We have a problem."

~

Anton West acknowledged Eckman's report and ordered him to await further instructions.

What are you up to, Driscoll?

After going to so much trouble to rescue Colback and enlist Naser's help, she wouldn't abandon them now.

Or would she?

160

Driscoll's brother had been part of Colback's unit, so her reason for teaming up with the ex-soldier might be purely personal. If she had been simply looking for the reason the former colleagues had been marked for death, she might already have everything she needed. If that were the case, she would have no further use for the two men in the hotel room.

In this business, there was no time for personal attachments. Did Driscoll feel the same way?

No, that didn't add up. Naser had stolen millions from the CIA accounts. Why choose to hang out in a sleazy hotel in Louisville with that kind of cash at his fingertips? And why would he still be accessing the CIA network if they already had everything they needed? Was it to keep tabs on the investigation, or were they still looking for answers?

They were waiting for Driscoll to return, he was sure of it. The question was, when would she come back?

"Those hotels take payment in advance," West told Eckman. "Find out how long they're planning to stay."

"Roger that."

"Sir," Pearson said, "Eagle Three is in position. That's everyone on site."

"Good." Sixteen against two. Hardly fair, but life was often like that. Colback and Naser were going nowhere, and if Driscoll were to make an appearance, then all the better.

"They're due to check out at ten in the morning," Eckman said over the phone.

Decision time. Take them out now, or wait for Driscoll to show?

Colback had always been the main target, and taking him and Naser out of the equation would make things simpler. For one, Driscoll would no longer have access to the databases of the intelligence agencies, leaving her blind.

On the flipside, if he ordered his men to go in now, someone might report a firefight and that would mean police on the scene when Driscoll showed up. Which would only scare her off and make her more vigilant.

Prudence dictated he play it safe—wait for her to turn up, then take them all out—but he had no guarantee she'd show. They might have arranged to meet somewhere else, in which case his men would end up trying to tail their quarry again. He also had to keep in mind that his superiors were becoming increasingly frustrated with his lack of success. Taking out Colback and Naser would appease them to some degree; he could then focus on Driscoll. Better still, he could take the pair alive and torture Driscoll's location out of them.

"Hit them at four," West told Eckman. "But take them alive."

CHAPTER 33

"Nice neighborhood," Sonny quipped as Len Smart followed Eva's instructions and pulled up outside the derelict-looking building.

Eva ignored the younger man's endless joking, as she'd tried to do for most of the journey. She'd used the drive to get to know them, and while Len Smart appeared mature and professional, Sonny had been infuriating in the extreme. His style was to reduce everything to jokes or innuendo. That said, her respect for Smart had only increased: if he could put up with Sonny for so long, his patience must be endless.

"Keep your eyes peeled," she said as she climbed out. "I'll just be a couple of minutes."

When she rapped on the door, it took a minute for DeBron's guard to answer it. He opened the door and rubbed his eyes, his attire adding to the impression that he'd just woken up.

Eva went through the pat-down procedure and walked up the stairs as the security door buzzed open. DeBron was sitting behind his desk, sporting the same clothes he'd been wearing on her last visit. Even the smile was the same, in spite of the hour.

"Sorry to wake you," she said, "but I couldn't wait. I need to get going as soon as possible."

DeBron rose and picked up a couple of black canvas bags that had been at his feet. He placed them on the desk.

"That's everything you asked for."

Even though their association had been long and cordial, Eva still needed to check the contents. She opened the first bag and pulled out four Sig Sauer SIG16 assault rifles and the same number of suppressed Glock 17s. They all looked to have been well maintained.

"Ammo?"

"Four hundred rounds of 9mm for the Glocks and a thousand 5.56 for the rifles."

Eva could see plenty of spare magazines for the weapons in the second bag, as well as a couple of cleaning kits and latex gloves so that the weapons and ammo could be handled without leaving fingerprints or traces of DNA. As usual, DeBron had thought of everything.

"Is the vehicle ready?"

"I told Tyrone to bring it around when you got here."

"Great. If you could get him to take the Ford back to the rental office, I'd appreciate it. My friends paid for it in their name, and I don't want them being flagged."

"Consider it done."

"Thanks again. I'll let you get back to sleep."

"Always a pleasure. Give my condolences to the other guy."

Eva smiled and picked up the bags. She carried them downstairs and out the door, where a Dodge Grand Caravan had parked behind the Ford. She would have preferred something with a little more under the hood, but she'd make do.

Tyrone tossed her the keys, and she ordered Len and Sonny to switch vehicles, telling the larger man to drive. She got in the front seat next to him.

"Sonny, make yourself useful and fill those magazines. Wear the gloves."

As they pulled away, she looked in the mirror and saw Tyrone getting into the rental.

"Take a left at the end of the street," she said. "Once we've picked up Rees and Farooq, we'll head for D.C. I suggest we stop at a motel overnight to catch up on sleep."

"Sleep sounds good," Sonny said. "I've been awake for about thirty hours."

We all have, thought Eva.

Smart had managed a couple of hours' sleep in the back seat on the drive from Atlanta, but they could all do with a good rest before the mission proper.

Eva directed Smart onto 7th Street Road, and soon she could see the hotel in the distance.

"That's the place," she said. "Park outside the entrance. I'll go up and get them."

Smart pulled up to the curb and left the engine running as she entered the lobby.

Still dressed in her old lady garb, she once again felt out of place, this time in an establishment run purely for the sex trade, but at least any description the receptionist gave would be useless in a few hours' time.

The youngish man behind the desk didn't glance up from his phone until she was standing right in front of him, and he looked beyond her to see if she'd brought along a companion. "Can I help?" he asked, his tone suggesting it was the last thing he wanted to do.

"I'm looking for my friends," she told him. "One's black, the other's Arabic. They've been here a couple of days."

"Four eleven," the man said, and returned his attention to his phone.

Eva turned to walk to the stairway, but froze when the receptionist added, "Popular guys . . ." under his breath.

"What's that?"

"Oh, just some guy was asking about them a couple of hours ago. Said he was a friend too."

Eva went immediately on edge. "Is he still here?" she asked, working to keep her voice even.

The man shook his head, still concentrating on his phone. "Came and left, just like the rest of them." He smirked at his own joke, but Eva didn't notice.

Somehow, West's people had managed to find Colback and Farooq. The "how" would have to wait until they were clear of the area and could take stock.

She walked to the stairs, her hand gripping the Glock in her purse. Tempted as she was to look up and scan for threats, she kept her eyes on the steps as she climbed to the second floor. The hallway was clear, so she continued her act and made it to the third. Again, no sign of danger, but she sensed that the enemy was close.

On the fourth floor, she took the gun from her purse and kept it out of view. When she reached room 411, she put her ear to the door. Hearing nothing, she knocked twice, then stood off to the side.

The door cracked open a couple of inches and Colback's face appeared in the gap.

"Yes?"

"It's me," Eva whispered, and his eyes widened as he recognized the voice. He slipped the chain and let her into the room.

Farooq was asleep on the bed, a shark documentary playing on the television, the volume low.

"You look—"

Eva held up a hand, and in a harsh whisper said, "Grab everything. We're leaving. They found you."

Colback started to speak, but she cut him off again. "Move!"

Farooq shot upright and stared at her, confusion on his face.

"Eva?" he asked after a couple of seconds.

"We have to go," she told him. "You've got thirty seconds to get your shit together."

The men quickly began stuffing their belongings into their bags and throwing on jackets. Colback took the Glock from his waistband and checked the chamber.

"There's a Dodge Caravan outside. The guys in it are with me. I'll leave first and check the area. If it's clear, I'll signal you. I want you both to run to the vehicle and get in. You hear me?"

They both nodded and she led them out of the room and down the hallway to the stairs.

They reached the lobby without incident, and Colback dropped his room key on the reception desk as Eva headed for the door.

She was halfway to the entrance when two men strode in.

Not Sonny. Not Smart.

Trouble.

They wore identical dark jeans and leather jackets, and they looked wired. One of them glanced past Eva and saw Colback and Farooq standing at the reception desk. He nudged his companion and spoke into his throat mic, at the same time reaching inside his jacket.

Eva continued to approach them in her old woman's gait, but the killers only had eyes for her friends at the desk.

That made her job much easier.

She put her hand in her bag, head down as if looking for her keys, all the while aiming to pass between them. As she drew level with the leather jackets, she brought her foot up and smashed it into the knee of the one on her left. Bone crunched and the man yelled in pain as he collapsed, but Eva was already moving onto the second target. She spun to her right and struck him at the base of the neck with the butt of her pistol.

Temporarily incapacitating them wasn't going to be enough. They would soon be back in the fight—at least one of them would—and Eva had a feeling there'd be plenty more outside to contend with. The one with the shattered knee grimaced as he reached for the pistol he'd dropped, and Eva put him out of his misery with a shot to the temple.

She dispatched the other in an equally clinical manner, feeling only the slightest remorse at having to kill agents whose work was much like hers had been.

She looked to Colback, who'd barely had time to draw his own weapon before it was all over.

"Let's go," Eva said as she made for the exit.

She poked her head around the door and saw four more men appear around the side of the building. They had weapons ready and were heading for her.

"Four more coming this way," she told Colback and Farooq. "Get in the van. I'll cover you."

But Sonny Baines had his own plans, emerging from the Dodge with a rifle in hand. He crept along the side of the van until level with the front passenger seat. He paused and looked back and forth between the approaching quartet and Eva. When she nodded, he brought the rifle to his shoulder and laid down suppressing fire. One of the targets staggered and fell, and the others dived for cover.

"Go! Go! Go!"

The moment Sonny shouted the order, Eva grabbed Farooq's collar and dragged him to the van. He scrambled inside and Eva followed, Colback close behind.

"Time to go!" she shouted to Sonny, who jumped back into the front seat, then rolled down the window as Smart hit the gas. Tires squealed as they sought purchase, and the van shot forward.

The incoming fire was immediate and ferocious. The windscreen spiderwebbed as rounds struck the glass, and Eva gave thanks that they faced only pistols.

Sonny leaned out of the window and fired three-round bursts, taking another two men down and forcing the last operative to scramble for cover around the side of the hotel.

"Sonny!" Smart yelled. "Two o'clock!"

Sonny looked ahead and saw two black SUVs race out of a parking lot and swing to a stop in the road, blocking it. Doors flew open and armed men piled out. Pinpricks of light preceded bullets slamming into the front of the Dodge.

"Hold on!"

Smart spun the wheel to the left to give Sonny a better angle, and his friend emptied his weapon at the blockade.

"Switching," Sonny said as he ejected the spent magazine and rammed home a fresh one.

Smart bounced up a curb and raced down the side of a car dealership, the van's tires fighting for traction in the loose dirt. The incoming fire had ceased for the moment, but seconds later headlights appeared in his rearview mirror. He kept his foot to the floor, the rear axle fishtailing at every opportunity.

A fence appeared in front of them, but Smart didn't lift his foot. After yelling for everyone to hold tight, he smashed through the woodwork. The nose dropped two feet as the ground disappeared beneath them and they hit the railway track hard. Everyone inside was thrown around like balls in a lotto machine, and Smart momentarily lost his grip on the wheel. He finally regained control as the bouncing stopped and they found themselves at the end of a residential street. Smart punched it once more, and seconds later they came to an intersection with a two-lane highway, one that paralleled 7th Street Road.

"Any suggestions?" he called out.

"Don't stop for hitchhikers," Sonny deadpanned. "Apart from that, just lose the bastards."

"We need to think about satellite coverage," Farooq said. "If they're watching us now, we haven't got a chance."

"One thing at a time," Eva said. "Len, get us clear of the area."

Smart turned right onto the two-lane. The road was clear, but not for long.

A Jeep screeched to a halt at the next junction, then accelerated straight for the van. Smart was having enough trouble seeing through the shattered windshield, and the oncoming high beams made it doubly difficult. He was about to ask Sonny to clear a path, but his partner was already on it.

As Sonny blasted away at the fast-approaching Jeep, Eva followed his lead and emptied her rifle out of the right-hand side of the van. The SUV jinked to evade the onslaught, but the fire was too accurate. One of Sonny's rounds struck the driver and the Jeep lurched to the right, hitting the curb hard and bouncing twice before embedding itself in the corner of a tire shop. There was no blinding explosion, only a jet of steam from under the hood. Eva pumped a few more rounds into the stricken vehicle as they passed, then began looking for new targets.

The road remained clear for the next minute, giving Eva time to tear Farooq a new one.

~

"Boss."

Castleton nudged Eckman and pointed to the hotel. A Dodge van had pulled up. An elderly woman got out.

Eckman snatched up his binoculars and focused on the entrance to the Beechwood. As the woman walked inside, he put the glasses down. "It's not her, unless she put on a hundred pounds and aged forty years in the last few days." He looked at his watch as the seconds ticked toward four in the morning.

The arrival of the van made no difference to the mission. Hopefully it would be gone before the countdown expired, but if not, no big deal. The plan was to take Colback and Naser out the back exit, so any activity at the front of the hotel was irrelevant. Everyone was in place and they were just awaiting his word.

The moment to issue the go order finally arrived. Eckman gave the command over the closed comms and watched as two of his men walked around the side of the building and headed for the main entrance. Out of sight, Eckman knew that six of his men would be making their way in through the back, with four more covering the outside in case the targets managed to slip past the vanguard.

The two-man team at the front disappeared inside and, seconds later, Eckman's comms squawked into life.

"Eagle Three. Eyes on Colback and Naser."

Damn. That soon?

Eckman hadn't expected them to be in the reception area. They were supposed to be tucked up in their beds, oblivious to the snatch squad coming for them.

The chances of this going down quietly were fast disappearing.

"Take them, but try not to cause a scene," Eckman ordered.

He waited for an acknowledgment, but none came.

"Eagle Three, did you copy last?"

Nothing.

"Rook One, Rook Two, targets sighted in the reception area. No response from Eagle Three. Check it out."

Eckman saw the four men creep around the side of the building and head toward the entrance to the Beechwood. He also saw someone emerge from the van with an assault rifle at his shoulder.

"Rook One—"

The gunman opened fire before he could get his warning away, and one man staggered and fell. The others dived for cover as three figures ran from the hotel entrance to the Dodge. Two of them were Colback and Naser, and Eckman was surprised to see an old woman with them.

Too late, he realized that he'd been fooled by a simple disguise.

"All units, they're at the entrance! Driscoll's with them! They're getting into the van!"

The target vehicle was already on the move. Eckman could only watch as two more of his men were hit, and that spurred him into action. He ordered Castleton into the driver's seat of his Jeep as he continued to issue orders.

"They're moving! All units, mount up. They're heading north on 7th Street Road."

Castleton gunned the engine and the Jeep roared onto the street to give chase. They were the only pursuers for the moment, as the rest of the men ran back to the parking lot to retrieve their vehicles.

Eckman's phone chirped and the caller ID told him it was West.

"I need satellite," Eckman said. "They've taken off and we're pursuing, but she's got a head start."

"The bird's not available," West told him. "It's tasked with an anti-terror operation in California. We're tracking Naser's phone though. Stay on the line and I'll give you updates."

Eckman was glad West hadn't asked how the operation had gone pear-shaped. That conversation could wait.

Eckman saw the van go off-road and told Castleton to follow. He hung on tight as the Jeep bounced up the curb and onto dirt. The Jeep had better traction and was gaining rapidly, but the cloud of dust being thrown up made it difficult to see. He almost soiled himself when the road suddenly disappeared, and Castleton brought the Jeep to a skidding halt inches from the drop onto the railway track. He could see the van pick up speed as it made it onto asphalt.

"Back up!" Eckman ordered, and got onto the radio to let the others know where Driscoll and her team were heading.

Eagle Four responded to say they were on an intercept course, while the teams he'd sent south to cut Driscoll off gave their ETAs.

Castleton reversed at speed and bounced back onto 7th Street Road, then headed north to the next turn, but by then they'd lost contact with Eagle Four.

Castleton stopped the Jeep at the next intersection, where the intercept team's crumpled vehicle was clearly visible, embedded in the corner of a tire shop.

"Where are they?" Eckman asked West.

"Heading east. They turned right onto West Oak Street toward Limerick. Wait one . . . Shit! We lost the signal."

~

"It's impossible," Farooq insisted. "There's no way they could have traced my phone or found my back doors."

"Someone did," Eva said. "The guy who was asking about you at the hotel wasn't trying to sell you insurance. Ditch the cell, right now."

Farooq sighed as he activated a program on his phone that wiped all data from the handset, then removed the battery and SIM card and tossed the components out of the window.

"Satisfied?"

"No."

Once more, they'd been caught on their back foot. She preferred to be hunter rather than prey and intended to reverse their roles as soon as possible.

"Did you check the comms file every ten minutes like I told you?"

"Yes. There was nothing," Farooq said.

"And I checked them while he was asleep," Colback added. "It was just chatter. No mention of us."

"They must have found your worm," Eva said. "They knew we were listening in and let us think we were in the clear. My guess is they'll be communicating by phone or closed comms instead. Len, take a right and then the next left. We'll spend some time in residential streets. If they're watching from above, we'll know soon enough. If they don't hit us in the next couple of minutes, we'll ditch the car and find new wheels."

"And if they *are* watching?" Farooq asked, the only one in the van unaccustomed to firefights.

Colback handed him a pistol. "Kill as many as you can." He showed Farooq how to switch magazines and ready the weapon. "There's no safety on a Glock, just point and squeeze, don't pull."

Farooq handled the weapon as if it were a poisonous snake, its purpose clearly at odds with his world of ones and zeros.

"Next right," Eva said, reading from the satnav app on her phone. To Farooq she said, "Don't hesitate if you get one of them in your sights. They're not here to invite you to the prom."

After another minute of driving around, this time heading east, Eva told Smart to pull into the parking lot of a Dollar General and park in back. The store was closed and they had three exits to choose from should West's men make an appearance.

After five minutes, it was clear they weren't being tracked from the sky. That didn't rule out choppers showing up at any moment, and Eva wanted to be on the move and clear of Louisville before that happened. She tucked her pistol into the waistband of her skirt. "I'll find a new vehicle. You guys stay here and get acquainted."

"How long should we give you?" Smart asked.

Eva liked the way he thought. "Fifteen minutes. After that, you're on your own."

She was back in twelve.

Eva parked the newly boosted Toyota Highlander next to the van and helped to transfer the bags, then told Sonny to take the wheel with Len riding shotgun. The rest of them hunkered down in the back seat as the onboard navigation system directed Sonny to the freeway.

~

Eckman told his men to report in, and the news wasn't good. Of the sixteen that had started the mission, six were already dead. They still had seven vehicles though, and they were all out patrolling the streets in search of Driscoll and her cronies. He'd given West the plate number and it had been added to an alert, but Driscoll had probably stolen another car by now. He'd also informed his boss that Driscoll's complement had been boosted to four, and that at least one of the newcomers knew how to handle an assault rifle.

The clean-up teams were en route, but too late to prevent local attention. Police and news teams were already at the Beechwood, and the scene of Eagle Four's crash had been cordoned off too. The only good news for Eckman was that West would be the one to deal with the fallout from above.

Eckman checked the screen on his tablet and saw the positions of all seven vehicles, his included. Since most of the men were in new vehicles, he'd redesignated them, assigning the name to the car rather than the men. He retained the Eagle Two call sign for himself.

Driscoll had doubled back on herself after the encounter with Eagle Four, which suggested she wanted to keep going east. That made sense, as that was where several freeways wound together like strands of spaghetti. She could travel in any direction from there, which was why Eckman had sent a couple of vehicles to the area to keep an eye out for her.

He wasn't optimistic.

Driscoll had proven time and time again to be as slippery as they came. Finding her would be no mean feat, but he had to try. There had been no word from Hannagan since his blue rinse, and Eckman didn't want to be the next one to disappear into the void. But his allotted time was quickly ticking down.

His remaining men were now spread out south of the river, checking out parking lots and back alleys—places Driscoll was most likely to have abandoned the van.

The break he needed came minutes later. Eagle One reported finding the abandoned Dodge behind the Dollar General, and Eckman immediately called West for assistance. He gave his boss the store's address and asked him to scour closed-circuit cameras in the area to see if they showed anything. Three minutes later, Eckman had the make, model, and license plate of a vehicle that had driven behind the store and come back out two minutes later. It'd had one person on board initially, but it had left the parking lot with two up front.

It had to be Driscoll.

West's team back at the control center hadn't been able to identify the driver or passenger when the Toyota left the parking lot. They had the perfect angle into the cab, but both were wearing baseball caps with the brims pulled down to conceal their faces. The only thing they could discern was a marked difference in size, and that both appeared to be male.

Still, it was a start. And two minutes later, things got better.

"They're eastbound on I-64," West said over the phone. "They just passed exit twelve. I've got a chopper in the air, but it'll take twenty minutes to get to you."

Eckman used closed comms to redirect his remaining six vehicles in the direction of I-64. The two units that had been watching the freeway on-ramps were closest and had a five-minute head start on the rest of them.

The ideal scenario would be to get ahead of them and block the highway, so Eckman radioed the closest unit, Eagle One, with instructions.

~

"Heads up," Smart said from behind the wheel. "We've got a vehicle closing fast."

Eva and Sonny flicked off the safeties on their rifles. Through the rear window, they could see headlights reining them in.

"Wait for my signal," Eva said, and no one argued.

The approaching Jeep was two lanes over, and the driver flashed by without so much as a glance in their direction. First impressions suggested someone in a hurry to get home, but Eva didn't like it. The second big Jeep of the evening seemed more than a coincidence.

As the taillights fled into the distance, she decided to play it safe.

"Wait until he's clear, then pull over and kill the lights. I want everyone out of the vehicle and under cover the moment we stop."

Seconds later, the Jeep crested a rise in the highway and was swallowed up by the darkness.

"Now."

Smart pulled onto the shoulder, doors flew open, and all five occupants piled out, a couple of them carrying bags as they ran into the trees. Ten yards in, Eva dropped her bag at the foot of a tree and stood behind it, her rifle raised and pointing toward the abandoned Toyota.

Silence descended, and as the seconds ticked by, her eyes grew accustomed to the darkness. To preserve her night vision, she closed one of them as a white beam hit the concrete median wall that separated the highway. The light brightened as a vehicle approached, its engine tone telling her it was slowing.

Eva realized she hadn't warned the others not to open fire unless she did. Now it was too late and all she could do was hope they kept their nerve. In the time she'd spent with them on the long road trip from Atlanta, Baines and Smart had talked a good game, and in the last hour they'd proved they were the real deal. She hoped they didn't spoil their reputation in the next few seconds.

A new, black Jeep stopped ten yards behind the Toyota, and Eva saw a man get out. He held up a suppressed pistol in a two-handed grip as he carefully approached her vehicle. Seeing it empty, the figure turned his attention to the woods. He said something inaudible into a mic, clearly calling in backup.

The man waited by the side of the road, pistol pointing into the darkness, until an SUV pulled up and decanted its two occupants. The new pair had flashlights and they played the beams into the trees.

As the light inched toward her position, Eva opened fire. One of the men holding a flashlight spun and fell, and by the time he hit the ground, three other rifles had joined in and found targets.

"Move!" she shouted, picking up her bag and running to the Toyota. She used the butt of the rifle to smash out its taillights, then got behind the wheel as more headlights appeared in her rearview.

"Are you sure this is a wise move?" Smart asked. "The one who passed us will be waiting ahead."

"More coming from behind," said Eva with a shrug, as she gunned the SUV back onto the highway. "If we stay in the woods, we're dead. We have to clear the area, and fast."

"Then why not take one of the Jeeps? They're a lot faster."

"They'll have trackers installed," Eva told him. "Now, roll your windows down and get ready to blast anyone who gets in our way."

She coaxed the fully laden vehicle up to ninety, and as she reached the high point in the road, flicked on her brights.

Two lanes of the freeway were blocked by the Jeep that had passed them earlier, and the man taking cover behind the engine block was already firing in their direction. Rounds pinged off the grille and took out one of the headlights, but Eva kept her foot on the accelerator as Sonny, Smart, and Colback returned fire, peppering the Jeep with lead, blowing out the tires, and destroying the windows. The shooter had to take cover from the barrage, and Eva swung around the stricken SUV doing more than a hundred. She turned off the headlights and weaved from lane to lane, making the Highlander a difficult target, but they didn't escape unscathed.

Farooq's scream filled the car and Eva looked at him in the rearview mirror.

"What's wrong?"

"I'm hit." He grimaced, clutching his left shoulder.

She could see a dark liquid oozing between his fingers. "Len, check it out."

Smart moved Farooq's hand and used a knife to slice the shirtsleeve so that he could see the wound. "It's a nick, that's all. It missed the bone."

"It hurts like a bitch," said Farooq.

"It will, for a few days." Smart tore off the rest of Farooq's sleeve and used it to stem the flow. "Keep pressure on it. We'll have to clean it up as soon as we get the chance."

The pinpricks of light from the shooter's rifle ceased as Eva took them out of range, but they weren't safe yet. She spotted the headlights of another vehicle in her mirror and it was quickly followed by another.

"How many are there?" Sonny asked as a third vehicle joined the chase.

"Three," Farooq said. "Make that four now."

"We have to split them up if we can," Smart said. He took out his phone and opened up the map application, allowing it to pinpoint their current location. "Get off at the next exit, then take a right. There are plenty of side roads to disappear into."

"If the satellite's watching, hiding won't do any good," said Farooq.

"It's better than trying to outrun them on a straight road," Sonny said.

"I agree," Colback said. "I'd rather choose the battleground and make a stand."

Eva took the next off-ramp and blew through a set of red lights, heading south.

"Take the second right," Smart told her. "After a hundred yards, take a left. There's a dirt road that leads into the woods."

The pursuing vehicles were still on the freeway when Eva spun the wheel onto the side road, and moments later she was forced to reduce their speed to a crawl as they bounced onto a dirt road in pitch darkness.

"There," Smart pointed. "See if you can get in among the trees."

Eva eased between a couple of oaks and managed to get a few yards farther in before the woods became too dense to continue. As soon as she cut the engine, Smart, Sonny, and Colback got out and took up positions at the tree line. She took a rifle from the bag and inserted a fresh magazine, then stuffed a spare into her waistband and jogged over to join Smart.

"Get Sonny to gather some branches and hide the car," he said without turning. "I'll take first watch with Rees. You guys get some rest."

Eva nodded. "Let's give it an hour. If they've got overhead coverage, they'll be here by then. If not, wake me and I'll take a walk into town to get some new wheels."

Eva went to pass on instructions to Sonny, then got into the car and lay across three seats, listening for sounds of approaching danger. All she heard was the morning chorus of songbirds and the remnants of a cricket choir.

As the adrenaline from the chase faded, fatigue hit her like a train. Seconds after closing her eyes, she was asleep.

~

Eckman saw the needle on the speedometer slip past 130 as Castleton coaxed every ounce of power from the Jeep's giant engine.

According to his tablet, they were still six miles—three minutes— from Eagle One's location. Eckman had ordered the driver to pass Driscoll's vehicle while other units closed from behind. Once in position, Eagle One would block the road and take Driscoll and her people out.

A simple plan, which they had quickly managed to fuck up.

Eagle One had passed Driscoll's stolen Toyota and stopped across two lanes a few miles down the road, giving the others a chance to close in. Only Driscoll hadn't taken the bait. Rooks One and Two had stopped to investigate the apparently abandoned Highlander before suddenly going quiet. As Castleton drove past their stationary vehicles, it was clear why they were no longer responding. All three men lay dead by the side of the road and the Toyota was gone.

"Eagle Two, Eagle One. Eyes on!"

Eagle One, the blockade vehicle, had Driscoll in sight, which meant they were less than ninety seconds down the road.

"Stop them if you can. If not, at least slow them down. We'll be there in one minute."

The wait for a reply felt interminable.

"Eagle One, respond."

"They got through and my car's shot to shit. Stop and pick me up."

Eckman saw the shredded Jeep moments later. The driver was waving his hands in the air, but there was no time to pick up passengers.

"Don't stop," he told Castleton, and the ruined vehicle flashed past in a blur.

At least he now knew where Driscoll had been for the last day or so. Somehow, she'd managed to recruit a couple of new faces and acquire a powerful arsenal. He wondered what other surprises she had in store.

The sign for the next exit loomed in the distance.

Eckman was down to four active vehicles, including his own, and Driscoll could head north, south, or continue east on the freeway. The latter was unlikely, given the power advantage the Jeeps had over the Toyota. No, she would take to the quieter rural roads and try to lose them.

"Rook One, Rook Two, one of you pick up Eagle One, then take exit 28 and head north. Eagle Three, you and I go south. She'll go to ground at the first opportunity, so think like her and check out any likely hiding places."

Castleton hit the off-ramp doing eighty, then slowed to fifty as he turned right onto an unlit road. The speed increased once more as he put his foot to the floor, but the road ahead remained empty.

After a few minutes, Eckman received news that the helicopter was overhead. He got a direct link to the pilot and told him to back up the units to the north, while he and Eagle Three continued their own search.

It proved fruitless.

After an hour and constant calls of no joy from the others, he told them to abandon the search. Driscoll had obviously turned off the main road soon after leaving the freeway, but there was no way they could cover every possible route. Even with a dozen cars it would be a pointless exercise.

Eckman reluctantly phoned West once more and asked that he circulate the Toyota's plate with local law enforcement. He listened as West threatened his very existence if Driscoll weren't eliminated by the end of the day. He told West that four vehicles had zero chance of success, and involving the local police was the only option now. His measured tone had the desired effect. West promised to put out an APB on the Highlander with orders to report sightings only: no attempts were to be made to apprehend the occupants.

"We've still got the plate linked to the traffic camera network, but my people tell me coverage in that area is sparse."

No shit.

He had to hand it to Driscoll. She'd become the proverbial needle in a haystack.

Eckman ended the call and radioed his men to rendezvous at a motel he'd passed a little earlier. There was little they could do until local police reported a sighting, apart from taking on food and grabbing a little shut-eye.

CHAPTER 34

Anton West screwed up his eyes as the early evening sun, barely above the horizon, burned into his retinas. After three days of napping in his office chair, he'd decided to drive home for a shower, shave, and change of clothes. A few hours in his own bed didn't seem like a bad idea either.

The satellite had finally been freed up and placed under his control, but so far, no sign of Driscoll's Toyota Highlander. Kentucky police hadn't seen it, and the alert he'd put on the traffic camera system had also reported no hits.

It was obvious by now that Driscoll had found new wheels, and with every passing second she was putting distance between herself and his men. He'd ordered his team at the control center to research every vehicle theft in the state, as well as any car sales within fifty miles of Driscoll's last known location, but that had yet to yield results.

The more concerning development was that Driscoll had managed to find some hired help. Neither of the two men seen in the stolen Toyota had been identified, due to their crude disguises. The only thing known about them was that they knew how to handle weapons and vehicles. He'd considered instructing his team to contact every security company looking for recent hires, but it was a task that would take far longer than they had, and learning the men's names would do nothing to advance the search. He'd have to wait until Driscoll was finally captured before learning their identities.

When he pulled into the cul-de-sac and up to his house, he saw that the light was off in the living room. That meant his wife had done as he'd asked and canceled her bridge evening. The last thing he wanted was a gaggle of women keeping him awake.

West put his key in the door and opened it.

"Janine?"

It immediately struck him that it wasn't just the living room light that was off: the whole of the first floor was in darkness.

Guessing that she was sulking in bed because he'd canceled her card game, he dumped his briefcase by the door and took off his jacket. He threw it over an armchair, then turned toward the stairs.

Driscoll stood ten feet away from him, the Glock in her hand pointing at his chest.

West froze, and it felt like the blood in his veins followed suit. "How the hell did you get in here?" he asked. "And where's my wife?"

Driscoll said nothing. Instead, she took two steps to the right and motioned with the gun toward the kitchen.

With his arms raised to shoulder height, he walked down the short hallway, privately thankful that she was sending him in this direction. In a cupboard just inside the kitchen door, he had a 9mm Sig Sauer Pro, the safety already off. If he could remain a few yards ahead of her, he should be able to run in, grab the weapon, and have it trained on the doorway by the time she came through.

His gait became more confident as he quickened the pace slightly, but when he drew level with the basement door, Driscoll ordered him to halt. He was tantalizingly close to the kitchen and decided to risk it. If she was there to kill him, she would have done it by now. She wanted him alive, and he was willing to bet his life that she wouldn't shoot.

He managed two more steps before a blond-haired man appeared in the kitchen doorway. He had the Sig in his right hand, and the barrel was pointing at West's legs.

"Back up or lose a kneecap."

West recognized the accent as British, and the no-nonsense look on the gunman's face made him stop in his tracks. Deflated, he slowly turned around and walked back to the door to the basement. Driscoll had already opened it, then taken a couple of steps back, remaining out of his reach.

Halfway down the basement stairs, he stopped when he saw Rees Colback and a balding man standing by a metal chair that had been brought in from the garden. Sitting on a box to the side was Farooq Naser.

"Keep going," Driscoll said.

West turned sideways on the step. "So you can torture me? I don't think—"

A round from Driscoll's suppressed Glock slammed into the side of his knee, sending him tumbling down the remaining stairs. When he hit the bottom, Colback and the other man took an arm each and dragged him to the chair. He could only offer token resistance as they used rolls of duct tape to secure his wrists and ankles to the furniture. West screamed as they bent his injured leg into place.

Driscoll descended and rifled through his pockets. She found his phone.

"What's the PIN?"

The initial shock of being shot was wearing off, and waves of pain began to wash over him.

"The PIN," she asked again.

When he didn't answer, Driscoll pressed her thumb into the wound.

West screamed in blinding agony until she stepped back.

"I can keep this up all night, or we can try waterboarding, if you prefer."

West flinched and, too late, realized that his involuntary response would be his undoing. He'd experienced that method of interrogation during training many years earlier. It had lasted just a few seconds, the purpose being to show him how effective it was. The fear and panic he'd felt all those years ago came flooding back, compounding the pain in his leg.

"Four-nine-one-eight," he said through clenched teeth.

Driscoll entered the number into the handset and began scrolling through his call logs. "Who's your contact at the ESO?"

West was about to argue that he would be a dead man if he gave her that information, but it dawned on him that there was no way he was leaving the basement alive. The two strangers with Driscoll hadn't tried to cover their faces to hide their identities, so Driscoll was hardly likely to allow him to go once the interrogation was over.

If there was the slightest chance he could extricate himself from this predicament he would have fought for his life, but facing four armed opponents while restrained was never a winning position. The remainder of his life would be spent waiting for Driscoll to deliver the fatal shot.

"I don't know his name," West said truthfully. "I'm too far down the pecking order to be given that information."

Driscoll's expression said she believed him.

"Tell me where your computer is. You must be able to log into the network from home."

"First, tell me where my wife is."

"Upstairs," Driscoll told him. "Once we're clear of the area, we'll call the police and they can untie her."

"And me?"

Driscoll raised an eyebrow. "Seriously? You sent your men to kill Rees, then me. You're also responsible for my brother's death. The best you can hope for is a clean, quick kill, and you know it. Now, where's the computer?"

West's head dropped. Believing the end was coming and having it confirmed were two different things. Suddenly, he no longer felt prepared for it.

He could try to hold out long enough for his team to become worried and send someone to investigate his disappearance, but that could be hours away. He'd already told them he'd be back early in the morning, giving Driscoll half a day to inflict pain.

And she would. Her record spoke for itself, and her personnel file made for scary reading. Spending twelve hours trying to defy her didn't even warrant consideration.

"Rees, go upstairs and get a bucket of water and a towel."

"No!" West's head snapped up. "There's a laptop in my briefcase by the front door."

Driscoll nodded to Colback, who ran up the stairs and returned moments later with the leather case. He took out the laptop and handed it to Naser.

"Password?"

West gave Naser an eleven-character code. Before inputting it, Naser looked to Driscoll.

"If that's the duress code that sends an alert and wipes the hard drive, you know what I'll do to you."

West had hoped she didn't know about that security measure. He'd been prepared to claim that Naser must have entered the incorrect password, shutting down the operating system. Unfortunately, they'd both known better.

West sighed, and gave Naser the real password.

"What's the password to get into the system?" Driscoll asked.

West told her, and moments later Naser gave her a thumbs-up. She read out a phone number from West's cell, and Naser tapped at the keyboard.

"No registered owner. I'll see if I can get a location."

"Why?" Driscoll asked West. "Why kill my brother and Bukowitz, and why go after Rees?"

West stared back at her. "Orders."

"I remember a group of people used that excuse about seventy years ago. Didn't work out too well for them. Your superiors didn't give you a reason?"

"You know that's not how things work. We're given instructions and we carry them out, bigger picture be damned. You of all people should understand that."

"So you don't know that this was all to silence those who knew about Hank Monroe's involvement in CIA drug running?"

"Who the hell's Hank Monroe?"

"He's the governor of Nebraska," Driscoll said.

"No wonder I've never heard of him."

"Few outside his state have, but the ESO has him penciled in as the next president. His drug-related activities in Afghanistan were the only blemish on an impeccable record, and if his name hadn't been mentioned in the Adrian Holmes piece, it probably never would've come to light."

"Then blame Elphick and Holmes for this mess. I was just doing my job."

"I've located the phone," Naser interrupted. "It's at a house on Greenbank Road, off I-66, around forty miles west of D.C. Just bringing up the details . . . It's called Gray Rock and is owned by a corporation based in Nassau. They paid twenty-six million dollars for it six years ago. Twelve bedrooms, eleven bathrooms, thirty thousand square feet."

"Find out who owns the business," Driscoll instructed him, "and get schematics, security details, everything you can."

"I'll bet you anything it's linked to Henry Langton," Naser said as he worked feverishly.

"That's far too obvious," said Driscoll.

"Who's Henry Langton?" the blond man asked.

"He's the head of the richest family on the planet," Naser told him, "though it's run more like a business, with him as the CEO. He controls every central bank in the world, except three, and he's the real power behind the governments of the world. He was the architect of the financial crash back in 2008, and the austerity measures we're seeing around the globe are his way of pushing his privatization agenda. If a country needs a bailout—Greece being a prime example—it's Langton who decides how much they get, what it can be used for, and what it'll cost. In the case of Greece, national assets such as airports, ports, railways, and waterworks have been earmarked for sale to German business interests under Langton's control, and once he's squeezed the country for everything he can, he'll move on to the next one."

"It's all conspiracy theory nonsense," Driscoll reiterated.

"Why doesn't anyone stop him?" the blond guy asked, ignoring Eva's comment.

"Because he's untouchable," West interjected. "The law can't touch you when you make the laws. You, me, we're just pawns in their game. You kill me, they'll just send someone else to take you down."

"You also think Langton's behind all this?" Driscoll asked.

West shrugged. "Who else? You need unlimited funds to control a government and get it to kill its own citizens. Langton has hundreds of billions, maybe trillions. More than enough to make anyone abandon their morals."

"The current president doesn't seem to be dancing to their tune," Colback said.

"A temporary setback. Anything that's hurt them will have gone through as an executive order, and those'll be undone by Monroe when he wins the next election. The people will see democracy in action for a couple more years and their faith in the system will be restored, but come the next election, it'll be business as usual."

"Bingo!" Naser exclaimed. "I was right about the Langtons, but the house is occupied by Edward, the oldest son. I've downloaded the layout to a flash drive and I'm searching for security measures."

"If you're thinking of storming the place, you're crazy," West said. "He's bound to have the latest in security, and a small army to back up the technology. You might as well just shoot yourself in the head now and get it over with."

"He could be right," Naser sighed. "The corporation recently paid nineteen million dollars to Armcorp International, a security firm in Washington. No details about what they purchased, but when you spend almost as much on guarding a house as you do purchasing it, I'm guessing it's state of the art."

"See if you can—"

West's phone chirped in Driscoll's hand, indicating an incoming call.

"If I don't answer that, the protocol is to trace the cell and send a team to look for me."

Driscoll stared at West for a few seconds, then raised her weapon and pointed it at his forehead. "One wrong word and your wife dies too."

Driscoll pressed the Connect button, put it on speaker, and held the phone closer to West.

"West."

Pearson began giving him updates received from Eagle Two, but West could scarcely focus on the words his underling was saying. Despite Driscoll's threat, he knew his wife would already be dead. He'd have done the same thing.

All that remained to resolve was his own demise. If he played along with her, she might finish by exacting revenge for her brother's death, and that would mean an agonizing final few hours. Better to get it over with.

Anton West swallowed, then closed his eyes.

"Driscoll's here—"

CHAPTER 35

Henry Langton stormed past the Calico Club employee waiting to take his coat and burst through the door to the meeting room. He shucked off his Burberry and threw it over the back of a chair, then stood facing the screen that had been set up on the table, ignoring the others in the room.

Attending these meetings by video call was highly irregular. The technical wizard who'd set up the link for his son had insisted it was impossible to intercept, but Langton paid little heed to such assurances.

Death was the only guarantee worth a damn.

At his insistence, the face on the screen was pixelated and the voice scrubbed through various filters to make a match impossible.

"You'd better have made progress since you called me this morning." Henry Langton's tone matched his mood: dark and vengeful.

"As I said, we sent the nearest team to check his house, but West was already dead and Driscoll was long gone. West's wife was found upstairs, trussed up in a linen closet. She's hysterical, but we've got someone taking care of her."

"I don't give a damn about his bitch. What did he tell them?"

"I've had the cyber-crime unit working to identify everything he accessed before his death. He was tied to a chair when she killed him, and his laptop was still logged into the network. It looks like he was tortured for the password."

Langton gripped the back of the leather chair in front of him. "What were they looking for?"

Edward Langton swallowed. "Us," he said. "They managed to trace my phone to Gray Rock. They downloaded the blueprints and discovered an invoice from Armcorp. I think they're planning to come after us."

"After *you*, you mean."

Though he'd nurtured the boy for more than four decades, Henry Langton often wondered if there'd been a mix-up at birth. His son should have wrapped this up a long time ago, but his incompetence was on a par with West's. Still, it had created an opportunity to end things once and for all.

"Obviously, I'll move out of Gray Rock until she's been dealt with," Edward said.

"You'll do no such thing," said Langton with heat. "We've spent days chasing her all over the country. It's time to let her come to us. I want you to stay in the house and act as if nothing's changed. If she suspects we know her plan, she'll crawl back into the woodwork."

"But what if she attacks?"

Henry could smell his son's fear—even over the video link—and his contempt for his heir threatened to overwhelm him.

"Oh, she will. I'm counting on it. And we'll be ready for her."

Henry poured himself a coffee and took his seat at the head of the two-hundred-year-old oak table. He lit a cigarette and blew a cloud toward the ceiling.

"What exactly are the current security arrangements at Gray Rock?"

"We've got twenty men rotating on eight-hour shifts, seven days a week. Never fewer than twelve on duty on a given day. Another eight men are on standby to cover holidays and absence."

"So, in any eight-hour period, you've got only four men on duty?"

Edward nodded. "It's all we've ever needed. Most of the time they deal with passers-by looking to get close enough to take photographs of the house. There's never been a serious threat."

"Until now," his father said. "What about early-warning systems?"

"Motion sensors around the perimeter, backed up by CCTV. All of them are virtually impossible to detect unless you know where to look."

"Let's assume she does. What else have you got?"

"That's it," Edward said.

It might have been enough to keep out tourists and the curious, but Driscoll and her team—which had recently increased by two—would have little trouble getting in.

And Henry Langton intended to let her do exactly that.

Farooq Naser was a noncombatant, but the two newcomers would have been brought in for precisely this kind of mission. Even if Naser took part in the assault, it would be five against . . . well, as many as he wanted.

He took out his phone and looked through the contacts for the CEO of Stormont International. Various hedge funds controlled by Langton owned 90 percent of the shares in the company, and the CEO was paid a million dollars a year more than he was worth. The extra compensation was to ensure compliance in situations such as this. Langton had only ever had reason to call the man once before, and that had been to order him to allow Libyan rebels access to one of Stormont's clients in the region. The bodyguards had dutifully stood back when the client had been ambushed and kidnapped, and as a result one of Langton's oil companies had managed to secure a twenty-billion-dollar contract weeks later.

"It's me," he said, aware that the software in his custom-made phone was scrambling the voice to make it unrecognizable. To the recipient, he sounded like a vinyl single played at forty RPM instead of forty-five, with all inflection removed, creating a monotone delivery.

"Yes, sir. What can I do for you?"

"I want a hundred of your best men and I need them in the next six hours."

"That's no problem. What's the mission?"

"I'll send someone to give you that information in a couple of hours. I'll need them for two weeks. Have an invoice ready when my man arrives."

"Yes, sir."

"And when I say your best men, I don't just mean those who are available. Pull people off other assignments if you have to."

"Understood."

Langton ended the call.

"Driscoll killed West about twelve hours ago, so my guess is she's already in the area," he thought aloud. "How do we get a hundred men into Gray Rock without her noticing?"

"We have regular food deliveries," Edward said. "We could cram them into the back of the truck."

"Not only a hundred men," Langton said. "They'll also need weapons and other equipment."

"We could bring them in separately, in a cable van or something like that. Plus, it's almost time to rotate the guards, so we could send in a bus but have most of them lying on the floor, with just eight men visible. We can send eight men out again, so it doesn't look like we're beefing up security."

Finally beginning to use your brain, huh? Now that your ass is on the line.

"Okay, Joel here will organize the trucks and liaise with Morrison at Stormont to get them to Gray Rock. Once they arrive, keep them out of sight. I don't want Driscoll being scared off by the sight of a small army. Get them to deploy within the house, covering all the entrances. And make sure you leave four men patrolling the perimeter. It has to look like business as usual. Once Driscoll gets into the house, take her down."

"Understood," Edward said. "Who've we got lined up to replace West?"

"No one, at the moment. There's no rush though—she's coming to us."

Langton stubbed out his cigarette and lit another.

"You also need to consider your own security, Henry," Joel Harmer said. "If she's identified Edward as being behind the kill order, it's no great leap to implicate you too."

Langton waved off the warning. It wasn't that he didn't trust Harmer's judgment, but anyone who knew the ins and outs of his personal arrangements could be made to talk. Henry Langton had decided long ago to compartmentalize his own security and had handpicked Willem Klaasen, a South African expert, to oversee the project.

Klaasen was handsomely paid for his services. At three million a year, he wasn't cheap, but for a man earning a couple of billion a day, it was pocket change to Langton.

The high salary meant sacrifices. Klaasen went everywhere with Henry Langton, without exception. He was never more than two doors away, and was currently sitting in the driver's seat of the armor-plated limousine parked outside the entrance. Langton simply had to touch a button on his million-dollar watch and his bodyguard would be with him in seconds.

In public, Klaasen appeared to be just another servant, but when they were alone, he was one of the few people on the planet that Langton treated with any sort of respect. A celibate teetotaler, Klaasen holidayed with Langton, slept in the next room, and never so much as took a dump unless his trusted deputy was there to sub in for him.

It was Klaasen who'd set up the security arrangements for Langton's sprawling estate south of Washington. Set on its own seventy-acre peninsula, the fifty-thousand-square-foot home boasted fifteen bedrooms, twenty bathrooms, and every luxury a man could dream of. He had a swimming pool the length of a football field, half a dozen reception rooms lined with a billion dollars' worth of art, and a three-thousand-foot runway for his private jets.

If it was security-related, Klaasen had thought of everything. Sonobuoys ringed the peninsula and would alert them to anything larger than a seal approaching land. The surrounding trees had been cut back so that anyone looking to assault the house would have to cover two hundred yards of open lawn, and the entire estate was bristling with motion sensors, thermal-imaging cameras, and standard CCTV coverage. The thousand-square-foot control room was constantly manned by three personnel; another fifty armed guards occupied an annex the size of a small mansion.

Officially, the residence didn't exist. Anyone looking at the outcrop of land on Google Earth would see nothing but trees, and air traffic control ensured that no aircraft flew within thirty miles of the peninsula.

Even if someone attempted to breach the formidable defenses, Langton had only to reach one of ten elevators that led to the sub-basement, where it was a short walk to his safe room. The elevators ran via their own power supply and could be manually operated if necessary, and the bunker was designed to withstand a nuclear blast. It was stocked with enough provisions to last a month and would maintain communications with the outside world.

And when it came to Langton's personal protection, Klaasen had a few tricks up his sleeve.

Literally.

In short, no one was getting near Henry Langton.

"You said yourself, we shouldn't underestimate her," Harmer warned. "We expected her to roll over days ago, and now it looks like she's bringing the fight to us. I wish you'd let me have some input on your security measures."

"As I told you years ago, that is something I will always handle personally. The subject is closed. Now, if there's nothing else, I have work to do."

"There is something," Edward said. "We found the Highlander they stole in Louisville. It was dumped in the woods a few miles out of town. There was blood on the back seat and we matched it with Farooq Naser's DNA. There's no telling if he's alive or dead though."

"He was probably laughing so much at your incompetence he gave himself a nosebleed," Langton said. He stood up, picked up his coat, and draped it over his arm. Without another word, he left the club and strolled across to where Klaasen waited by the open door of the limo.

"Home?"

"Yes," Langton replied as he got in and made himself comfortable.

The car glided into traffic and Langton pushed a button that activated the intercom. "When we get back, I want a full review of security. Make sure every sensor is working and tell your men to be extra vigilant for the next few days."

"Yes, sir. Any specific threat?"

Langton considered keeping him out of the loop—the fewer people who knew about the issue, the better—but Klaasen would be hampered in dealing with the problem unless he knew all the details.

"Her name is Eva Driscoll. I think it's best that you know everything about her."

~

"What happened to Anton West?" Carl Huff asked when Bill Sanders answered his call. "I was trying to reach him but got no answer, so I checked his file for an alternative number and saw the deceased flag."

"It was Driscoll. She was waiting for him when he got home. She took him down to the basement, put a bullet in his knee and another in his head."

Exactly what Huff had assumed. "I did warn you that she'd go on the offensive," he said. "I assume she got information from him before he died."

"That's correct. His network account was accessed minutes before he was killed. We analyzed the activity and we know what she was looking for."

"The people who ordered her death," Huff said, "did you pass my concerns on to them?"

"I did," Sanders replied. "That was a couple of days ago, and I got the impression they didn't take it too seriously. It seems they do now."

"Yeah? What makes you say that?"

"They told me to pull the existing teams back."

Huff's first impression was that it was a strange decision, but the more he thought about it, the clearer the picture became, like a blurry image coming into sharp focus.

"They don't want anyone to get in her way," he said. "They *want* her to come. They're waiting for her."

"That's exactly what I thought," Sanders agreed. "They're setting a trap, and she's going to walk right into it."

Huff took a few moments to process the information. "When they said to pull the teams back, did that include me?"

"No," Sanders told him. "My instructions to you still stand."

"In that case, I'll need to be on the inside. Make a call."

CHAPTER 36

For Eva Driscoll, the hardest aspect of surveillance was the mind-numbing boredom. She was itching to storm the house and take down Edward Langton, but to do so without properly scoping the place out would be reckless at best.

In the eight hours since they'd been in position, they'd noted the guards' routines and taken pictures of them all, using the camera Len Smart had purchased. She'd sent the Brits to do the shopping, as neither were on any watch lists.

Yet.

They'd come back with a Canon EOS 80D and a lens that brought the faces of the guards into sharp focus from a mile and a half away. That equipment hadn't been cheap, and nor had the four sets of night-vision glasses they would use for the assault.

Eva put the camera down on the shelf of earth in front of her, then rubbed her eyes and stretched her legs as best she could. Smart and Sonny had done an excellent job of creating the observation post. They'd spent five hours digging and had fashioned a seat in the rear from dirt. While they did the hard work, Colback had built the roof, using branches lashed together, packed with dirt, and topped off with the grass that had sat atop the original hole. The roof sat on two legs at the front, allowing whoever was on observations to look through an eight-inch gap at the house, which was nearly 2,500 yards away. At the rear was a gap big enough for the team members to enter and exit.

"You're early," she said as she heard footsteps in the undergrowth behind her.

"Only a few minutes," Sonny said, lying on his stomach so he could see her.

Eva turned to face him and saw the same come-hither look he'd been giving her since she'd ditched the old lady disguise.

"I thought we could chat for a few minutes before you knock off."

"Great idea." Eva favored him with a smile.

Sonny's grin spread across his face, but only until Eva picked up her notebook.

"At 14:12, a bus arrived. There were eight people on board, not including the driver. It left forty minutes later with a different eight men on board. I know, because I took photos as it came and went."

"It could be the guards rotating on and off duty," Sonny suggested.

"I thought the same thing, except it was a huge bus for eight people. They could have used a minibus, but that thing could easily seat forty."

"Maybe that's all they had available."

"Yeah, that was a possibility, but to be sure I took pictures of the front and rear wheel wells as it arrived, and again when it left." Eva found the images in the camera's memory and showed them to Sonny.

"It looks to be riding low," he noted.

"That's it coming in." She took the camera and flicked to the picture of the bus as it left the house. "Take a look now."

"That's a hell of a difference. So they know we're coming."

Eva nodded. "I'm guessing there were at least fifty others on that bus, plus weapons and the rest of their gear."

"So they offloaded in the courtyard."

Viewed from above, the house was shaped like a top hat, with an eighty-yard facade and three other wings surrounding a courtyard with an ornate fountain in the center. Vehicles entered via an archway that was secured by ten-foot wooden gates.

"They did," Eva confirmed. "Tight squeeze for a bus that size, so you have to ask why they didn't just offload at the front door. They didn't have any other visitors who might have been inconvenienced."

"So, are you still planning to go ahead with the assault?"

Eva stared at the house. She'd been asking herself the same question for the last hour. The original idea had been to strike at three in the morning, two days from now. That would have given them plenty of time for observation and to fine-tune any details, but with the suspected new arrivals, that plan was now moot.

"Keep watching for now," Eva said as she climbed out of the blind. "I'll go discuss it with the others."

Sonny slithered into the hole to begin his two-hour stint, while Eva jogged back to the main camp a dozen yards away.

They'd chosen a heavily wooded area atop a hill, so their comings and goings wouldn't be noticed. There was always the possibility that a satellite's infrared camera could pick up their body heat, but Len Smart had considered this on his shopping trip.

Eva ducked under the thermal tarpaulin that had been strung up between four trees. It hung four feet off the ground and had originally been designed to cover and mask the heat signatures of battle tanks. Smart had also picked up a solar-powered cooler, sleeping bags, and enough food and water to last them a few days.

"You should be sleeping," she said to Smart, who was lying on top of his sleeping bag, reading a Kindle.

"I've had an hour. That's fine for now. Besides, I want to finish this book before it all kicks off."

Eva was intrigued. "What is it? A military handbook on close-quarter battle?"

"Hardly," Smart said. "It's *Walking with Shadows* by Luke Romyn. A famous fiction author and a ten-year-old boy are the only survivors of a plane crash in the Amazon rainforest, and standing between them and civilization are vicious mercenaries and drug runners. You should try it."

"Thanks, but I get enough action in real life."

"Oh, it's much more than just a shoot-'em-up."

Eva took a bottle of water from the cooler and drank half of it. "Much as I'd like to participate in your book club, there's been a development."

Farooq was fast asleep, while Colback was making a sandwich from a packet of cold cuts.

"Rees, we're going to have to rethink our approach."

She told the pair what she'd seen during her two hours on duty and they were visibly disheartened by the news.

"It was already a challenge when we thought we were facing a handful of men," Colback said. "Now it's more like fifteen-to-one in their favor."

"The odds aren't great," Eva admitted.

"It sounds like a trap to me," Smart said. "If they wanted to deter an attack, the extra men would be out in force. They want to draw us in."

"Agreed. The question is, do we take the bait?"

"The way I see it," Smart said, "he's going nowhere. The longer we sit tight, the more frustrated Edward will become, and that might lead to the mistake we need."

"They might also flood the area with troops," Colback suggested, "and that would be the end of us."

Both men made valid points. If they were going to bide their time, they couldn't hang around the house. It would be better to withdraw and pick the ideal moment, preferably when Edward Langton was in transit. He had to be taken alive, otherwise they might never discover who else comprised the ESO. Langton's father Henry was undoubtedly involved, but Eva wanted them all, not just the man at the top. Even he could be replaced. She wanted to end the ESO, not temporarily halt it. According to Farooq, though, there was no official residence listed for him anywhere. Simply finding his home looked to be a near impossibility.

"Okay," Eva said, "we pull back. He has to leave the house at some point. When he does, we'll be waiting."

"That could be days, or even weeks," Colback said.

"I don't think so," Eva told him. "They'd expect us to watch the place for a couple of days at the very least. If we don't hit them soon, they'll start to wonder what's going on. I'd say another three days, max, before they send people out to check the perimeter."

"So, what about the blind? Leave it where it is, so they know we were watching?"

"No, let's keep them guessing. Rees, wake Farooq and pack everything away. Len, you come with me."

Eva led Smart to the hide, where Sonny was watching the house through the viewfinder of the camera.

"Just in time. We've got another visitor," Sonny told them.

"It doesn't matter," Eva replied. "We're bugging out. Let's demolish this thing and make it look like we were never here."

Sonny snapped off a couple of shots of the newcomer anyway, then turned the camera off and put it back in its case. He wriggled out of the hole, then helped Smart remove the roof.

"Take the turf off gently," Smart said. "We're going to cover our tracks."

"No problem. I'll handle the delicate work; you get shoveling."

~

Carl Huff maintained a sedate pace as he cruised up the pristine white gravel driveway toward Gray Rock. The house and manicured gardens stank of money, and the building itself looked as if it had been plucked from an English country estate.

He pulled up to the steps leading to the huge double doors that formed the main entrance, then switched off the ignition and got out of the silver Ford. He suspected it was by far the cheapest car to have ever parked on that particular spot.

Huff turned away from the house and looked off into the distance. The front lawn extended for at least three hundred yards, and on either side the ground steadily rose a hundred feet, the hillsides thick with trees.

The perfect place to sit and observe.

You're out there, Eva. I can feel it.

Huff turned at the sound of the ostentatious doors opening: an ex-army type in a flak jacket appeared at the entrance, automatic rifle aimed casually in Huff's direction.

"Name!" the man barked.

"Carl Huff."

The man lowered his weapon. "You were supposed to use the rear entrance."

"Is that right?"

"Yeah. Follow the road all the way until you see the big gates."

Huff flipped off a lazy salute, then got back in the car. He drove around to the back of the mansion and found the gates to the courtyard open.

Four armed men were waiting to meet him. They instructed him to halt a few yards from the entrance and one signaled for him to get out. Huff did so, slowly, and a fifth man appeared with a dog on a leash. The canine sniffed around the exterior of the car, followed by the interior. When it had finished, it sniffed Huff for good measure, then returned to its handler.

"Clear," the man said, and motioned toward the entrance. "Inside, there's a garage on the left. Park in there."

Huff drove through the gates and followed the instructions. The garage took up the entire first floor of the east wing, with enough space for at least a dozen more cars. Huff found a spot, then walked back out into the sunshine.

Before he had time to admire his surroundings, another armed guard beckoned for him to follow. He led Huff through an archway and down a hallway, then into a reception room.

The interior of the house was as opulent as the outside. Huff guessed the art on the wall probably cost more than he could hope to earn in a lifetime, and every stick of furniture screamed wealth and privilege.

"You were supposed to go straight to the rear entrance. Why did you stop outside the front door?"

The question was asked by a middle-aged man wearing dark slacks and a dress shirt. He was holding a tall, clear drink and sitting on a leather sofa facing an inlaid coffee table. There were also two guards in the room, standing in positions that allowed them to cover all three exits.

"I did it to help protect you," Huff replied. "If Driscoll's out there, she saw me arrive. It's important she knows I'm here."

"Why is that?" Edward Langton asked.

"Because she knows me and I know her. I know how she thinks. Right now, she'll be dumping her original plan because she knows I have it covered. She'll be forced to come up with something more daring, and that comes with higher risk."

Langton jumped out of his seat. "I don't *want* her to have second thoughts. I want her to think I'm an easy target so that she waltzes in here and gets her ass blown to hell!"

Huff remained calm in the face of the outburst. "That was never going to happen," he said. "Let me guess, you beefed up security in the last twenty-four hours."

"I did," Langton replied, "but it was done discreetly. We just had another forty men arrive in the last couple of hours."

"You brought men in while she was watching?"

"Obviously, they were hidden."

"Hidden how? Under a blanket?"

Langton stiffened. "Remember who you're talking to."

205

"With respect," Huff said, "when she puts a gun to your head and pulls the trigger, the bullet will have the same effect as it would on a street urchin in Mumbai. You're powerful, but not immortal. Don't forget that."

Langton took out his phone and scrolled through the contacts. "I told Sanders this was a bad idea. I should have refused his offer."

"You can get rid of me if you want." Huff shrugged. "But if you do, I'll give you a week alive at the most. You need me more than you'll ever know."

Langton looked up from his phone. "I'll have over a hundred men here soon. I don't need you at all."

Huff raised his hands in mock surrender. "Hey, you want me gone, I'm gone. If you change your mind, I'll be at the Four Seasons in town until nine tomorrow morning." He turned and took a few steps toward the door, then stopped and turned back. "When did you say the reinforcements arrived?"

"A couple of hours ago, if it's any of your business."

"Two hours? Then she's already gone. Send a couple of men to check out the hills out front. Exit the house, at their one o'clock. She was probably between a mile and two miles away. When they report back in, you know where to find me."

Huff walked back to his car unescorted. As he drove past the front of the house, he looked once more at the hills in the distance. Driscoll would be gone, but where to? Hitting the house was pointless now, so she'd look to get to Langton in some other way.

He performed a mental calculation: Langton's men would need two hours to find traces of Driscoll, then add another hour for the spoiled asshole to swallow his pride. That meant Huff had three hours to scope out the only road leading to the house, plus possibly grab a bite to eat, before one of the richest men on the planet began begging him to come back.

CHAPTER 37

Carl Huff woke to the familiar smells of body odor, nocturnal farts, and gun oil. Gray Rock boasted numerous bedrooms, but none had been allocated to the men guarding Edward Langton. Instead, the second-floor hallways in the east and south wings had been turned into vast dormitories, with seventy-five men sleeping in each at any given time.

Langton's personal army had grown to three hundred in the three days since Huff had arrived. Thankfully, a hundred of these were now camped out in the surrounding woods, rotating every twelve hours. Huff dreaded to think what the sleeping conditions would be like if they were all still stationed in the house. As it was, he'd set up a perimeter a shade over half a mile from the house in all directions, with the men located sixty yards apart. Each one reported in every twenty minutes and any delayed acknowledgments would result in a rapid response team heading to their location to investigate. So far, everyone had reported in on time.

Huff stood, stretched, then went to the toilet he shared with the rest of the south wing crew. He'd had the foresight to bring along a few changes of clothes, so he freshened up before going to see the client.

Edward Langton's foul mood had not improved since Huff's arrival. His latest grievance was his wife's decision to take her leave until the crisis was over. While she was sunning herself in the Caribbean, Edward was stuck at home waiting for a highly skilled assassin to strike. Their two children had been due to return from their Swiss boarding school a few days earlier, but they had joined their mother instead.

"How long am I going to remain a prisoner in my own home?"

"Preparations to draw her out are almost complete," Huff assured him. "In the meantime, the security measures I put in place are keeping you safe."

"I may be safe, but I have work to do, and most of the conversations I need to have are too sensitive to discuss over the phone or via video calls."

"I appreciate that. If all goes well, you should be able to go about your business tomorrow."

"Well, what about a helicopter?" Langton asked. "If you're right that she wants me alive, she's hardly likely to blow me out of the sky."

"No, you need to stick to your normal habits and take the limo. We need to make her think she has an opportunity to get to you."

"That's the part I'm not comfortable with," Langton said. "What if she actually *does* get to me?"

"She won't."

The new limo Huff had selected was so heavily armored, Eva would need a tank just to scratch the paintwork. Plus, her ambush points were severely limited. She wouldn't try to attack on the freeway or in D.C., so her only option would be to strike on the road between Gray Rock and I-66, a distance of just over two miles. A small section of it passed through a wooded area, but the rest was open road with nowhere to hide.

"Are you sure she'll strike as we drive through the woods?"

"I'm counting on it. The replacement limo will be here first thing in the morning, and the choppers with the rapid response teams are set to go. They'll be in the air, holding position two miles away. The moment she attacks, we'll call them in. Flight time is about thirty seconds."

"That sounds like a long time to be under fire." Langton was clearly unhappy with the arrangement, and Huff noticed the slight hint of fear in his voice.

"It will seem a lot at the time, I'm not going to lie to you. However, the new limo is state of the art. It can withstand multiple RPG hits, and the glass in the windows can take over a thousand rounds of automatic fire from a range of six feet. Driscoll and her friends won't fire half that before the cavalry arrives to mop up."

Langton still looked skeptical, and Huff thought it ironic that a man who was responsible for the deaths of millions of people in the wars he'd helped create should now be worried about his own well-being. Langton had lived an insulated life, never knowing hunger or fear, and he wasn't coping well, faced with the prospect of being in the crosshairs. He was still barking orders as if his biggest concern was deciding which thousand-dollar bottle of wine to have with his lunch, but Huff could see past the facade. Langton was scared, and because it was Driscoll gunning for him, he had every right to be.

"I'm in no particular hurry to die," Huff said, "so if I were the slightest bit uncertain, I wouldn't ride along with you. If she does attack—and I'm sure she will—we'll be sitting comfortably in the limo, drinking expensive champagne, while she spends the last minute of her life wasting ammo."

His words seemed to hit the mark. Langton's posture relaxed a little, and he took a seat before waving a hand to indicate that the meeting was over.

Huff took his leave, walking to one of three kitchens in the house. This one had been assigned to the security personnel, and breakfast was well underway. A dozen men were sitting at a huge dining table, tucking into bacon, eggs, hash browns, and pancakes. Huff decided to forgo the saturated fat and loaded a bowl with granola and banana.

He stood by the window and ate, trying to put himself in Driscoll's shoes. Despite what he'd told Langton, there was no way she would attack at such an obvious ambush point. A desperate amateur might, but not Eva Driscoll.

Having taken on the role of Langton's head of security three days earlier, Huff had told his principal only what he needed to know. He'd kept certain arrangements to himself, such as the spotters that would be stationed near the on-ramp for I-66. If any suspicious vehicles were waiting to tail the limo once it got on the freeway, Huff would know.

The original plan—to draw Driscoll out—hadn't changed, but he planned to go about it a different way.

CHAPTER 38

Eva stared out the window of the two-bed apartment and willed Edward Langton to make his move. She'd booked the place on Airbnb with a prepaid credit card supplied by DeBron. Given the alerts that the authorities would have sent to all major hotel chains, booking via Airbnb made for a much safer option.

Farooq was cleaning the breakfast dishes while Colback had his eyes glued to the laptop screen. The ex-soldier hadn't shaved since the day he'd been jumped in New York, and his new beard helped disguise his features.

It had been four days since they'd abandoned the observation post overlooking Gray Rock, and the waiting had begun to grate on her nerves. The only time Eva had been out of the apartment had been two days earlier with Len Smart, shopping for a few select items. One was a motion sensor and the other was a discreet video camera. Eva had taken them to the woods a mile from Gray Rock that night, placing the motion sensor by the side of the only road leading into and out of Langton's estate, and the camera three hundred yards back.

Over the next couple of days, there'd been a few alerts from the sensor, but when they'd checked the live camera feed, none had been Edward Langton leaving his mansion.

Eva took out her phone, one of a handful Smart had picked up on another shopping expedition. It was an unregistered, prepaid cell, and as with the others, she'd installed WhatsApp and set up fake accounts. As long as they chatted between themselves in code, it would be impossible to link back to them.

She banged out a quick message:

HOW'S SALLY? *[STATUS REPORT.]*

The reply was almost instantaneous:

SAME OLD, SAME OLD. *[SITUATION NORMAL.]*

Any other reply would signal that Smart was compromised, and Eva would abandon him to his own fate. Both had accepted this arrangement up front and, to their credit, done so without complaint.

Eva fired off a similar message to Sonny, who also reported back in the affirmative. He was the lucky one, sitting in a hotel room overlooking the road where 522, the road leading from Gray Rock, crossed I-66, the freeway that Edward Langton would have to take to get to D.C.

Smart, on the other hand, had drawn the short straw today. He was sitting in a newly purchased, well-used Toyota Camry in the parking lot of a mall twelve miles closer to the capital and near an on-ramp for I-66.

"Maybe he'll never leave his house again," Colback said, sitting back in his chair and stretching.

"He will," Eva replied, without turning around. "People like Edward Langton are all about power. He'll want to demonstrate his control of the situation sooner rather than later. The fact that we haven't tried to get to him will just add to his confidence."

"Well, he'd better make a move soon. Otherwise I'm likely to die of boredom before he shows his face."

Twenty minutes later, Colback got his wish. The app on Eva's phone beeped twice to indicate a hit on the motion sensor, and she rushed to the laptop to see which vehicle had triggered it.

The vehicle looked familiar.

"If I never see another black Jeep Cherokee with tinted windows—"

The app beeped twice more, then again as two other vehicles passed the sensor. They waited for them to come into view, and it wasn't long before they saw the stretch limo that had arrived on a flatbed that morning, followed by another Jeep. The windows on all three vehicles were tinted black, but it seemed clear who rode in the middle car.

Eva opened WhatsApp and composed a quick message for Sonny: SENT YOU AN EMAIL. CONFIRM RECEIPT. *[HE'S ON HIS WAY. CONFIRM WHEN HE JOINS I-66.]*

~

"It's now or never," Huff said as the limo reached the stretch of road where a thick belt of trees lined the asphalt. He glanced over and saw Edward Langton tense up, his jaw taut.

"Alpha One, Alpha Two, report status."

Both chopper pilots declared themselves airborne and ready to rock and roll.

Huff checked his seatbelt once more and turned to comfort his nervous client. "If she's got any sense, she'll have given up and taken a boat to China by now."

Langton ignored the comment, edging slightly away from his door as the first of the trees flashed past.

Huff stared out the window as they reached the densest part of the woods. They were traveling at sixty miles an hour, which meant they'd be out of the gauntlet in another fifteen seconds.

The trees began to thin out, eventually giving way to a vast sea of green.

"I told you," Huff said, watching Langton let out a breath he'd been holding for the last half-minute. "She knows she can't get to you, so she's given up."

"I still want the men at the house until further notice," Langton said.

"Of course." The cost of the security operation ran to almost half a million dollars a day, but that was nothing to a man who earned as much by the minute.

Huff radioed the helicopters and told them to stand down, then informed the spotter near I-66 to keep an eye out.

The limousine arrived a minute later, halted by a red stop light, then took the turn that led onto the freeway. Two minutes later, the lookout reported that no suspicious vehicles had begun to tail them.

Huff hadn't really expected Eva to make such a foolish move, but he had to demonstrate to Langton that he was doing his utmost to keep the man alive. He took a bottle of water from the cooler and broke the seal, then settled back for the journey to D.C.

Len Smart picked up the cell and tapped the WhatsApp notification at the top of the screen.

SENT YOU A PACKAGE. SHOULD BE WITH YOU SHORTLY. TRACKING CODE T11 3CE. [*Langton's heading your way. License plate T11 3CE.*]

Smart knew he had about ten minutes from the moment he received Sonny's message. He finished the coffee he'd been nursing, then got out of the car and took the empty cup to a trash can, glad to stretch his legs. He got back in the Camry and drove out of the parking lot, following the signs for I-66 East. He joined the freeway a minute later and settled into the slow lane.

The plan was simple: let the limo containing Langton cruise by, then tuck in behind and see where it went. Their overall objective, Eva had explained, was to discover the identities of the other members of the ESO. She'd originally wanted to get that information from Edward Langton, but as he'd surrounded himself with a small army, they'd have to do it another way.

Smart had asked whether the ESO conducted any of their meetings electronically but, according to Eva, the group's discussions were so sensitive that anything besides face-to-face communication posed too great a security risk.

Eva's new goal was to identify the group's meeting place and see who attended.

Smart gradually let his speed decrease, spending the next fifteen minutes ignoring the flashing headlights and blaring horns behind him. When Langton's three-car convoy appeared in his side mirror, he increased his speed from forty-five to fifty-five, still slower than the vehicles in the middle lane, but fast enough to stop drawing attention to himself. As the SUVs and limo passed in the fast lane, he compared the plate with the code Sonny had sent.

Bingo!

Smart pulled into the middle lane, his car one of hundreds in the nondescript, metal stream flowing toward the capital. He waited until the rear SUV got two hundred yards ahead, then eased into the fast lane. That left seven cars between the target and him, but the tall profile of the second SUV was easy to spot.

Twenty minutes later, they crossed the Theodore Roosevelt Bridge, then drove past the White House before taking a left. Smart was only four cars behind them at this point, but he saw nothing to suggest they'd picked up his tail.

A few blocks farther on, the three black cars turned onto M St. NW. Smart had his phone on his lap as he made the turn, and he saw the limo and its escorts pull up outside a brick building that looked out of place among the modern structures that surrounded it. He clicked Record on the camera, then held the phone to his ear as he slowly drove past the entrance. Two people had exited the limousine and were heading to the door that was being held open by a liveried doorman.

One of them was Edward Langton. Smart recognized him from the picture Eva had shown him. The other man's identity would have to be determined later, once they had a chance to study the footage.

His task completed, Smart turned at the next corner. He pulled over and composed a cryptic message to Eva, then tapped the address of the hotel he shared with Sonny into the vehicle's satnav system.

Apart from the skirmish on his first day in-country, the mission had been a lot less exciting than he'd anticipated. Not that he was complaining. Three grand a day for surveillance work was easy money, and now that they'd identified one of Edward Langton's haunts, it looked as if he could expect more of the same. Smart was under no illusion though: at some point the action would come thick and fast. Once they'd identified the members of the ESO, Eva would have Sonny and him doing a lot more than conducting surveillance.

As yet, she hadn't shared her endgame with the rest of the team, as was her prerogative. The decisions she'd made so far had been sound, so Smart didn't expect she'd be asking them to undertake a suicide mission.

He pulled into a gap in the traffic and followed the directions of the electronic voice, wondering how this was going to play out.

~

Edward Langton stopped in the doorway and turned to face Huff. "Wait in the car."

"I think it might be wise—"

"If you did as you were told." Edward turned on his heel, knowing the doorman would prevent the bodyguard from following. Huff might be good at his job, but he was hired help, and that didn't grant him a place at the big table.

Langton entered the meeting room and took his usual seat. Pots of fresh coffee had already been prepared, and two members of the group were already in attendance.

"Joel, George."

Harmer and Carson both nodded as Edward poured himself a cup.

"I take it you had an uneventful journey this morning," said Joel Harmer.

Harmer's role as head of security didn't extend to protecting the ESO members themselves, for which he was grateful. A failure of that kind would cost him his life. Harmer's focus was, instead, on the international front, fomenting unrest in areas of the world not yet controlled by the ESO, then coordinating with the joint chiefs and State Department to ensure America's interests were promoted.

"I think she realized that trying to get to us is a waste of time," Langton said. "She had the perfect opportunity to strike today. My best guess is they're halfway around the world by now. I'll speak to Bill Sanders and get him to alert all embassy chiefs to be on the lookout for them. Sooner or later, one of them will slip up and we'll have them."

Before the others could offer their opinions, the door opened and Alexander Mumford strode in.

"You made it." The man responsible for the ESO's finances smiled at Langton.

"I was just saying, Driscoll is no longer a personal threat, but we still need to silence her as soon as we can."

"That means finding a replacement for Anton West," Mumford pointed out.

"The most experienced member of West's team, Willard Eckman, has assumed control until we can find a permanent replacement. I was thinking of giving the job to Carl Huff."

"Isn't he the maverick West was complaining about?" Harmer asked.

"A clash of personalities, nothing more," Langton assured him. "Huff knows Driscoll inside out. He should have been in charge from day one."

"The benefit of twenty-twenty hindsight," Mumford said.

"Yeah, well, as I was saying, we'll focus the manhunt abroad. I—"

All talking ceased when Henry Langton entered the room. He threw his coat over the back of his chair, then slammed his briefcase on the table with such force that even the coffee pots jumped.

"Why did you disobey my orders?" He glared at his son, who flinched at his father's anger like a scolded teen. "You were supposed to draw her in and finish this, but no, you had to screw that up too?"

Edward had spoken to his father a few times while holed up in his mansion, but this subject had never come up. No doubt the old man had waited until now in order to embarrass him in front of the others.

"It wasn't anything I did." He tried to remain calm, but it came out as a half shout. "We all agreed on the plan, but Driscoll saw through it. I brought in someone who knows her, Carl Huff, and he correctly guessed that she'd abandoned the surveillance of Gray Rock. I have no idea what spooked her, but Huff told us where to look and we found the remains of her setup."

"So where does this expert think she is now?"

"Gone," Edward said. "Probably out of the country by now, but unless she's in North Korea, there's nowhere to hide."

"She can still do damage from the other side of the world," his father said. "That is, if she's even left. She doesn't strike me as the quitting type."

"She's gone," Edward insisted. "If she tries to revive the story, we'll kill it again."

He looked at Alexander Mumford, who nodded in agreement.

Henry Langton slapped the desk with more force than any of them could have imagined. "In the last two weeks I've heard could, should, can, and will—yet she's *still* out there! This started as a simple hit on Rees Colback and now we're looking for at least five people—who are looking for you! At least tell me you've identified the two men she recruited."

All heads bowed, each person suddenly engrossed by the table's highly polished surface.

"That's just great. We've got access to every security service database in the world but we can't put names to these guys?"

"Willard Eckman, West's replacement and the man in charge of pursuing them, only got a brief glimpse of one of them. We have CCTV footage too, but all they could determine was that one was bigger than the other."

"Brilliant! Just fucking brilliant! Instruct all law enforcement agencies to be on the lookout for two men who aren't the same height! We'll have them in no time!"

Henry launched into a coughing fit as he slumped into his chair. He was purple in the face from his exertions, and a casual observer might have expected him to keel over at any moment, but Edward had seen many such outbursts in the past. That didn't make them any more welcome. Experience told him to remain silent and let his father get it out of his system, and the others in the room clearly had the same idea. No one spoke until Henry Langton broke the silence.

"We've tried subtlety and it didn't work. Colback and Naser have sisters, correct?"

"That's right," Edward confirmed. "We've got people watching them in case they try to get in touch."

"The time for watching is over. Use them to smoke out Driscoll and her friends."

"How?" Edward asked. "We can't exactly call Colback and tell him we have his sister."

"I'm not asking you to think. Or even try. I'm telling you what to do. Just follow my instructions. To the letter. You understand?"

Edward hated being spoken to like a child, especially in front of the other ESO members, but until he could replace his father, he'd have to put up with it.

It took Henry Langton a few minutes to spell out his plan. Based on the level of detail, Edward was sure he'd been working on it for some time—it wasn't the kind of idea that just popped into someone's head, not even his father's. It certainly wasn't the kind of thing that could be discussed over the phone, which was why he'd waited until now to share it.

"That's a lot of collateral damage," Mumford noted.

"More die when we instigate a regime change," Langton replied. "A lot more."

"But we've never done anything like this on home soil," Edward pointed out.

"There's a first time for everything." Langton's tone declared the matter settled. "You have your orders."

Langton picked up his briefcase and coat and walked to the door. With his hand poised on the handle, he turned and fixed his gaze on Edward.

"Don't fuck this up."

CHAPTER 39

"That's the guy I saw at Gray Rock right before we cleared out."

Eva looked from the screen to Sonny. "Are you sure?"

"Positive. I got some photos."

"I take it you know him," Smart said.

"I did," Eva admitted. "A long time ago."

Eva had thought she'd seen the last of Carl Huff, but fate obviously had other ideas.

She watched the video once more, seeing him emerge from the limo after Edward Langton and look around confidently. A decade might have passed, but he looked no different than he had during training. His hair was a little neater, if the shaky video could be trusted, and time had been kind to him.

"His name's Carl Huff. At least, that's the name he adopted when he joined the CIA. We were . . . involved for a while."

"Looks like he went over to the dark side," Sonny said.

"We were always on the dark side, we just didn't know it. When we signed up, we were sold a dream. America's invisible protectors, keeping the country safe from enemies foreign and domestic. Certain people couldn't be taken to court for fear of exposing secrets vital to national security. It was our job to make those problems go away."

"Only it wasn't America's problems you were eliminating, it was Henry Langton's."

"It's obvious once you know the full story," Eva admitted.

An uneasy silence fell over the room. She'd told Sonny and Len about her involvement in the death of Adrian Holmes, and she was glad they didn't bring it up now.

"Does it change things, Huff being around?"

"He thinks like me, so he'll be able to anticipate my moves. That's going to make planning tricky."

"More so for him," Smart said. "It's clear they want to draw you in, though Huff knows you won't take the obvious options. But—and it's a huge hairy *but*—he'll have to plan for the obvious too. He has to cover all bases while still giving you a window of opportunity."

Eva thought about Smart's statement. "That's only true if *he* knows that *I* know he's on their side."

"He knows," Sonny said, and went to get the camera. He hit a few commands, then scrolled through the images in the Canon's memory.

"Here," he said, handing it to Eva. "He's looking straight at the camera. He's even smiling."

Eva studied the photograph. It did indeed look like Huff was posing for the snap.

"It's like he knew exactly where we would be," Sonny added.

"And given all the possible locations for an OP, that makes him as good as you suggested," Smart told Eva. "He's confident you know he's on the case, so how do we play it?"

"Good question."

How indeed.

No matter how audacious her plan, Huff would have contemplated and covered it.

"We might still have the advantage," she said. "He's expecting us to try to get to Edward Langton. He might even see Henry Langton as a possible target and have him covered too, but there are more than two people in the ESO. Let's stick to the plan and find the weak link."

"And Carl Huff?"

"His time will come."

CHAPTER 40

Sonny Baines kicked open the lid of the cooler and leaned in to get a bottle of water. The food he'd brought with him the previous day was gone, the last sandwich polished off for breakfast at five in the morning. For the next few hours, he'd be reduced to a liquid diet. He looked at his watch: 177 more minutes until Len was due to relieve him at midday.

A pigeon startled him as it flapped noisily onto the ledge outside the open window, and he resisted the urge to shoo it away. It wasn't interfering with his view of the entrance to the Calico Club, six stories down and ninety yards to his left on the opposite side of the street.

The bird viewed Sonny from a variety of angles, and with no threat detected, began to peck at unseen morsels. Sonny watched it for a few moments, until movement outside the Calico caught his eye. The fifth limousine of the morning pulled into the no-parking zone in front of the huge red awning. Sonny put his eye to the tripod-mounted camera and snapped off a series of shots as the driver opened the rear door for the passenger.

Sonny couldn't tell if it was Henry Langton, but it was the closest match they'd had over the last three days. He was the right stature, but the fedora prevented Sonny from catching his face. He'd have a better view when the subject left the building, and then he could compare the man's face to the photograph he had on his phone.

Sonny desperately wanted it to be Henry Langton. His son Edward had arrived twenty minutes earlier, accompanied by Carl Huff, so it made sense for the other members of the ESO to turn up too. While it was nice to be earning good money for sitting in a rented office taking photos, Sonny wanted to see some action.

He'd said the same to Len Smart on the last handover, but his long-time friend had begged to differ. Smart could hold his own against the best, even though he was no longer in his prime. The few extra inches around his waist meant he wouldn't be beating endurance records any time soon, but his responses were still razor-sharp. The pair regularly practiced at Minotaur's training facility and were equally skilled in close-quarters combat. The main change in Len was that he'd mellowed over the years. While Sonny never felt more alive than when he had a weapon in his hands, Smart's idea of a good time was a glass of red wine and a book.

In the end, it took an hour before the man in the fedora reappeared. Sonny silently urged him to look up and show his face.

His wish was granted.

The target glanced up at the heavens as rain began to bounce off the sidewalk, and Sonny got a dozen decent shots before he disappeared from view, safely ensconced in the limo.

It was Henry Langton, no doubt about it. And if the head of the ESO was here, then the other members would probably still be inside. Langton was the first person to leave the club; the others would probably soon follow.

A month earlier, if anyone had tried to convince him that the ESO existed, he'd have told them to take a happy pill and have a nice lie down in a padded room. The days he'd spent with Eva Driscoll had changed that.

It wasn't so much the stories she'd told, but the fact that she'd done their bidding. She hadn't gone into detail about the individual hits, but they fitted neatly into the bigger picture she'd painted.

It was sobering to think he was going up against such powerful people. They controlled the government, security services, police, courts, and everyone in between. Still, there was a certain satisfaction in knowing he'd do his bit to bring them down.

Sonny had always been a soldier. He'd joined the Junior Leaders at fifteen and moved to the regulars a couple of years later. Four years on, he'd passed the grueling SAS selection course and had been straining at the leash to see his first action. He'd been prepared to put his life on the line to protect his country, but now he realized it hadn't been the UK's interests he'd been fighting for. The wars in the Middle East—dating back to the first Gulf War in 1990—had been fought for the benefit of a handful of people, all of them represented in the figure of Henry Langton.

Millions of people had died or been displaced in similar war zones around the world so the ESO's interests would be protected. Gadhafi was ousted for daring to move away from the petrodollar in favor of a gold-backed dinar. Assad's decision to block plans to build a gas pipeline through Syria—a move that would have threatened Russia's domination when it came to supplying Europe's needs—resulted in yet another long-running war aimed at installing a new leader whose ideals were more aligned with those of the ESO. All those years in uniform, thinking the people he killed were a threat to freedom and democracy, while he was simply furthering Henry Langton's agenda . . .

Sonny was still dwelling on his role in a few such disasters when Len Smart turned up at midday to relieve him.

"Anything to report?" Smart asked as he placed a bag of groceries on the table.

Sonny caught a whiff of hot pastrami and his stomach reminded him that he hadn't eaten in seven hours.

"Plenty," Sonny said, reading from his notes. "Henry Langton finally showed, and so did his son. All in all, seven people arrived before Henry, and four of them, including Edward, left shortly after him. I've downloaded the images to my phone and I'll send them to Eva on the way back to the RV."

"Sounds like we've got the people we're looking for. I'll keep watching just in case we missed anyone."

They chatted for a few minutes, until the smell of food forced Sonny to go in search of some sustenance of his own.

"I'll message you if Eva wants you to come in," Sonny said.

"No worries. I'm not going anywhere."

CHAPTER 41

"This isn't good."

Eva was staring at the television screen. The news all morning had been dominated by the explosion at an elementary school in Gaithersburg, Maryland. The anchor was recapping what was already known: the bomb had gone off at 10:14 in the morning, and twenty-four children were still unaccounted for.

Images from the scene showed smoke still pouring from a two-story building as firefighters from half a dozen fire trucks dealt with the aftermath. At least ten police cruisers were on the scene, as well as a handful of people with "FBI" emblazoned on the back of their jackets.

"Those poor kids," Farooq said for the fifth time in the past hour.

Eva felt for them too, but what concerned her the most was the speed with which the news networks had gotten hold of CCTV coverage. It was normally hours after an attack that such information was released, but the grainy image of the woman walking across a parking lot with a large canvas bag had hit the screen within eighty minutes.

The moment it played, she knew it was her.

"It's Lee Harvey Oswald all over again," she said.

Now, almost two hours after the explosion, she was waiting for the others to finish packing their gear. It wouldn't be long before her face appeared on every news channel, and she wanted to be clear of the apartment before that happened.

Fortunately, she'd spent the last two days working on her appearance. Her black hair was now bleached blonde, and the makeup she'd applied in the last hour had darkened her complexion.

There wasn't much the boys could do to alter their looks. Both had grown beards over the last couple of weeks and that would have to do.

"All set," Colback said.

Farooq nodded that he was ready too. His shoulder injury had healed nicely after they'd cleaned it out and closed the wound with surgical glue, but he would carry the scar for the rest of his life.

There was little point in wiping the place down. If any of the neighbors recognized her picture, getting rid of any prints would serve no real purpose.

Eva opened the apartment door and looked up and down the second-floor landing. There was no one in sight, so she ushered the other two out and closed the door quietly behind her. They made it to the car without coming across anyone else from the complex, and Eva opted to drive.

"We should have joined up with Len and Sonny sooner," Farooq said.

"Woulda, coulda, shoulda. How could we know the ESO would kill a bunch of kids just to get my picture all over the news?"

Eva had to admit that the ESO had won this round. The staged attack would so incense the American people that everyone would be looking for her. And it wouldn't stop there. Colback and Farooq would no doubt be named as accomplices soon, making it important that they all disappear as soon as possible.

Sonny had rented an RV the previous day, and Eva had intended for the Brits to handle the recon alone, but now she had no option but to join them.

She tossed her phone into the back seat and Farooq caught it. "Message Sonny," she said. "See if there's news from the Calico Club."

Before Farooq could open WhatsApp, the phone vibrated to signal an incoming message.

"Speak of the devil. Sonny has some more pictures for us. He says he's on his way to the RV now. He just paused at a truck stop to get something to eat."

"Tell him we'll see him at the RV," Eva said. "See what he sent us."

Farooq downloaded the images and thumbed through them. The last one was of Sonny's notes, indicating the times the subjects arrived and left.

"Both the Langtons are here," he told Eva. "I also recognize Alexander Mumford. The others I don't know. I'll have to search for them. It looks like we've got the main players though."

"Then Len can pull back. Find a quiet spot on the map and tell them to meet us there with the RV. Make sure it's a place we can ditch this car."

Farooq searched on his phone, and after a few minutes he found a suitable area for the rendezvous. He told Eva where to drive, then sent the coordinates and instructions to Sonny and Len.

Half an hour later, Eva pulled off the freeway outside Manassas, Virginia, and turned onto a residential road. The houses were set back from the street, behind sturdy gates. The dwellings were widely spread along the verge of the lush woodland that surrounded the subdivision.

"There should be a fire road coming up on the right," Farooq told her.

Eva spotted it moments later and turned off. The car was immediately shrouded in twilight as the sun fought a losing battle to penetrate the canopy. Eva drove on until the trees thinned out and she entered an open area that was a hundred feet in diameter.

Parked off to one side were the RV and Len's rental car. Both men emerged from the woods with automatic rifles in their hands when Eva got out of the throwaway Ford.

"You're not a very popular lady right now," Sonny said.

Eva noticed the absence of his usual smile.

"I'm sure there's no need to tell you I wasn't involved."

"We didn't think you were," Smart said. "The ESO trying to smoke you out?"

"That's about the size of it. With my face all over the news, it'll be difficult to go anywhere."

"They also had Rees's sister on TV, asking him to hand himself in. Farooq's too."

Exactly what she'd feared, although worse—the use of the men's siblings being a particularly naked threat by the ESO.

"So, they're desperate enough to kill kids in order to get to you," said Sonny.

"They are, and they're going to pay for it. Farooq identified another likely member of the ESO, and we're going to pay him a visit tonight."

"What security does he have in place?" Smart asked.

"I don't know, and we haven't got the luxury of scoping his place out for a couple of days. If they're willing to wipe out a bunch of kids to force our hand, who knows what they'll do next."

"Agreed," Sonny said. "Now they've implicated Rees and Farooq, it's going to be difficult for any of you to move in public."

"Another reason we need to move quickly and finish this."

Eva led them into the RV and saw that Sonny had stocked it with enough food and drinks to last at least a week.

"Farooq, find out where Alexander Mumford lives, then work on ID'ing the others. The rest of you—weapons check, then get some sleep."

CHAPTER 42

The weather couldn't have been more accommodating. After more than three weeks of glorious sunshine, the thunderstorm was welcomed by both farmers and trained assassins alike.

The pounding rain helped drown out the sound of Eva's approach to the house, an expensive and expansive replica of a Mexican hacienda. It was all terracotta tiles and archways, and she could see the two guards taking cover from the storm. They were patrolling the first floor, letting the second-floor balcony protect them from the downpour. Eva had been watching them for a couple of hours, and their drill remained constant: one covering the east side and the rear of the building, the other watching the front and west. It took each of them two minutes to cover their half of the house, then another two to walk back and meet up on the corner. She noticed that they never spoke, only acknowledged that the other was still alive and doing his job before the patrolling started once more.

Eva had no idea when the shifts would change, but guessed it would be at the top of the hour. She decided to strike at 2:20 a.m. That would give them fifteen minutes to make their way through the trees that surrounded Alexander Mumford's villa and get to the back of the house, where she would make her entry. She'd scouted it out already and identified a way in through the door at the rear: it was the perfect place to launch the attack.

She was a hundred yards from the house, ten yards inside the tree line, so Eva wasn't worried about being seen by the guards. If there were any motion sensors or CCTV cameras in the woods, they would have known about it by now.

She had the rest of the team in place with three minutes to spare, only Farooq sitting this one out.

The guard reached the corner of the house and met his companion, then turned and slowly retraced his steps, his eyes always on the trees. Eva waited until he turned the corner then broke cover and ran across the manicured lawn. It took twenty seconds to reach the back wall, and she leaned against it for a few seconds as she brought her breathing under control.

The guard would reach the corner again in around a minute. Eva crouched as she crept past a window, then straightened as she reached the end of the wall. She heard the approaching footsteps just as the guard's shadow came into view, and tightened her grip on the rubber-handled knife. Her pulse raced as adrenaline surged through her body, every sinew poised to strike.

The guard appeared, but not where Eva expected him to be. He was half a yard farther away than she'd anticipated, and she had to adjust her feet as she lunged at him. The knife was inches from the man's throat when he twisted sideways, bringing his rifle up in the same movement. Eva missed his neck by millimeters, but followed through with her elbow and felt the satisfying crunch of cartilage as the guard's nose imploded. He staggered backward and tried to bring his weapon up again, but Eva was too quick for him. The top of her boot connected with his groin and, as he doubled over, she reversed the knife and plunged it into the base of his skull.

Spinal cord severed, the man went limp and collapsed to the ground, his rifle clattering onto the tiles. Eva pulled the knife free and ran as silently as she could to the far corner of the house to intercept the other guard. She'd lost precious seconds in the skirmish, and it was about to prove costly.

Eva was still five yards from the corner when the other guard appeared. His rifle rose to his shoulder in an instant and the sharp crack of a round reached her ears. The fact she heard it meant she was still alive, which was more than could be said for the guard. His head jerked sideways as a bullet slammed into his temple, and he dropped like a sack of rocks.

Much as Eva was relieved to still be breathing, the noise was a disaster. Police or other reinforcements would soon be on their way, so her plan to interrogate Alexander Mumford was blown.

She could still make a statement though.

The rear doors flew open and two men rushed out, weapons searching for targets. Eva took one out with a pair of rounds to the head, while Colback's rifle claimed its second victim of the night.

Sonny and Len ran from the trees, rifles slung and silenced pistols in hand, but Eva didn't wait for them. She ducked inside the house and found herself in a reception room. An open door in the opposite wall led out to the hallway, which was bathed in artificial light. Hurried footsteps approached, and Eva waited until the figure was framed in the doorway before putting a couple of rounds into the silhouette's head.

Sonny and Smart joined her in the room. Eva stepped over the dead body and the other two followed her into the hall. No more guards in sight, but Eva didn't want any sneaking up from behind. She motioned for Sonny and Len to clear the first-floor rooms while she stood guard. Normally she would have gone in herself, but Sonny had been a close-quarters battle instructor in his SAS days, making him better qualified for the job.

Sonny stood to one side of the first door while Smart took the other. He turned the knob and pushed it open a few millimeters, then waited for gunfire. When none came, he stepped back and kicked the door wide open, then spun 180 degrees and put his back to the wall again.

The last movement saved his life, as two automatic rifles opened up. Bullets flew out of the room and across the hallway, destroying a giant mirror and shattering a priceless vase.

Sonny used hand signals to tell Smart what he had in mind. After getting a nod in acknowledgment, Sonny started to count while his friend unslung his rifle and held it above his head.

On three, Smart started spraying the room blindly with lead. As he did, Sonny crouched and darted inside, taking cover behind a high-backed chair. When Smart's magazine ran dry, two figures popped up from behind a desk and let loose at the doorway. Sonny crept around the side of the chair and hit the first just above the eye. By the time the second one had a chance to identify the new threat, it was too late. A double-tap sent a puff of red mist into the air and he collapsed next to his colleague.

"Clear!" Sonny shouted, and exited the space to repeat the process with the next room.

They encountered no more bodyguards on the first floor, so Eva led them up the marble staircase, which branched off to the left and the right at the top. She was choosing which way to go when the decision was made for her. A burst of automatic fire from the left missed her head by inches, and the shooter disappeared around a corner.

Eva gave chase. She reached the same corner and dived to the floor before looking around it. The guard had to adjust his aim, and she pulled her head back just as bullets tore chunks out of the plaster. He'd fired from the second doorway on the right: likely the room where Alexander Mumford was hiding.

Eva hand-signaled Sonny and Smart to her side and motioned for them to cover her, letting them know where the shooter was. Smart already had a fresh magazine in place as he got into position. Eva tapped him on the shoulder, and he stuck the barrel of the rifle around the corner and began laying down covering fire. As he did so, Eva crouched and rushed to the first doorway, halfway to the guard's position. She threw herself to the floor and brought her pistol up. As Smart stopped firing, Mumford's man took his turn. He only showed Eva a couple of inches of his profile, but from five yards away, it was all she needed.

Eva was up and running before the guard hit the floor. She paused as she reached the bedroom, then put her head around the open doorway. It was only there for a fraction of a second, but that was enough to take in the scene.

Alexander Mumford was kneeling down behind his enormous bed, wearing silk pajamas and pointing a pistol at the door. He hadn't had time to get a shot off because she'd been too quick. If she planned to incapacitate him, she'd have to expose herself for longer.

A better idea came to her.

Eva pulled Sonny close and whispered in his ear. "Get me the biggest flashlight you can find."

While he went to fulfill her request, Eva kept Mumford occupied.

"I guess you know who I am," she said loudly.

"You're a dead woman, that's who you are. This place will be surrounded in a couple of minutes. You fucked with the wrong people, Driscoll!"

Mumford fired twice at the wall next to the door frame, more for show than in expectation of hitting anyone on the other side. Eva didn't flinch, knowing that no one with Mumford's money would live in a house built with drywall.

"I know you're part of the ESO," she replied. "I want the names of the other members. Henry and Edward Langton are two. Who are the others?"

Mumford replied with an expletive-laden diatribe as Sonny returned with a large Maglite, which Eva gave to Smart, sending Sonny back downstairs with further instructions.

"If you give yourself up, you might save your friends' sisters," Mumford said.

"No thanks, I have—what the hell?"

The house was suddenly enveloped in darkness.

"Too late," Mumford called out. "The cavalry's here—"

Smart flicked on the flashlight and Mumford put his hand up to shield his eyes from the dazzling glare. At the same time, Eva stepped into the doorway, got a bead on Mumford, and shot him in the shoulder. His pistol slipped from his grasp, and Eva ran into the room as the lights came back on. She kicked Mumford in the chest, knocking him onto his back. She landed a heavy knee on his torso and the other on his good arm, then jabbed her thumb into his bloody puncture wound. Mumford howled in pain, and she waited a few seconds before relieving the pressure.

"I want the names," she said. "I was planning to gently tease them out of you but there isn't time for that." She drew a knife from the scabbard in her boot and held it up so Mumford could see its six-inch serrated edge. "I'll give you five seconds to start talking. It'll save you a lot of pain. I already know about the Langtons and you. I'm guessing Joel Harmer, right?"

Those were the only people Farooq had been able to identify from the surveillance photographs, but Eva figured there had to be others involved.

"Fuck you." Mumford spat at her, missing her face but hitting her jacket.

"Okay, we'll play it your way."

Eva adjusted her position and sliced through Mumford's pajama pants. She gripped one of his testicles in her left hand, then began to squeeze.

He screamed, an animal sound that told her she had his attention.

"Talk." She eased the pressure but placed the razor-sharp edge of the blade against his scrotum.

Mumford squeezed his eyes shut, then shook his head. "It's pointless," he said. "You kill me, they'll have my replacement by lunchtime."

"Wrong. When I'm finished with you, no one's gonna want to take your place."

She sliced upward, then dropped a bloody mass on Mumford's chest. "You've got one left. Tell me the names."

Mumford was too busy screaming to hear. With limited time, she'd been forced to take the extreme route, and it had backfired. Mumford was now a blubbering wreck and it was long past time to clear out.

"Last chance to talk," she said, but when Mumford didn't acknowledge her, she decided the time had come to make a point.

Eva turned to the doorway. Sonny had come back from turning off the breakers for those ten crucial seconds.

"Get to the rendezvous point," she told Sonny and Smart. "I'll be right behind you."

Both men nodded and disappeared, and Eva turned back to Mumford.

"How does it feel to reap what you sow, huh?" She knelt and put her lips to the wounded man's ear. "The only reason I'm here is because you created me. You needed someone to do your dirty work, so you trained people like me to do things you wouldn't dare try yourself. While you and your friends sat in your clubhouse, I was out killing anyone who threatened your balance sheet. I thought I was doing something noble, protecting my country and keeping America safe, but it was never like that. I was murdering the innocent. I took the lives of over thirty people, and I lived with it because I thought it was for the good of the country. Now I have to spend the rest of my life knowing I was just a hired killer, and their blood will be on my hands forever."

Mumford gurgled and spluttered but Eva was far from finished.

"And how could you kill all those children just to get to me? What kind of monster does that? Sure, target me, but . . ." Her voice cracked, and she had to pause. As she gathered herself, she saw that Mumford was losing a lot of blood, his end near.

"I wish I had another twelve hours with you, but that's not going to happen, so I'll make it brief. You killed my brother because you wanted to be one of the most powerful men on the planet, but that's not how people are going to remember you. All they'll see is the sad old man who choked to death on his own cock."

Eva castrated him with one slice of the knife, then pinched his jaw to force his mouth open and stuffed his manhood inside. She put her hand over his mouth to prevent him spitting the bloody flesh out and held his nostrils closed.

Mumford bucked with all his strength, but Eva had anticipated it and held firm. She stared into his bulging eyes as his face grew crimson and his thrashing more frantic.

His face was blue by the time he stopped moving. Eva kept her hands in place for another minute in case he was feigning death, then wiped her hands on his pajamas and stood. She used her phone to take a few photographs, then jogged out of the house to meet up with the others.

CHAPTER 43

Eva lay in her bunk and stared up at the ceiling of the RV. She'd woken a few minutes earlier, but the dream she'd been having was still with her.

It had been about Carl Huff.

Eva hadn't dreamed about him in years, although she had thought about him from time to time. She wanted to think that the dream was a response to seeing him in the recent photographs, but wasn't convinced. She certainly wasn't one to put much stock in her nocturnal imaginings. Dreams weren't portents any more than black cats or broken mirrors were harbingers of misfortune.

She got up and walked out of her room. The others were still sleeping, so she took a bottle of water from the refrigerator and went back to bed. She lay back and tried to put Huff out of her mind.

The real issue she faced was how to get to the other ESO members. Mumford had died only eight hours ago, but Henry Langton would already know about it. All members of the inner circle would be on an even higher level of alert, making her job all the more difficult. Even the lesser lights in the organization would be upping their security arrangements.

Going after individuals was no longer an option. Each would have an army protecting them by now, and she simply didn't have the resources to take them on. What she needed was an opportunity to get to them all at the same time.

Eva wondered if perhaps that was why she'd been subconsciously thinking about Huff. He had access to the Langtons, although she noted he hadn't been allowed into any of their meetings at the Calico Club. At least, so far as Smart and Sonny's surveillance indicated.

What are you doing with them, Carl?

Was it too much of a coincidence that he should turn up to protect the people she was gunning for? It made sense for Langton to pick personnel from the CIA's clandestine services program.

But why Huff?

Was he the only one available at the time? Perhaps. It wasn't as if they churned out hundreds of operatives every few weeks, so there weren't that many to choose from. Still—Carl Huff?

Eva wanted to take a walk and clear her head, but even in their remote location, there was a chance that hunters or hikers might happen upon their vehicle. She remained in bed, staring at the white ceiling and trying to make sense of Huff's involvement.

She gave up when she heard stirring outside the bedroom. The answer wasn't going to fall into her lap, so she would have to get it from the only reliable source: the horse's mouth.

Eva picked up the camera that had been used to take the surveillance photographs of the Langtons at the Calico. She flicked through the Canon's memory, looking for a shot she'd seen previously. It was of Edward Langton's limousine after he'd been dropped off at the club. She looked at the subsequent pictures, and an idea formed in her head.

Eva used the mapping app on her phone to zoom onto the street where the Calico Club had sat for a couple of hundred years. She used the app's street-view function to go to the next corner, then took a left as the driver had done in the photographs. As she passed a metal barrier she rotated the image to the left and saw three limousines parked one in front of the other. The license plates were obscured, but she knew this had to be the place the chauffeurs parked while waiting for their bosses to call them back to the front entrance.

That was where Huff would likely wait the next time he dropped Edward Langton off at the Calico. Given what she'd done to Alexander Mumford, that next meeting would take place soon.

Eva walked through to the kitchen and put a pot of coffee on. Smart and Sonny were awake already, and she shook Colback and Farooq from their slumber.

"I have to go meet Carl Huff," she said, once everyone had shaken off the last of their sleep.

"Why the hell would you want to do that?" Colback asked.

"Because he's not here by chance. He can't be."

Sonny also looked unsure. "It's a huge risk. What do you plan to talk about? The good old days? Or are you going to ask him nicely to step aside while you fillet his client?"

"I just want to know why he's here."

"To stop you from killing Edward Langton," Colback told her. "Plain and simple."

"I'm not buying it." Eva poured herself a coffee. "Of all the people in the world, why him?"

"To get you thinking like this," Smart suggested. "Make you second-guess everything, lose focus, you name it."

"And it seems to be working," Colback added.

"I agree," Sonny chimed in. "Either that or it's purely coincidence. Either way, I wouldn't read anything into it. If he gets in our way, he goes down."

Eva looked around the room, but their faces backed up their words: none of them supported her idea.

"Okay, then how about a compromise? I'll meet up with him in a public place, and if he reaches for a weapon, you can take him out?"

The men regarded each other.

"Anything you try to do in public is extremely risky," Smart said. "You're public enemy number one, and Rees and Farooq are right behind you."

"Also," Colback added, "if he's as good as you say and manages to get the drop on you before we take him out, where does that leave us?"

"Sneaking up on him isn't the issue: I've got that covered. As for him getting the better of me, it's not gonna happen."

"Ego aside," Colback persisted, "what if he does? What are we supposed to do then?"

"Scatter," Eva said. "Sonny and Len can just head back to England. You two, you'll have to change identities. I'll give you the names of my contacts. A new passport will get you to South America, where you can get plastic surgery and different papers. There's money in the account to last you a lifetime. Just don't draw attention to yourselves."

"In that case, would you mind paying us up to the end of the week?" Sonny asked. "Not that I don't have every confidence in you, but . . . you know."

"I'll do that before I leave," Eva promised. "Now, are you all on board?"

Smart spoke for all of them. "When do you want to do this?"

"In the next couple of days. I need to prepare a couple of things first. We've still got the lease on the office overlooking the Calico, so I want Len and Sonny to resume surveillance on the club. I'll be in place each morning, but if they don't show by 9:30, we'll wait till the next day."

"How're we supposed to cover you?" Colback asked. "I assume you're thinking about a sniper?"

"Exactly, but it's an unnecessary risk for you to be out in public. Sonny, are you up to it?"

"Sure. I take it you're going to source a decent weapon."

"I will. Any preferences?"

Sonny shrugged. "As long as it's suppressed, I don't mind. I'd rather not draw attention to myself if I'm forced to use it."

"No problem. You and Len will be doing the shopping anyway, so choose whatever you want. I'll call ahead and let my contact know to expect you."

"Are you sure?" Farooq said. "The reward for information that leads to your arrest is now at some quarter-million dollars. That's serious temptation."

"Not my guy. He's got too much to lose. If I even suspected he'd turned me in, I'd drop the dirt on him before they got to me. I'll just explain how mutually beneficial my continuing freedom is and he'll play ball. Plus, he knows I'm not capable of blowing up a school full of kids. As for the call, I'll make it just before we move to our next location."

"Where will that be?" Farooq asked.

"On the Potomac."

CHAPTER 44

Edward Langton waited for Huff to get out of the driver's seat and walk around the limo to open the door for him. He took a deep breath before he got out of the car, but the sniper's round he'd been expecting never arrived. Still, he moved more quickly than usual to the front door of the Calico Club and was safely inside within a couple of seconds of leaving the safety of the armored car.

He'd been skittish since the moment he'd heard about Alexander Mumford's death. The newspapers were reporting it as a heart attack, but he doubted that was the case. Hopefully, his father would be able to shed some light on the matter.

He entered the room and saw that a couple of the others had beaten him in once more. Joel Harmer was already there, as was Mumford's replacement. Dale Naughton was a Wall Street giant that few people had ever heard of. He ran his own consultancy firm and advised the boards of every Dow Jones 30 company. He'd been groomed to succeed Mumford for the last decade, and now that he was sitting in the dead man's seat, he looked ready to take on the responsibility.

Naughton was in his mid-fifties, young for an ESO member. He wore a two-thousand-dollar suit and his hair showed not a hint of gray. His physique was impressive for a man of his age. He had billions to spend and many more billions yet to be earned, and he was looking forward to a long and healthy life.

The ESO had expected that Naughton would spend another ten years preparing for this role, but Mumford's death had forced the elder Langton to accelerate the process. Naughton had handed over the reins of his company to the man who would eventually replace him at this very table, his focus from this day on the needs of the ESO and nothing else.

Edward shook Naughton's hand. "Good to see you again, Dale. Sorry it had to be under these circumstances."

"Same here. Alexander was a fine man."

Edward poured a coffee and took his seat as his father entered the room.

Henry Langton nodded to those present, then made himself comfortable and lit a cigarette before addressing them. "Joel, please fill us in on what you know about Alexander's death."

Edward saw Naughton recoil from the cigarette smoke floating toward him.

Better get used to it.

"Driscoll attacked his home at around 2:30 in the morning. She took out his full complement of eight bodyguards, then proceeded to torture him. It isn't known how long she had with him, but backup arrived within seventeen minutes of the call going out. We have no idea if Mumford talked before she killed him. Death was caused by asphyxiation. She cut his cock and balls off and stuffed them down his throat."

Edward and Naughton winced as they heard the news for the first time.

"So, it wasn't a heart attack," Edward said.

"No," Langton said. "Driscoll killed him. And what matters now is discovering how she knew that Alexander was one of us."

"She must have been watching us here," Edward said.

Langton favored him with a curt nod. "I have people checking out every room for rent in a one-mile radius over the last two weeks. She wouldn't have been standing across the street from us, so she must have hired a place to watch from."

"And what if we do find the place? It's a little late now, don't you think?"

"Think, man! Think!" Langton looked on the edge of one of his infamous meltdowns. "How do you suppose she paid? Cash? Unlikely in this neighborhood. She must have used a card, and that's something we can trace."

"She might be there right now, looking to see who's replaced Alexander," Harmer said.

The remark didn't sit well with Naughton, who looked pale as he fidgeted in his seat.

"Perhaps. Dale, I suggest you invest in a little extra personal security from now on. Just to be on the safe side. Let me call my man at Stormont and get the ball rolling."

~

After Edward Langton entered the Calico Club, Huff got back behind the wheel and drove around the corner. The club had its own private parking lot at the back of the building, with a manned entrance to ensure only members gained access.

As Huff approached the lot, he slowed to let an old woman pass. She was on the sidewalk, directly in front of the barrier, making slow progress with her walking stick. Huff blocked traffic while waiting for her to move out the way. A few drivers hit their horns to encourage him to move. The woman's head snapped up at the sound. She was in mid-stride, and she overreached with her stick. Huff watched as she tried to regain her balance, but she was unable to recover. She hit the sidewalk hard, blocking Huff's entry completely.

Horns continued to blare as he got out of the limo to help the fallen woman. The nearest driver gestured his displeasure, and Huff responded by opening his jacket just enough to show the butt of the Glock in his shoulder holster. He walked over to the prostrate lady and took a knee beside her.

"You okay?" he asked.

She rolled onto her back, revealing the barrel of a small handgun. "Just peachy, honey."

Huff immediately recognized the voice.

"How about you help me into your car so we can catch up on old times?"

Facing the business end of her pistol, Huff had no choice but to help Driscoll to her feet. She covered up the weapon so it wasn't visible to the other drivers waiting impatiently behind the limo, then gingerly got to her feet. She told Huff to pick up her stick and hand it to her, then let him help her into the front passenger seat of the car. He walked around the car and got in beside her.

"Drive around the block a few times," she said.

Huff got the vehicle moving and took a left at the next corner. "What took you so long?" he asked. "I thought you'd have been in touch days ago."

"I've been a little busy trying to stay alive," she replied, keeping one eye on Huff and the other on the road ahead. She didn't put it past him to cause a deliberate crash while she wasn't concentrating. Just to be sure, she put her seatbelt on.

"You're looking good, kid."

"You too," Driscoll admitted, "but this isn't a social visit. I want to know why you're here."

"For you, of course."

The smile on his face took her back a decade. He'd been handsome back then, but if anything, he was even more of a looker now. An ancient memory stirred in the pit of her stomach, but she willed it away. This was not the time.

"I guessed that, but do you plan to help me or kill me?"

The smile remained in place as he turned his head to face her. "If I told you, would you believe me?"

"Try me."

~

Sonny stood a few feet back from the open window and watched the target get back into the limousine. He'd already alerted Eva to Huff's presence and had kept the M24 sniper rifle trained on the operative.

As the car pulled away, Sonny let the rifle drop from his shoulder. There was nothing he could do now but wait until the vehicle returned to the same spot and hope Eva got out unscathed.

It made for a tense twenty minutes.

He saw the vehicle pass by a couple of times, which he took to be a good sign. Huff wouldn't drive around all day if he'd managed to incapacitate Eva. Nevertheless, Sonny wouldn't be happy until he saw her.

After one more lap, Huff pulled the car over at the point Eva had chosen. Sonny watched the limo pull back into traffic and take the next left, then go through the barrier to the Calico's rear parking lot.

Eva waited until the black car had disappeared, then crossed the road and got into the Chevy Express van parked opposite the Calico. As soon as Len Smart drove the Chevy away, Sonny dismantled the M24 and put the parts into the briefcase it had come in. It was the perfect accessory to his suit and no one batted an eyelid when he emerged onto the street a minute later and walked to the Metro station.

~

When he heard the familiar *beep! beep!* and the light on his dashboard blinked, Huff turned the key in the ignition and drove around to the front of the Calico Club. He was there within one minute of receiving the signal that Edward Langton was ready to leave, and the front door to the building opened as he glided to the curb.

Once Langton was settled in the back seat, Huff asked where he wanted to be taken. The answer was the airport.

"I have to be on Wall Street by lunchtime. I want you to come with me."

"I think it'd be better if I stayed behind and planned the attack on Driscoll. She just paid me a visit."

Langton's head snapped up from his phone. "What? When?"

"She came to see me while you were in the club."

"What? Where is she now? Did you kill her?"

"No, she's gone."

"Stop the car!" Langton shouted.

Huff ignored the order. "There's no point looking for her. She'll be out of the city by now. Killing her would have solved nothing anyway. If I'd taken Driscoll down, Colback and the others would have vanished."

"But you can't just let her go! If my father hears about this . . . We have to at least make a show of trying to find her."

"As I said, that's pointless."

Huff looked in his mirror and could see Langton trying to cope with the unexpected news. The heir to the ESO, destined to become the most powerful man in the world, looked panicked, out of his depth. Perhaps it was the knowledge that his nemesis had been in the same car a few minutes ago.

"What did she want?"

"A truce," Huff said. "She wants you to back off, cancel the witch hunt, and let her walk away."

"Never going to happen," Langton said. "She has nothing to trade."

"I suggested that to her, and she said that Mumford is what she has to offer. If you keep coming for her, she'll do the same to all of you."

Langton swallowed hard.

Huff was glad to see he was taking the threat seriously. "She told me what she did to him," he said, enjoying the sight of his principal squirming. "Not a nice way to go."

"She tried once and gave up." Langton tried to hide the fear in his voice and failed miserably. "She knows better than to come after me again."

"She managed to get the drop on me. If she hadn't come to make her offer, you'd be in pieces by now. And so would I."

Huff let the statement sink in, then pulled Langton back from the brink of panic. "However, we have the upper hand. I think I know where she is."

Langton pushed forward in his seat. "You do? Where?"

"In a cabin on the Potomac, opposite Quantico."

"She told you?"

"Not in so many words," Huff said. "When we were discussing our past, she said the place she was staying held lots of memories, all of them good. She and I used to stay there when we were training for clandestine services." He let Langton consider what he'd said in silence, then elaborated when his charge couldn't make the connection on his own. "We were romantically involved."

Langton threw his hands in the air. "You were sleeping with Driscoll? And you didn't think to share that with me earlier?"

"It was irrelevant. Ancient history. Until now. Now, we have a strong lead. Do you want to accept her offer, or should I take a team and check out the cabin tonight?"

Langton made a call and told his PA to cancel his meeting in New York.

"I can arrange a hundred men for you. More if you need them."

"A hundred should be more than enough," Huff said.

"Good. I'll let my father know we've got her."

"I wouldn't," Huff said. "It's not guaranteed she'll be there. She could have said it just to mess with me. Maybe she booby-trapped the place, hoping to take out half of your security. No, I'd wait until she's dead before you give your father the good news. Otherwise you risk disappointment."

Langton nodded. "That's true. I'll wait until you've confirmed her death."

"It's the right decision," Huff said. "What kind of proof do you want? Photographs? Her head in a box? Or . . ."

"Or what?"

"Or do you want to do it yourself?"

"What do you mean? Are you suggesting I go to the cabin with you? Are you crazy?"

"No, that would be dumb. I was just wondering if you wanted me to bring her in alive. If the opportunity presents itself, obviously. It might be a good idea to learn exactly what they know."

Huff watched as Langton played with the idea in his head.

"You could even invite your father along to watch, if you like."

A smile crept onto Langton's face. "Yes, I'd like that very much."

CHAPTER 45

Huff pulled the night-vision glasses over his eyes and studied the cabin seventy yards away. It was a two-story affair with a porch out front, and like the other houses in the region, was constructed entirely from wood.

It was also occupied.

A faint light shone through what Huff recalled being the living room window. He'd sketched out the internal layout for the rest of the team, and although the dimensions might not be 100 percent accurate—it had, after all, been ten years since he'd seen the interior—he was confident that the floorplan was correct.

Huff had chosen five men to help with the assault, with another ninety circling the area at a distance of three hundred yards. Each had NVGs and enough weaponry to fight a small war. Huff thought it over-kill, but Edward Langton had insisted on sending as much firepower as possible. At one point, he'd even suggested helicopters and amphibious landing craft, but Huff had talked him out of it. This operation called for subtlety, not a tribute to D-Day. Or *Rambo*.

The strike team consisted of some of Langton's permanent security detail, while the other men on the perimeter were the recently hired help. Their task was simple: shoot anyone who came running toward them. They didn't know for sure who the target was, and Huff wanted it to remain that way. The fewer people who knew the true nature of this mission, the better. His plan was to take Driscoll's team alive, but if anyone made it to the outer perimeter they would be taken down hard.

Huff spoke to the operative at the Homeland Security control center and asked for the latest movement report. They had a live satellite feed from directly overhead, and could see the infrared profiles of himself and the other five members of the strike team. It also showed the heat signatures of the cabin's four occupants.

"I've got eyes on four people," Huff heard over comms. "One in bedroom one, two in bedroom two, one in the living room."

"Roger that. We're going in now."

Nothing had changed in the last three hours, apart from the targets' positions within the building. Anton West's replacement Willard Eckman had wanted to know who the targets were, but Edward Langton had made it clear that it was need-to-know.

Huff switched channels and updated the strike team. He gave each man an assignment, then told them to move out.

The other five members of the assault team acknowledged his instructions. It wouldn't be a dash to the building. Huff had decided on a quiet approach and a noisy entry.

Dressed in ghillie suits to blend into the landscape, the six men inched their way toward the cabin, which lay some two hundred feet from them.

Five minutes later, they were in position. Throughout that time, Eckman had been feeding Huff live updates, and now that he'd stopped at the side of the building, the latest news came through: all four targets were still in the same locations.

Huff used hand signals to remind the men which rooms they'd been assigned, and all nodded that they understood their roles. He led them around to the front of the cabin, then counted down on his fingers.

Three . . .

Two . . .

One!

Huff's shotgun exploded and a hole appeared where the doorknob and lock had been. Another member of the team kicked the door open and they piled in, four men peeling off to secure the bedrooms.

"Hands where I can see them!" Huff shouted, and a short guy with blond hair froze, still holding the deck of cards he'd been using to play solitaire. Next to him was a Glock 17 and his eyes strayed toward it.

"Don't even think about it! I'll blow your fucking head off! Stand up and take three steps toward me!"

The man did as he was told.

"Drop the cards and put your hands out where I can see them."

Again, the blond guy complied. One of Huff's men produced a set of handcuffs and slapped them on the man's wrists, securing his hands behind his back. He was then thrown to the floor and patted down.

"Clear!"

The other team members emerged from the bedrooms with three more prisoners in tow, including Eva Driscoll.

"Where's Naser?"

"Dead," Driscoll said. "He was hit in the heart near the Beechwood Hotel. We buried him in the woods."

"Show me."

Huff motioned for another man to join them, and the trio marched out of the cabin. Driscoll led the way, with Huff clutching her arm. They walked for around fifty yards, then Driscoll nodded at a patch of earth that had recently been disturbed.

"How deep is he buried?"

"About four feet."

Huff looked at the grave for a moment, then took out a device and recorded the GPS coordinates for later investigation. He turned and dragged Driscoll back to the cabin. As they neared it, the three other prisoners waited outside, looking thoroughly dejected, as if they knew the fate that awaited them and were resigned to accepting it.

Not Driscoll.

She planted a foot and aimed a headbutt at Huff's skull, but only managed to connect with his shoulder. In return, she got backhanded across the mouth.

"Still as feisty as ever," Huff said.

Driscoll spat blood in his direction but missed. "You should kill me now. If you don't, you'll live to regret it."

Huff laughed. "You know, Ed Langton's dying to meet you. I'll let him decide how you die."

Driscoll shook her head, as if disappointed. "What happened to you?"

"I'll tell you what happened. Money. Money and power. Taking on Henry Langton was the biggest mistake of your life. You should have mourned your brother and gone on with your life, but you had to push it. You put your head in the lion's mouth and now he's gonna start chomping. When you're gone, I'll be Langton's blue-eyed boy and I'll get all the riches that go with it. By the time I'm forty, I'll have fifty million in the bank and the rest of my life to spend it."

"I can give you fifty million if you let us go right now."

Another chuckle escaped Huff's lips. "Nice try."

Four vehicles pulled up. One prisoner was loaded into each, accompanied by three of Huff's men.

Huff contacted the team on the perimeter and told them to pack up and return to base. He shrugged off the ghillie suit and threw it in the trunk of an SUV, then dressed in jeans and a T-shirt. He got in beside Driscoll and put her seatbelt on, then took out his phone.

"That's mission accomplished . . . Yes, we got 'em all except Naser. He took a bullet a few days ago and . . . Yes, sir. Thank you, sir. We'll be there within a couple of hours. May I suggest you dismiss the extra security? Now that Driscoll is contained, the fewer witnesses, the better . . . Yes, sir. I will."

Huff put his phone in his pocket.

"Don't you realize you're on the losing side?" Driscoll asked. "The Langtons and their cronies may have gotten away with it for years, decades even, but that was before the Internet came along. People are waking up, and one day this will all come crashing down."

"That's where I have to disagree. The Internet has been around for decades, and what difference has it made? Absolutely none, except maybe to polarize the nation. Citizens are too busy fighting among themselves to see the bigger picture. Even if someone offers a glimpse of the truth, they just keep scrolling down until they find a funny cat video. No, I picked a winner, Driscoll."

It took more than two hours to reach Gray Rock, during which time Driscoll and Huff occasionally bickered but mostly fell into silence. When the house came into view, Huff called Edward Langton for instructions.

"Park next to the west-wing entrance," Huff told the driver. The three hundred-plus men Langton had hired were now gathered in the courtyard. A few had already been shipped out and the rest were waiting for transport. By entering via the west wing, he could get the prisoners into the basement without being spotted.

Huff got out of the SUV and undid Driscoll's seatbelt. He pulled her from the vehicle and she barely managed to keep her balance as she slid out the door.

"You're such an asshole."

"Maybe, but at least I'm not the dumbass in the cuffs."

He led her through a door and down a hallway. Although he'd seen plenty of the opulent surroundings, Driscoll was clearly in awe.

"Nice, huh? I'm hoping to get a place like this one day. Langton told me I can have half of any money I manage to recover from you, so that should be a good start. Then just another ten, maybe fifteen years as his right-hand man and it'll be time to retire."

"It'll never happen," Driscoll sneered. "Anyone on Langton's payroll is cursed. In ten years, you won't be looking at real estate, you'll be banged up in prison. The only luxury you can look forward to is a little lubricant before Mr. Big fucks you up the ass."

Huff burst out laughing. "You always paint such vivid pictures, Driscoll. It's a shame we can't hang out a little longer. I'm gonna miss you."

They turned a corner and walked into a large kitchen. It was all chrome worktops and industrial-sized appliances, the kind of setup seen in most high-end restaurants.

Huff pulled a door open and pushed Driscoll ahead of him. She walked down the straight set of stone steps and into the basement.

It was huge, with half the space occupied by tall racks full of wine bottles. The other half was empty, apart from five chairs that had recently been installed. They were bolted into the floor, and metal rings were also set into the concrete, one in front of each chair and one behind.

Huff pushed Driscoll into the middle chair and unlocked her cuffs. He reattached the cuffs behind the back of the chair, ran a metal chain from them, and looped it through the metal ring before securing it with a padlock. He then got another set of handcuffs from a table and used them to shackle Driscoll's ankles to the ring in front of her.

The other prisoners were brought downstairs, and five minutes later, they were all chained up.

"I'd relax if I were you," said Huff. "The main man will be here soon enough."

CHAPTER 46

Willem Klaasen walked down the stone basement steps ahead of Henry Langton and his son. When he reached the bottom and saw the four prisoners chained to the chairs, he gestured for his boss to wait while he checked their restraints. Finally satisfied that the chains and padlocks were secure, he stood back and let Henry Langton take center stage.

"Where's the other one?" he asked.

"Naser's dead," Huff told him. "He took one in the heart when they fled Louisville."

"Good. One less problem to deal with." Henry Langton focused on Driscoll. "You gave us quite a chase," he said to her. "You should have stayed out of it."

"And miss this moment? Not a chance."

Langton chuckled and signaled for a chair. Klaasen brought one over and the old man sat down a couple of yards away from his enemies. He looked at Sonny. "Have you identified these two?"

"Not yet," Huff said. "I'll run their prints and DNA when they're dead."

"What's your name?"

"I'm Fuck," Sonny said, and nodded toward Smart, "and he's You. Fuck, You. You, Fuck."

Langton left the bait on the hook and instead took out a cigarette, lit up, and blew smoke in Driscoll's direction. "I imagined you would be taken down by one of my teams, but this is an unexpected and most welcome turn of events."

"Don't expect me to beg for my life," Driscoll said. "You've killed so many people to put Hank Monroe on the throne, you should be the one facing the bullet."

"My dear, I would never contemplate anything as simple as shooting you. No, that's far too quick. For the aggravation you've caused, this is going to be a long-drawn-out affair. For all of you. As for Hank Monroe, I'm afraid you've got it all wrong."

Driscoll's forehead furrowed. "You didn't kill my brother to keep Monroe's CIA dealings secret?"

"Oh, that's true enough. Your brother, Danny Bukowitz, Adrian Holmes, they all died to stop that news from leaking. But it wasn't to put Monroe on any throne. It was to *stop* him from becoming the next president of the United States."

Driscoll angled her head, clearly confused.

"Two years ago, I did everything I could to ensure that Appleton became president. I funded his entire campaign through endless businesses, paid millions to find dirt on his opponent, greased all the necessary palms and, of course, I had the mainstream media on my side throughout."

"And he still lost."

"Yes, he did, and the swing in the polls when the news about his indiscretions broke was phenomenal. He managed to turn a twenty-point lead into a fifteen-point defeat in a matter of days. Which made me think—rather than looking for skeletons in the opposition candidate's closet next time around, why not ensure that the best candidate has some of his own?

"The reason I had your brother and his colleagues killed was that I didn't want the story about Monroe's drug-running activities breaking too early. The plan was—and still is, now that I have you—to wait until a week before the election and then leak the whole dossier to the news channels I control. I've already got witnesses lined up, sworn affidavits from people he worked with, reams of paperwork and more images than the newspapers will know what to do with. As soon as the story breaks, Monroe will be out of contention, leaving my real choice of candidate to clean up. The only way to be sure of a winner in a two-horse race is to own both horses."

Driscoll seemed about to speak, but Langton held up a hand to stop her.

"Monroe's a fine man, but I need someone who'll end North Korea. The question's been put to Monroe a few times, and he favors a diplomatic approach, whereas the other guy can't wait to wipe the DPRK off the map."

"That'll start a nuclear war."

"No, it won't. It'll prevent one. The North Koreans are still three or four years away from being able to launch a nuclear attack on the US. We intend to strike before they get that far. Kim and his cronies will be gone, and I'll ensure that whoever takes over is eternally grateful to me for saving their country."

"You're not concerned that your people with all the evidence against Monroe will leak it before you're ready?"

"Not at all. These people are realists. They've been well paid to stick to the script, with guarantees of future windfalls and cushy jobs for life. Who would risk that when they know the alternative? We only live once, Miss Driscoll, and most people tend to choose a comfortable existence when option B is an early demise."

"Is that the offer you made to my brother?"

"Heavens, no," said Langton. "He was far too insignificant."

"He fought for his country," said Driscoll.

261

"He fought for *me*. I decide which wars we start. Not a single soldier leaves these shores unless it suits my purpose. You name a conflict in the last forty years and I can tell you how I benefited."

"Someday this will all come out and you'll get the death penalty—all of you."

"And just how is that going to happen? I control the media. They don't even consider running a story about me unless my office approves it. Sure, I let them play off against each other—this newspaper supports the right, this one loves the left—but ultimately, they run for my benefit. The people of America, and the rest of the world for that matter, are too dumb to be given the truth. Or the vote. No, the media won't run anything negative about me. I could be filmed shooting a nun in the head and it wouldn't even make the eleven o'clock news in Bumfuck, Alabama."

"Instead, you bomb children to death and tell the news I did it."

"And the police, and the FBI, NSA, you name it. One call and they all do as they're told." He started counting off on his fingers. "The judiciary, the military, the Senate . . . all of them."

Driscoll shook her head. "All that money, all that power . . . you could have done so much good in the world. Instead, you peddle hate and death, just to make another buck."

"Actually, it's trillions of bucks. And yes, people have died. But you know what? People die every day. The world is already overpopulated, so consider it my way of bringing the numbers down. Do I feel for any of them?" He shrugged. "I didn't even shed a tear when my parents died. Do you know why?"

"Because you're a sociopath?" Sonny suggested.

"Hardly." Langton chuckled. "Even sociopaths have a conscience, no matter how weak. I'm not afflicted with inner voices telling me to feel guilt or remorse. I'm a realist, that's all. Everyone dies, no matter how rich or poor. I'm going to die someday and there's nothing I can do about it. What's the point in crying about something you can't change?"

"It's what makes us human," Driscoll said.

"You're wrong again," he said. "It's what makes you weak." Langton rose from his chair. "I've wasted enough time on them. Get on with it."

"Anyone in particular?" Huff asked.

Langton pointed to Sonny. "The comedian."

"How about we start off with a nice decapitation?"

"Whatever. Just leave Driscoll till last."

Huff removed a knife from his belt and walked behind the line of prisoners until he was standing behind Sonny. He grabbed a clump of blond hair and leaned in close. "You ever seen someone decapitated with a knife?" he asked. "It isn't like using an ax or guillotine. You have to saw back and forth, slicing the tendons and muscles until you reach the spinal column. I'll save your windpipe until last so you can tell me how painful it is."

While talking, Huff placed the key to the cuffs in Sonny's hands. When he'd finished his little act, Sonny said a single word.

"Ready."

Huff stood upright and transferred the knife to his left hand, then reached into his jacket and pulled out his Glock. He pointed it at Klaasen. "Take it out, nice and slow."

Henry Langton's bodyguard stiffened, then reached into his own coat and took out a pistol using a finger and thumb. He tossed the weapon at Huff's feet.

"What the hell are you doing?" Edward Langton asked.

"Bringing you down," Huff said.

Sonny released the handcuffs securing his ankles, then got up and freed Driscoll, who picked up Klaasen's weapon.

Huff took his phone from his pocket and glanced at the screen. "If you look closely at the corners of the room, gentlemen, you'll see the cameras I set up yesterday. Every word you've said has been captured for all time."

Langton took a step toward Huff. "Are you a total moron? Weren't you listening to a word I said? I *control* the news. No one's airing any recordings you make. If you put it on a website, it'll be taken down in minutes."

"Not quite," Huff said. "Ever heard of Facebook?"

Langton refused to dignify the question with a response.

"I thought so. Then you might be familiar with Facebook Live. It lets you stream video to your friends in real time."

"Then you've just killed your 'friends.' I'll wipe them off the planet before the week's out."

"Not just our friends," Driscoll said. "I'm afraid we lied when we said Farooq Naser was dead. He's also familiar with Facebook and how to reach its two billion users. A lot of them are online at this very moment, watching. Farooq worked his magic and managed to stream this video on the feed of every active account. Carl, how many people are watching us right now?"

Huff looked at the screen of his smartphone and smiled. "Just short of four hundred million, including twenty-six White House staff accounts. We've got forty-one British MPs, seventeen in Germany's Bundestag, a couple dozen in the French Senate . . . the list goes on." He looked up at one of the cameras. "And if any of the news channels refuses to show this recording and air the full story, it means they were complicit in Langton's activities. Copies will be sent to your offices shortly, and I suggest the producers cut their ties with the ESO immediately and start reporting this. Help us to bring these people to justice."

While Huff was playing to the camera and Driscoll was preoccupied releasing Smart and Colback from their bonds, Klaasen saw an opportunity to strike. He raised his arms above his head and activated the gravity-fed valve sewn into the lining of his sleeve. A small metal ball slid down inside a tube filled with viscous liquid. Klaasen began the five-second countdown in his head.

On one, he started walking toward Henry Langton. "Sir."

Langton turned and saw what his bodyguard was doing. He in turn began to move, taking small steps away from Klaasen, who was still walking toward the center of the basement.

"Look out!" shouted Colback.

~

Eva looked up from unshackling Colback's feet and saw the big South African moving toward her. She also spotted Langton backing away.

As Langton twisted and covered his ears, Eva tried to shout a warning to the others, but the blinding flash and ear-splitting bang worked as intended. The improvised flashbangs that had been fashioned to look like pockets on the front of Klaasen's jacket had disoriented everyone in the room, with the exception of the big South African. Even Henry Langton, who had known to expect a blast, had been knocked off his feet.

Eva tried to clear her vision and the ringing in her ears, but Klaasen was on her before she had a chance to recover. He delivered a punch to the side of her jaw and she flew sideways into the chairs, landing on top of Colback and sending them both sprawling.

"Go!" Klaasen shouted to his boss, and Henry Langton grabbed his son by the collar and pulled him toward the staircase.

Klaasen went after Eva once more, moving for the gun in her waistband as she lay on her front, but before he could grasp it, she lashed out with her left hand and caught him in the temple with her fist. Klaasen shrugged off the blow, but now Eva had flipped over and onto her feet to face him. She brought a knee to connect with his jaw, but Klaasen blocked the attack and countered with another punch to her face. Blood exploded from her nose and Eva saw stars. She aimed a blow at his face but missed by a few inches, and Klaasen went for her abdomen, landing a combination of lefts and rights that knocked her onto her back. Eva brought her feet up to protect herself, then kicked out, catching Klaasen in the chest. He flew backward but steadied himself, then saw Huff's knife on the floor. He picked it up and launched himself at the supine woman in the same movement, the knife high and arcing down for her chest. Once more, Eva brought her knees up and planted her feet on his chest, using his momentum to flip him over her head. She moved to continue her attack but only managed to get onto one knee before Klaasen flipped himself upright like a gymnast and reversed the knife. He came at her again and Eva got to her feet just in time to block his attempt to ram the blade into her skull.

Her knee was halfway to Klaasen's crotch when the side of his head exploded.

"We haven't got time for that kung fu shit," Sonny said, lowering Huff's pistol. "Langton's getting away."

Smart staggered to his feet, while Huff remained on his knees, still clearing his head. Colback, who himself had blood dripping from one nostril, helped Huff up and checked he was able to walk.

Eva took out her gun and ran to the bottom of the stairs. She stuck her head around the wooden post, glanced up to the door, and was instantly met with a hail of bullets. They shredded the wood above her head as she backed away and took Huff by the arm.

"Is there another way out of here?"

Huff watched her mouth moving, and she guessed his hearing had been affected by the blast. He'd been standing closest to Klaasen and had taken the bulk of the flashbang's impact.

She wiped snot and blood from her nose and asked the question again, enunciating her words so he could read her lips.

"No," he shouted. "That's the only way in or out."

Damn. "How many men does Langton have in the house?"

"Twelve."

It wasn't looking good. All they had between them were two handguns, and the only way out of the basement was well defended by a dozen men with unknown firepower.

Eva pinched her bloody nose as she scanned the basement for something that might aid their escape. She saw the cardboard boxes that lined the walls and started rummaging through them in search of a weapon of any kind. Most contained paperwork, some faded yellow from years underground. One box was full of old sports equipment and another was home to an eclectic assortment of books.

Nothing useful, not even a bottle of alcohol to turn into a Molotov cocktail.

They were well and truly trapped. Langton's men simply had to wait them out, or perhaps call in Kevlar-clad reinforcements and storm the basement. They might even soften them up with more flashbangs or grenades . . .

An idea came to her. It was risky, and she would only have one chance at it, but there were no other options. She had to make her move before Langton got too far and the enemy count increased beyond a manageable number.

"We've got to get out of here before they start using grenades!" Eva shouted at the top of her voice.

Sonny ran over to her, waving his hands to tell her to stop. "What the hell are you doing?" he whispered. "You're giving them ideas!"

"I know," she said more quietly. "It's our only way out of here."

She waved him away and stood at the foot of the stairs, just out of sight of Langton's men. All she could do now was wait and see if her ploy had worked.

It wasn't long before the answer came.

The moment she heard the sound of metal bouncing on the stone steps, Eva switched the pistol to her left hand and took a couple of steps to the left so she was standing at the foot of the stairs. She fired off a few rounds at the door, but her focus was the bouncing grenade. She watched it ping off the seventh step from the bottom and caught it as it came back down. In the same movement, she tossed it back to the top of the stairs and ran for cover. A second later the explosion reached her ears, and she sprang into action.

"Go!"

Eva took the stairs two at a time, and Sonny was a couple of steps behind her. At the door, she saw the devastation that the grenade had caused. Five men looked like they'd been pureed in a blender, but she had another seven to contend with before they could get to the Langtons.

Eva stowed her pistol and replaced it with an M4A1 from one of the corpses. She ripped the comms from the dead man's ear and followed the wire to the transceiver clipped to his belt. Sonny did the same, and pocketed a couple of grenades and spare magazines at the same time.

He took the lead as they made for the kitchen door. On the way, he picked up a large cooking pot, and when he got to the doorway he stuck it out into the hall. Bullets immediately pinged off it, and Sonny hand-signaled the direction the gunfire had come from. Following his lead, Eva went high while Sonny crouched and stuck the nose of the rifle around the corner. He let off a burst, then ran from cover and took out one target who stuck his head out a little too far. Eva followed Sonny into the hallway and they ran to the next corner.

A couple of shots rang out from behind them, and Eva spun around to see Smart aiming a pistol at the other end of the hallway. Another of Langton's men was down, leaving five to deal with. Colback appeared from the kitchen, assault rifle in hand, Huff just behind him.

"Carl, on me!" Sonny shouted. "You two, that way!"

Huff sprinted to Sonny and relieved the dead guard of his spare ammunition.

"All the transport will be in the courtyard," Huff said. "Follow me."

He checked around the next corner, then set off at pace toward the double doors that led outside. He was just in time to see Henry Langton's limousine fishtail as the driver floored it through the gates.

The window next to him shattered, and Huff was spun around as a bullet slammed into his shoulder. Eva answered the gunfire with a burst of her own as he staggered to cover.

"How bad is it?"

"It hurts like hell but I'll live."

Sonny also opened up on the two shooters who were taking cover behind the ornamental fountain in the center of the courtyard.

"We need to flank them," he told Eva. "Keep them pinned down."

Sonny sprinted back the way he'd come as Eva's weapon chattered away. He raced up the main staircase to the second floor, then ran around to the east wing, where he found a door leading to a balcony overlooking the fountain. Two three-round bursts ended the standoff.

"Clear!" he called. "Get a vehicle. I'm on my way down!"

Sonny was breathing hard by the time he joined the others outside. Smart and Colback were also there, and Huff was looking through a valet keyboard. He found a set and pressed a button on the fob. The blinkers on a gleaming Range Rover flashed twice.

"Nice choice," Sonny smiled, as he snatched the keys from Huff's hand and got behind the wheel. "Buckle up, people."

The Range Rover was moving within seconds. Sonny gunned it through the gates, then spun the wheel to the right. The backend tried to get away, but Sonny easily corrected the slide and floored it. He kept it to a reasonable eighty miles an hour until the gravel gave way to asphalt, then pushed the Range Rover to its limit.

He soon saw the rear end of Langton's limo.

"What now?" he asked his companions. "Shoot his tires out?"

"They're composite runflats and the car's armor-plated," Huff said, applying pressure to his bloody shoulder. "Our weapons won't make a dent."

"We have to at least try," Colback said. "Try and ram him off the road."

"It won't work," Huff warned, but Sonny tried anyway.

"Whoa!"

Sonny had intended to tap the right-rear fender of the limousine with the nose of the Range Rover to send it into a spin, but he found the three-ton limo immovable.

"We need to try something else," Sonny said, reaching into his pocket. He came out with a grenade, which he tossed to Smart sitting next to him. "I'll get ahead of him; you give him the good news."

The engine roared as Sonny coaxed more power out of the big five-liter V8, and 550 horses pushed him ahead of the sleek black limo.

"A little to the left," Smart said.

When Sonny complied, he dropped the grenade out the window.

Apart from Sonny, they all turned to watch the explosion and collectively cursed as the small bomb disappeared under Langton's vehicle and exploded with no effect on the car. It remained on a true line and began to close in on the Range Rover.

The change in speed took Sonny by surprise, and before he knew it, the other driver had executed the perfect PIT—or Pursuit Intervention Technique—maneuver. Sonny tried to steer into the skid, but it was too late. The SUV performed a slow ninety-degree turn, pinned to the front of the other car, then the tires caught on the asphalt and the Range Rover flipped. It rolled twice, three times, then came to rest on its wheels.

Sonny fought off several airbags and tried to restart the engine, but it wouldn't catch. He turned his head in time to see the limo screech to a halt and reverse back toward them. It stopped fifty yards away, the rear doors opened, and two armed men dived out. The doors closed again as Langton's remaining bodyguards walked toward the Range Rover, their weapons up and firing.

"Incoming!" Sonny shouted, but the bullets pinging off the bodywork rendered his warning redundant.

Eva kicked at her door. The frame had buckled in the crash, trapping her inside. After a couple of attempts, she gave up. Instead, she took out her pistol and started returning fire through the rear window. She got one of the shooters in the sternum and he dropped to the grass, but the other got into the Range Rover's blind spot and continued to pump rounds into the vehicle.

Smart managed to get his door open and crawled out, using the body of the SUV for cover. He popped up from behind the hood and opened up on the remaining bodyguard, almost cutting him in half as he used the better part of a full magazine to end the battle.

"Len, help me with this door!"

Smart tugged at Eva's door, and between them they managed to get it open.

"Anyone hurt?"

Sonny, Colback, and Smart responded that they were fine, and Huff managed a groan as he kept pressure on his wound.

"Erm, I think we might be in deep shit." Sonny pointed into the distance.

A convoy of red and blue lights was soon accompanied by the sound of multiple sirens.

"Back down the road!" Eva shouted. "Into the trees!"

They'd passed the woods half a mile earlier. If they hauled ass, they might just make it. What they'd do once they got there was another matter.

Eva leaned into the car and unclipped Huff's seatbelt, then dragged him out by his good arm. "We gotta go," she said. "Do you think you can run?"

Huff looked beyond her, then shook his head and rested it on her shoulder.

Eva turned and, like the others, stared at the two AH-1 Cobra helicopter gunships bearing down on them.

The pressure of the last few weeks suddenly seemed to hit her all at once. It exploded in her gut and left a huge hole that quickly began to fill with despair.

Langton was going to get away with it. All her efforts had been for nothing.

The moment she'd learned of her brother's faked suicide, she should have realized the ESO was involved and backed off. But no, she had to push it, and even with the firepower hovering above her and the police barreling toward them, she felt it had been the right decision. She couldn't have lived with herself knowing that someone had murdered Jeff and she hadn't done anything about it.

The only thing she regretted was all the lives she'd taken under false pretenses. If she'd really killed those people to protect her country, she could have lived with it, but to have murdered so many simply to further Langton's agenda would haunt her forever.

Part of her wanted to make one last stand, but that meant certain death. Her own, she could deal with, but she would most certainly get the others killed too. After all they'd been through, she wasn't about to make that decision for them.

She eased Huff back onto the seat, then took the pistol from her waistband and tossed it away. She took a few steps away from the wrecked Range Rover, then got down on her knees and put her hands behind her head.

Seeing Eva admit defeat, one by one her companions relinquished their weapons and assumed the position.

~

Henry Langton watched Driscoll throw her gun away and fall to her knees. He checked the road ahead and saw that the police were around a mile away. They would be on the scene in approximately one minute.

He opened a compartment at the side of his seat and took out a silver pistol with a diamond-studded grip. It had been a gift from a foreign prime minister or president, Langton couldn't remember which—one of thousands of little trinkets he'd been given over the years. But this one he'd actually found a use for.

"Stay in the car!" Edward told his father as Henry put his hand on the door release.

"You stay if you like. I want to see the look on her face when they slap the cuffs on her."

He got out of the car and checked the progress of the cops. They were closing fast, but he still had time to say goodbye to Driscoll before they arrived.

The pistol was for his protection only. As he'd told Driscoll in the basement earlier, a bullet was too good for her. He'd already come up with an exotic way for her to go. Although he wouldn't be there to see it in person, he would make sure they filmed her death so that he could enjoy it in private later.

Langton strode over to Driscoll and could feel the hatred radiating from her. He made sure to keep the pistol in clear view so she knew not to make any foolish moves, and he came to a stop a few yards in front of her.

"Hear that noise?" He tilted his head at the approaching cavalry. "That's death coming."

Driscoll didn't answer.

"You think your little stunt back there was clever, don't you? Well, it was a waste of time. I've already made calls and Facebook's now offline. It'll be blamed on a malicious hack designed to discredit one of the most generous philanthropists the world has ever known. The news channels will wait a couple of hours, then quote senior intelligence sources who will conclude that the video was a staged performance by an anarchist group using lookalikes. Apparently, they wanted to make the nation think the entire government was corrupt in the hope of toppling it. A few known activists will be arrested, evidence planted as needed, and they'll spend the rest of their lives behind bars."

Driscoll looked away, her eyes coming to rest on the gun she'd dropped.

"I wouldn't if I were you," Langton warned her. "I may be an old man but I know how to use one of these."

"I'll take a quick death. And if it steals a little of your pleasure, it'll be worth it."

"Oh, I won't shoot to kill. In fact, I'll let the doctors patch you up before we really go to work on you."

Tires squealed as the first of the police cars reached the scene, and two officers got out with their handguns pointing at Langton.

"Drop it!"

Langton ignored the order and flicked the gun in Driscoll's direction. "Take her away."

"I said drop the gun, NOW!"

Langton now realized that both cops were focusing on him and ignoring Driscoll. His phone call requesting immediate help had obviously been answered, but the objective clearly hadn't filtered down to the front line.

The cops looked wired, caught in a situation that could quickly escalate. He decided to do as they ordered, knowing he could crush them at a later date.

He held out his arms and let the half-million-dollar weapon drop to the grass.

"Take three steps toward me and lie face down with your arms spread wide!"

Langton sighed and shook his head. He moved toward the cop and then got down on his knees. "This is a ten-thousand-dollar suit, you know." He lowered himself onto his stomach and put his arms out to both sides.

Six more police cruisers pulled up, with the occupants covering Driscoll and her four friends while the choppers hovered nearby. The two cops dealing with Langton cuffed him and patted him down, then pulled him roughly to his feet.

"I know you're just doing your job but I'm going to ruin you for this."

The first officer took out a Miranda card. "Henry Langton, I'm arresting you on suspicion of murder. You have the right to remain silent and refuse to answer questions. Anything you say may be used against you in a court of law. You have the right to—"

"You're arresting *me*? Are you fucking kidding?"

The cop ignored the outburst. "You have the right to consult an attorney before speaking to the police and to have an attorney present during questioning now or in the future. If you cannot afford an attorney, one will be appointed for you before any questioning if you wish. If you decide to answer questions now without an attorney present, you will still have the right to stop answering at any time until you talk to an attorney."

The two cops took an arm each and began to walk the protesting Langton back to their squad car.

~

What the hell are they doing?

Edward Langton watched his father lie face down on the grass as the two officers approached. One cuffed and searched him while the other covered his partner with his pistol.

He rolled the window down when he saw them tug his father to his feet and one of them started reading from a card. Moments later, he heard his father shouting at the top of his voice: "You're arresting *me*? Are you fucking kidding?"

This wasn't in the script.

Edward hit the button to close the window. "Lock the doors," he told the driver. When he heard the solid *clunk*, he sat back, knowing he had time to think. No one was getting in unless he let them.

Huff's video had clearly done more damage than he'd imagined. Someone had thought it prudent to act on it. A career-ending move.

This needed to be squared away as soon as possible. His father was being marched to a police cruiser, and the only way to get him out would be to speak to the right people. To do that, he would need to retain his own freedom.

A cop knocked on his window with his free hand, the other holding a pistol.

"Step out of the car."

Edward Langton knew that a few rounds from a police-issue pistol weren't going to be a concern, but the conversations he needed to have couldn't happen on an unsecure cell phone. If someone had the audacity to have his father taken into custody, they might even be foolish enough to follow up with phone surveillance. His number wasn't in any database but it wouldn't take long to add it.

"Give me your phone and take me to Winchester Airport," he told the driver.

No one would be listening in on a chauffeur's number, and for now he only needed to call the helicopter pilot to be ready to take off the moment he got there.

He looked up the number on his own phone, then dialed the pilot on the driver's cell and told him to power up the chopper. He also gave instructions to ready the Airbus A340-500 at his father's estate for a flight to Dubai.

Edward tossed the phone back into the front seat. "Why aren't we moving?"

"Sir . . . the road's blocked."

"Then unblock it!"

The driver started the engine, which drew gunfire from the police who had gathered around it. Edward heard rounds strike the doors and windows but they all bounced harmlessly away.

He managed a grin as he waved at the figures jumping out of the way, even though he knew they couldn't see him through the tinted glass.

Seconds later, the car juddered ever so slightly as it shunted two police cruisers aside like cardboard cutouts.

The local airport was just a few miles away. If the gods were kind, they should be able to get there before the police managed to get a decent roadblock in place. From there it was just a short hop to the jet, and he would use the secure onboard communications to get things in motion.

After making a mental list of people to contact to ensure his father's freedom, Edward Langton's thoughts turned to those who'd crossed him, and what he'd do to them.

It was the last thought he had.

An AGM-114 Hellfire missile flew from one of the Cobra helicopters, and the HEAT—high-explosive anti-tank—warhead punched effortlessly through the roof of the limousine. Edward Langton and his driver were instantly incinerated, leaving insufficient DNA material behind for the subsequent investigation to identify either of them.

CHAPTER 47

President Leo Russell looked out of the bulletproof window and over the plush green lawn below. From his office on the second floor of the White House, he could see the Washington Monument standing proudly in the morning sunshine, and he wondered if the nation's first president—or indeed, any of his predecessors—had been tasked with cleaning up such a godawful mess.

It was a question of where to begin.

When his son had shown him the tail end of the live Facebook feed, then pointed him to the full YouTube version, Russell had acted instinctively. He'd ordered an aide to send whatever resources were in the area to investigate, which turned out to be half a dozen police cars and a couple of Cobra attack helicopters on a live-fire training exercise out of New River, North Carolina.

If only he'd known the shitstorm he was about to unleash.

He'd been told about the ESO when he'd assumed office in January the previous year. Having been around politics all his life, the name had been whispered in hushed conversations a couple of times, but it wasn't until he'd achieved the highest office that the details began to emerge. Within days of taking up the position, he'd suggested investigating them but had been warned that anyone willing to take on the role of prosecutor would likely be in the ESO's pocket. Not only that: finding anyone willing to turn over evidence or testify would be a task in itself.

His first and only meeting with Henry Langton had been in the Oval Office. The staff photographer had taken a few snaps for posterity, then the room had been cleared and Russell had discovered just who the mysterious man really was. At first, all was cordial, but the real Langton soon came to the fore. He'd spoken to Russell in the same way that a grade school teacher addresses an unruly student, demanding a number of laws be left in place despite the president's campaign promises.

It hadn't ended well.

Russell had told Langton he would be sticking to his 'For the 100 percent' motto, and that any changes he made would be for the many, not the privileged few. Langton had stood and left without another word, and Russell had thought him a nuisance and nothing more.

It turned out he'd greatly underestimated the man.

If the revelations in the video seen by hundreds of millions were true, then the place to start was with the police and security services. He would have to remove the top few layers of management and hope the cancer hadn't spread beyond that. That done, he'd have to find untainted professionals qualified to replace them. In addition, he'd need a modern-day Eliot Ness to head things up and ensure that all authorities remained untouchable. But where would he possibly find a person like that in a town riddled with corruption?

Even if he managed that monumental task, he'd still have to find enough impartial judges to try any cases involving the ESO. They wouldn't all be in the ESO's pocket, but those in the Supreme Court would have to be retired and replaced with younger blood, people the ESO wouldn't have bothered recruiting because they were so far off influential positions.

After that, his focus would turn to Congress. What to do about the hundred members of the Senate and the 435 in the House of Representatives? He couldn't simply dismiss them all, as that would be a violation of Article One of the Constitution. He would have to get the lawyers to look into implementing term limits for all members, or perhaps calling a snap election, with no current serving members eligible.

That was sure to go down well. But then, extraordinary times called for extraordinary measures.

The more he considered the scale of the problem, the greater and more complicated it became. Military chiefs, heads of industry, the financial sector . . . they'd all have to be investigated.

Since becoming president, Russell had brought in a few of his own people. Secretary of State Dan Latimer was his own choice, but he'd taken advice on most of the senior appointments. Were they all secretly working for the ESO?

Russell sighed as he turned away from the window and took a seat at his desk. He couldn't even trust Latimer. Not after their last conversation. Russell had told his friend that he had to act on the information in the video, but the secretary of state's response had come across as a thinly veiled threat.

"In 2008, when the banks were on their knees, we had to bail them out. They were too big to fail. Now imagine that on an exponentially larger scale. You start tinkering with the status quo and you could cause the meltdown of the USA, maybe even the world. If they do control the banks, who's to say they won't suddenly call in all debts? Millions of Americans will be faced with the choice of paying off their mortgages within thirty days or losing their homes. And what about small business loans? If they all had their debts called in, the closures and job losses would be astronomical. And where would the blame lie? With the president."

Latimer hadn't stopped there. From military coups to the worst dystopian nightmare, every scenario had been laid bare in the one-hour meeting.

By the end, Russell had felt physically sick.

Yet here he was, contemplating the changes that would have to be made in order to rid the world of the ESO.

He rested his elbows on the desk and placed his head in his hands. He felt a migraine coming on.

The phone in his pocket rang, and he saw it was Latimer.

"Yes, Dan."

"Henry Langton's dead." No preamble, just straight to the point.

"How?"

"Heart attack. He was rushed to the hospital but pronounced DOA."

"Okay. Thanks for letting me know."

A nightmare scenario had just gotten a whole lot worse. The lead suspect in his world-changing investigation was dead. His son was already presumed dead in the helicopter attack on the limo, which meant they only had one name to work with, thanks to Eva Driscoll: Joel Harmer.

Eva Driscoll.

Yet another decision that had to be made.

She'd killed people and would have to face the consequences. He'd demanded transcripts of all police interviews with her. They made for interesting reading.

She claimed that if she'd gone to the police with her suspicions about her brother's suicide, she would have been blocked at every turn by the ESO. As it was, she admitted to killing several men, but claimed it was the only way to get to the people who'd ordered Jeff Driscoll's murder.

Russell believed her. Video evidence had already emerged showing that Driscoll couldn't have been involved in the school bombing. Instead, she'd been targeting those she believed to be heading up the ESO, along with the men who'd already been tasked with killing her. She'd had a strong case for self-defense . . . right up until the moment she castrated Alexander Mumford. You don't feed someone their own genitalia to stave off an attack.

Her case would also hinge on being able to prove that the ESO existed in the first place. The video was one thing, but a competent lawyer would be able to discredit it as a forgery. That left her word against that of Joel Harmer, who, even while incarcerated, probably still held sway with the judiciary.

The outlook was bleak.

For everyone.

CHAPTER 48

Day seven in the Bedford Hills Correctional Facility began the same as the previous six.

Eva Driscoll had done two hundred sit-ups and two hundred push-ups by the time the bell rang for breakfast. She stood by the door, waiting for the guard to open it from the safety of his reinforced glass booth. The bars eventually slid back, and Eva and her cellmate Dimalia joined the procession heading for the mess hall.

Dimalia was a young gang member from East New York. At only nineteen years old, she was one year into a ninety-nine-year stretch for a double homicide. Compared to Eva's sentence, it was a slap on the wrist.

As they ambled to the mess hall, Eva's eyes were everywhere.

On the second day, she'd been given an initiation. In the shower, one of the prison's lesser lights had been given the job of welcoming her to the facility. It was standard practice to show newcomers who really ran the place, but the message was lost on Eva. She broke the woman's nose with one blow and snapped her wrist before asking who had sent her. Armed with a name, Eva had sought out the woman the inmates referred to as Big Annie.

The meeting consisted of a brief discussion and extreme violence.

From that moment on, everyone knew what Eva was capable of and the sensible ones got out of her way. That left the dumb ones still to contend with. Those who wished to earn a name for themselves. Only one other person had tested her in that first week, and the doctors believed the poor sap might walk again someday.

It wasn't that Eva was out to terrorize people. She was by no means a bully; she simply wanted her time in Bedford Hills to pass peacefully. It was to be her home for the rest of her life, and she didn't want to spend the next sixty years looking over her shoulder. Of course, there'd be others who'd try for her crown. Big Annie still ran the prison but everyone knew Eva was the ultimate challenge. With each new intake, there'd be someone looking to build a reputation, but Eva hoped that, over time, they'd learn to leave her be.

Eva lined up and got her breakfast. Others with her reputation would have jumped to the front of the line, but she wanted to show that she was tough but fair. She wasn't intent on starting confrontations, only ending them swiftly.

She sat at a table with her back to the wall. Her only companion was Dimalia, who knew not to make small talk while Eva was eating.

Eva thought about Carl Huff as she chewed on a piece of bread. It had been ninety-three days since they'd surrendered, and although she'd seen him at the trial, she hadn't had much opportunity to speak to him. In fact, she hadn't really spoken to any of her team since the day Henry Langton had been arrested and Edward Langton vaporized.

They certainly wouldn't be visiting any time soon. Colback had received thirty years for his part in the assault on Mumford's home, as had Sonny Baines and Len Smart. Huff had been given twenty-five years for his role in the firefight at Gray Rock, even though the prosecution could provide no evidence to suggest the weapon he'd used had killed anyone. The prosecution had managed to convince the jury of his intent, and that had been enough to secure a conviction.

There'd been gasps in the court when the verdict and sentences had been read out. Many who'd followed the saga in the news considered Eva a hero, taking on the corrupt establishment against overwhelming odds.

The jury clearly thought otherwise.

A couple of hard cases walked by and gave Eva the look. Maybe they were doing it to let others know they weren't scared of her, or maybe it was the prelude to another encounter. Either way, they were the least of her problems.

Her biggest concern was the ESO.

She'd heard about Henry Langton's death and Joel Harmer's arrest, but she was under no illusions that the ESO had gone up in a puff of smoke. How many of the remaining members were intent on avenging the Langtons and Mumford? The truth about Hank Monroe was now public knowledge and his political career was over, so there was no need to silence her about that. Would they be satisfied with her incarceration and let it go? It was a nice thought, but Eva wasn't counting on it. It might be days, months, even years, but someday she expected someone to make a move on her. A gun might mysteriously make it through security, or the guards could suddenly disappear while she was in a room full of armed women. She could think of a thousand ways she would do it, which meant the ESO would never run short of options.

Eva finished her chow and took her tray to the cleaning station, then joined the line to await escort back to the cell. She would remain there for the rest of the day, only emerging to eat and shower. The chance to enroll for a prison job wouldn't come around for another few weeks, after she'd passed her probation period. With a couple of black marks against her already, she wasn't holding out much hope of finding something to take her mind off her predicament.

"Driscoll, front and center!"

She saw a hard-nosed guard known as Lott glaring at her. Eva did as the guard ordered, standing close to attention as the others filed past on their way back to the block.

"Turn around, hands behind your back."

Eva turned and felt handcuffs go on, and immediately wondered if this was the ESO making their move. They would know from experience to incapacitate her first but she would happily disappoint them. Getting out of cuffs was something she'd learned years earlier, and they would only hold for as long as she let them.

"Let's go," Lott said. "Warden wants to speak to you."

She led Eva out of the wing and through three manned security gates to a part of the prison Eva hadn't yet seen. They passed a few offices before they came to a door with "Superintendent Foley" painted on the window.

Lott knocked and waited to be called in. "Sir, this is Eva Driscoll," she said when told to enter. She maneuvered Eva to stand on a yellow line in front of the warden's desk.

Foley wore a five-hundred-dollar suit and had the air of a man who held power and knew it. He opened a file, read for a minute, then closed it and looked up at Eva.

"Looks like you're leaving us already," Foley said, holding the file out for Lott to take. "Apparently, you're considered too high-risk for this facility, which surprises me. In all my years at Bedford Hills, I've never had someone transferred for that reason. We specialize in reforming the worst of the worst, and if there's a better place to deal with you, I'd love to know about it. Unfortunately, for security reasons, your new home isn't listed. What do you make of that?"

Eva didn't say anything. Only one explanation came to mind: the ESO was behind it. Once in their custody, it would be game over.

Foley was waiting for a reaction, but when he saw he wasn't going to get one, he waved a hand at the guard. "Get her out of here."

Eva was escorted back to her cell, uncuffed, and Lott remained outside the door while she gathered her belongings. Lott then took her to the reception wing and Eva signed for her belongings. She was given the clothes she'd arrived in—black jeans, white T-shirt, and a pair of sneakers—and a manila envelope. Eva tipped out the contents and saw a couple of items she didn't recognize. One was a cell phone, which she knew for a fact she hadn't brought to the prison. The second was a small key. There was also a few dollars in cash and the gold necklace her brother had given her when she'd graduated from high school.

After Eva signed for her things, Lott put them back in the envelope and reapplied the handcuffs before escorting her to the main entrance. They made the long walk in silence. Above them, the October sky was gunmetal gray, a color Eva normally associated with misery and depression.

It had never been more apt.

As they neared the main entrance, Eva could see a large black Jeep waiting just below the watch tower. It was parked between the inner and outer gates, and the tinted windows were up, preventing her from seeing the occupants.

Every sinew in her body felt wired for action. Should she tell Lott she was being set up, and that the men inside were going to kill her? There was no point, and Eva knew it. Lott had spent her whole adult life at Bedford Hills, and she'd probably heard every brand of insane rambling in that time.

Lott led her through the inner gate, and when it closed, the doors of the Jeep opened. A man dressed in a leather jacket got out and handed Lott a clipboard, not once looking at the prisoner. The guard checked the details, then signed the form and handed over Eva's belongings.

Eva's heart bounced in her chest but she said nothing. When the man removed her cuffs and put them on again in front of her body, Eva closed her eyes in case her emotions gave her away. She felt her arm being pulled and let her body follow as she was put in the back seat of the vehicle. Leather Jacket got in beside her and closed the door.

Eva struck with lightning speed. She put her cuffed hands around the man's neck and kissed him with more passion than she'd ever managed in her life.

"Get a room." Sonny smiled from the front seat.

Huff broke free from Eva's lips and removed her cuffs. He immediately got a punch in the stomach.

"What the hell was that for?"

"For turning up in a black Jeep. You scared the shit out of me!"

"I did warn them," Farooq said from beside her. "I told them you wouldn't find it amusing."

Smart started the engine and backed out through the main gate while Eva tried to get over her initial shock. As prison breaks went, this was one of the smoothest she'd known.

"How did you organize the paperwork?" she asked.

"We didn't," Huff said. "The same thing happened to us yesterday. Some guy with transfer papers picked us up at the gates at Sing Sing and took us to a hotel. He said we should be here at ten this morning and to show this form when we got to the gate. That's all we know."

It was getting weirder by the second. If the ESO were behind this, it was their strangest play to date. Straight out of left field, a mysterious benefactor securing their release.

And then there was the phone that had appeared in her belongings . . .

Eva opened the envelope and took the cell out, and before she had the chance to scroll through the menus, it began to play a familiar tune.

"Isn't that 'Hail to the Chief'?" Smart asked.

"Yes, sir, it is," Colback said.

Eva stabbed the Connect button and put it on speaker.

"Hello?"

"Ms. Driscoll, this is Leo Russell. I see you got the phone I arranged for you. I expect you have a few questions, so I'll be brief."

The president? Sonny mouthed.

Eva nodded.

"I hope your time in Bedford Hills wasn't too traumatic."

"I've had worse," Eva admitted.

"I have to thank you for exposing Henry Langton," Russell continued, "and bringing the ESO to my attention. I'm just sorry that we couldn't meet in person. I appreciate that you sacrificed a lot and risked your own lives to bring this man to justice, and I intend to finish that job. Langton, as you may know, died shortly after his arrest, but I've instructed a new agency—set up and run by some close personal friends—to investigate his activities over the years so we can identify other members of the ESO and the people they've influenced. I'm afraid this is going to take a few years, but someday we'll be able to comprehensively say we've identified everyone involved."

"Thank you, Mr. President. It's gratifying to know that you're taking my claims seriously."

"Not at all, Ms. Driscoll. It's I who should be thanking you. Due to the matter's sensitivity though, any public outpouring of appreciation is out of the question. I've been able to arrange your freedom, but beyond that, my hands are tied. As far as your former wardens and cellmates know, you've been transferred to destinations unknown. As of now, you are free to go. It's my understanding that the money you managed to steal from the ESO was never recovered, so I'm trusting you won't be short of funds for a while. It should at least be enough to set you up in a new life for a few years."

Eva murmured her assent.

"If you look at the release form, in the top left-hand corner there's a serial number. In the bottom right-hand corner is the address of the printing company. Can you see them?"

Eva took the clipboard from Huff. "Got 'em."

"Good. The serial number is a locker number, and you'll find it at that address. I trust you got the key my man left for you. In the locker, you'll find passports, driver's licenses, and prepaid credit cards under your new identities. Mr. Smart, Mr. Baines, I've spoken to your prime minister and he has agreed to honor the pardon I've granted you. That document will remain sealed for the next fifty years, and even your own security services don't know the names on your new passports. You're free to return to the United Kingdom under your real identities or remain here as US citizens using the aliases."

"Thank you, Mr. President," said Smart.

"As I said, this is the extent of my intervention. From now on, you're on your own. I can't guarantee that the ESO won't try to find you, but you should have enough resources to disappear until I can make headway with the investigation. I wish you the best of luck."

"Thank you—"

The disconnect tone coming from the phone told them that POTUS had hung up.

"Well, there's one to tell the grandkids," Sonny said. "So, what's the plan?"

"Len," Eva said, "take us to Kansas City. Along the way, find a hotel where we can change our appearances and I can sleep with both eyes closed."

~

Henry Langton's bony hand reached out and clicked on the incoming message. The computer's built-in encryption software prompted him to enter his twelve-digit password, then began deciphering the seemingly random string of characters. It took a full minute before he found himself staring at the transcript of a telephone conversation.

So, Russell let you out, did he?

He lit a cigarette and blew a cloud of smoke at the screen. His plan to have the six of them killed in prison was now moot, but strangely he didn't feel any rage. Instead, a grin found its way to his lips.

Driscoll—indeed, the whole world—believed him dead. Armed with new papers, she'd soon begin to feel safe, and at some point, she'd get sloppy. When she did, he'd pounce.

Langton got out of his chair and walked around his office. It was adorned with some of his favorite pieces, shipped over from his house in Washington, but it still wasn't home. He had access to every luxury a man could possibly imagine yet was effectively a prisoner in his own residence.

He walked out of the room and leaned on the wooden railing overlooking the atrium below. Men in black uniforms were hauling boxes into his new command center, which would be up and running in the next few days. He would once again have access to every security database in the world, and the operatives at his disposal worldwide would number more than a hundred. More would be added over time, which was something he had a lot of.

Only a handful of people knew he was still alive, and his recent surgery meant even those below him had no idea who he was. As far as they were concerned, he was just some old guy charged with overseeing a project of national importance. Once they'd delivered all the equipment, he'd bring his own men in to set things up and run the operation from his private island.

Langton walked back into his office and looked again at the transcript. It would be impossible to compile a list of all the places in the US that had key-operated lockers. Even if they could narrow it down and they somehow managed to spot her on CCTV, they'd be powerless to catch her unless they happened to have personnel nearby.

It wasn't the end though. In fact, it was just the beginning. Now that he'd handed over the reins of the ESO, he could devote most of his time to tracking down Driscoll and her friends. In his spare moments, he would begin to prepare his grandchildren for their destiny. With their father gone, it fell to Langton to teach them the ropes so that someday they could take control of the organization. Langtons had led the ESO since its inception, and he wasn't about to let that tradition slide.

He minimized the message and stared at the desktop picture. It was Eva Driscoll's CIA file, and her face took up a quarter of the screen. Impatient as he was to get started, for him, the chase was almost as exciting as the prize at the end of it. She'd be a difficult beast to catch but catch her he would.

She couldn't hide forever.

He would flush her out eventually, and she would only have one option:

Run.

If you enjoyed this novel and would like to know about Alan's future releases, please email alanmac@ntlworld.com including "Driscoll" in the subject line. You can find the rest of his books at www.alanmcdermottbooks.co.uk.

ACKNOWLEDGMENTS

I would like to thank everyone at Thomas & Mercer for taking yet another chance on me. I'd also like to thank fellow (and vastly superior) author Keith Houghton for listening to my inane ramblings when things aren't going well. A final special mention goes to everyone who picked up one of my books, read it, and came back for more—you're the reason I still write!

ABOUT THE AUTHOR

Alan McDermott is a husband and a father to beautiful twin girls, and currently lives in the south of England. Born in West Germany to Scottish parents, Alan spent his early years moving from town to town as his father was posted to different army units around the United Kingdom. Alan has had a number of jobs since leaving school, including working on a cruise ship in Hong Kong and Singapore, where he met his wife, and as a software developer creating clinical applications for the National Health Service. Alan gave up his day job in December 2014 to become a full-time author. Alan's writing career began in 2011 with the action thriller *Gray Justice*, his first full-length novel.